Book 2

THE COMPASS

D. Henry

ISBN Paperback: 978-0-6450098-1-1
ISBN Hardcover: 978-0-6450098-2-8

Edited by Todd Barselow

Cover art by Erin Wong
http://www.littleeworks.com/

THE COMPASS

Legs buckled and knees crashed into hard packed dirt. The shockwave of pain was barely recognized. Everything his body felt his brain muted in a bid for self-preservation. If he allowed himself to feel, he would be overwhelmed by injuries covered in dried blood and caked-on dirt, worn down bare feet, and bruising from fractures and breaks in his wrist and chest.

Hands lifted him up and waited for weak legs to remember how to support him before letting him go. He rubbed his eyes, trying to get them to focus, but before he could make out any features, they stepped out of sight. When he tried to speak, his voice couldn't make it past his dry throat.

A gentle hand pushed against the middle of his back, urging him forward.

"Go give him our gift, Jayden."

When he glanced back, whoever had been there with him had vanished. How had the person disappeared so quickly? Why would they leave him alone?

Jayden stared at the open space in front of him. He wondered where he had come from. He wondered where he was. His body was stiff from exhaustion and no matter how hard he tried to remember, he couldn't come up with any answers.

Returning his attention back the other way, he spent a few confusing seconds staring at the city. Sleek high rise buildings circled around something large and blue with a jagged, pointed top. Surrounding those were single and double-story houses and mansions complete with well-kept gardens, and a lively forest.

The first step forward was completed with uncertainty but when he remained standing, he kept going. Every movement he forced his body to make felt like he was walking through thick sludge. There was something he had to do, and no amount of pain or exhaustion would stop him from delivering the gift to those in the city.

By the time he reached a main road, he could barely lift his head up and his feet were as heavy as lead.

A hand grabbed his shoulder and something inside of him snapped.

Gale force winds knocked everyone around him off their feet. The ground groaned and shook. Buildings swayed, glass shattered, poles, seats, trees, and more were toppled over. There was a rush of people using their Abilities in an effort to stay on their feet and shield themselves from the cacophony of wind and flying debris.

The air rapidly filled with foreign power and Jayden struggled to breathe through the panic. He had walked right into the middle of the war. People surrounding him wanted to kill him on orders from the Council of 8.

He cried out as he unleashed his Abilities on those around him. All he wanted was to be able to live in peace and to give Szantium his gift.

There was no ebbing the outpouring of his power. It was overwhelming and frightening. Something heavy crashed nearby, causing him to whip around, eyes frantically searching as he breathed heavily.

Jayden slammed his foot down and sent a ripple of power through the ground. Cement was ripped up until his Abilities came crashing into a building.

When the dust settled, the left half of a multi-story structure was leaning lazily away from the rest of it.

Soft green light bathed the city and wrapped Jayden up in a comforting warmth. He glanced around and any panic he felt was washed away. His eyes grew heavy and he yawned. As he succumbed to the need for sleep, gentle hands wrapped around him in a soft yet firm embrace.

The smell of disinfectant and an incessant beeping played with a headache pounding against his temples. When he opened his eyes, he was overwhelmed with inexplicable panic. Breath came in short desperate bursts and his heart was a jackhammer pounding against his sore ribs.

Jayden attempted to coax his limbs into cooperating in order to get out of the hospital bed.

"Jayden! Jayden, you need to calm down and breathe. You're safe, okay? You're safe."

He wanted to heed the familiar voice but something was stopping him. The hospital was dangerous. He knew he couldn't stay here. He had to keep running. He didn't know or understand why. He just knew that he had to. It was a matter of life or death.

"Jay, listen to me."

A symbol glowing green washed over his body, causing him to slump against the pillows. His heart slowed and his breathing evened out. The urge to run fled and confusion and exhaustion replaced it.

"You good?"

"Liz?" Jayden croaked, licking his dry lips.

"Yeah."

"Thank … you."

- **Chapter One -**

"Whoa!"

Jayden tripped over the edge of the mattress and thumped his forehead the hardwood floor. Now that he was sleeping without painkillers in his system, he was left at the mercy of nightmares instead of the deep, dreamless sleep the drugs had provided. The blue and green river of the In Between was a false comfort amidst the urgency of an invisible battle raging on all around him.

As he sat up, Jayden rubbed his bruised chest and took a deep breath. His heart was still thundering and his bare skin was lathered in sweat. Leaning his head against the mattress, he closed his eyes and focused on steadying his breathing.

It had been three days since he had been discharged from the hospital and given a room in the Laiyfe-Rain mansion. He had left the hospital with a multitude of injuries: bruised ribs, a twisted knee, a broken left arm in a cast, a bandaged right wrist, and stitches on a shoulder blade. All that was on top of a weakened body spotted with ugly fading bruises and abrasions.

The hospital staff hadn't been able to get close enough to him to use their Healing Wards, so he was left to naturally heal with human medication. It was a slow, painful, and tiring experience.

No matter how many times he tried to remember, he couldn't work out what had happened to him and no one else seemed to be able to give him any answers.

Jayden opened his eyes and slowly exhaled. In the darkness, he could still see the blue and green river.

It was suffocating.

It was terrifying.

Needing to get out, he eased himself up on his bed and reached out for his crutches. His fingers barely brushed against the walking aid before the pair toppled over and crashed on to the floor.

He growled in frustration.

Getting around was a nuisance. He looked at the wheelchair with resigned frustration.

A knock on the door caused him to jump involuntarily, which lead to a wince of pain.

"Ahh, sorry. I'm fine. Sorry," Jayden quickly said.

The light was switched on, blinding him briefly. When he was able to see, Aster was bending down to pick up his fallen crutches. With a warm smile shining in those tired black eyes, his grandfather handed them over and sat next to him.

Aster had aged since the last time Jayden had seen him. His dark gray hair was now lighter. There were more lines along his face and hands, which had a slight shake to them. He was dressed in a thick cardigan, plain t-shirt, sweat pants, and slippers.

"Can't sleep?" Aster asked.

Jayden shook his head. "No. Sorry for waking you."

"Don't worry about it. I've never been able to sleep well so I was already awake. Did you want to talk about it?" Aster offered.

Jayden grimaced. "It's fine."

Aster tilted his head and studied his grandson. "Okay. Let's go for a walk then. It's a nice night out."

"I'm supposed to be resting," Jayden pointed out.

Aster pushed the wheelchair over with a mischievous smile.

"I won't tell if you don't," Aster said.

He relented and eased himself into the chair. He really missed being able to maneuver around without aid. He missed having days where pain wasn't hindering. At least he was on the mend and should be free of the bandages and the cast soon.

Aster steered him outside and through the garden until they reached a bench. Jayden took the chance to stand out of the chair, wincing as the pain in his knee flared as he lightly stretched.

The garden bench faced towards the forest. Exploring the land was on the list of things he'd like to do once he was able to move around easier.

It was the first time since leaving the hospital that he had been able to get out of the house. Leeran and Taylin had kept a close eye on him and he couldn't step anywhere without being diverted back to a couch or to his bed to rest. It wouldn't have been a problem if he had something to occupy himself outside of napping.

"I like these nights the most," Aster commented.

Jayden blinked at his grandfather and shuffled around to sit down beside him.

"Sorry?"

"The sky is clear and there's a feeling of peace in the air. It helps clear the mind," Aster explained.

He glanced up at the sky and the unfamiliar stars. "Oh. I guess."

After a moment of silence, he fiddled with the bandage on his wrist. There was barely any nighttime noise, and after having grown up in the human suburbs, it was rather unnerving.

"Everything is different," he noted.

"Yes," Aster agreed.

"It's …"

"Too much and overwhelming?" Aster guessed.

"Yeah," Jayden nodded.

"Understandable."

"Dad? Jayden? What are you two doing out here?"

Jayden tensed. So much for a peaceful night.

Leeran came around and stood there with her arms folded across her chest. She stared at him with a cold judgment in her black eyes that made him squirm in his seat.

"Jay, you're supposed to be in bed resting. It's chilly out here, come on back in," Leeran said.

Aster gave him an apologetic look before standing and moving the wheelchair in front of Jayden.

He stood to his full height and looked to Leeran with an unimpressed look.

"It's Jayden," he grunted.

Despite Aster taking him inside and helping him get back into bed, Leeran hovered close behind them, watching their every move.

Stiff muscles tensed and he contemplated asking for pain relief but thought better of it. He wanted a clear mind. He didn't want to rely so much on drugs to help him through this.

"Sleep well, Jay," Aster said gently.

Jayden gave him a small smile of gratitude. From the corner of his eye, he watched as Leeran folded her arms across her chest with an unreadable expression.

Aster gently squeezed one of his shoulders before shuffling out. Leeran stayed in the doorway for a moment longer, watching him in silence, before closing the door.

Once alone, he stared up at the ceiling and sighed.

Judging from the last few days, he knew that living here was going to be a grueling test of his patience.

Jayden glanced at the door as more and more noise began wafting through the mansion. The morning sun filtered in through his window, blinding him for a moment. He had barely gotten a wink of sleep. Pain had escalated as the night wore on and he hadn't wanted to aggravate it by moving to get his painkillers.

With a sigh, he closed his eyes and tried to filter out the sounds in the hope that no one would come to see whether or not he was awake yet.

Unfortunately, the worst person in the house decided to pop their head in.

"Breakfast is ready," Mackenzie said.

He clenched his jaw and ignored his twin.

Mackenzie sighed, "Jay, everyone eats breakfast and dinner together. And you need to have food before you can have any of your painkillers."

Again, Jayden chose to ignore him. There was no way he wanted to interact with the person who had killed his family. There was nothing that would force him to do so and no one would ever change his mind on the matter. Every time he looked at Mackenzie, all he could see was his twin covered in the blood of his parents and it made him sick.

Thankfully, Mackenzie seemed to give up and left him alone.

He glanced to the door, shaking. He had to force his eyes closed to rein in his anger.

When there was a knock on the door, Jayden couldn't help the flinch. He prayed to any higher being out there that it wasn't Mackenzie back at his door.

To his luck, Iris was patiently waiting for him.

"Good morning, Jayden. It's time for breakfast," Iris greeted.

"I'm not hungry," Jayden murmured, sitting up.

"You need to eat," she pressed.

"I can't. He killed my mom and dad … and brother," Jayden argued.

His grandmother grimaced and sat down beside his legs on the mattress. She gently took his hand and ran a thumb over his bandaged wrist. There was a knowing, understanding look reflected in her blue eyes.

"I know and I'm terribly sorry, but please bear with it. At least for the meantime. When they leave for the day, the five of us will talk. I promise."

Jayden thought about it. He had no qualms with his grandparents. They had never dismissed the Lugians and they hadn't made any excuses for any wrongdoing.

With a sigh, he eased himself up and into his wheelchair. Iris smiled gratefully and stepped back as a man in a black and white suit came in and wheeled him out to the dining table. Jayden frowned and watched the man, unsure of whom he was. His dark hair was slicked back and he had an inquisitive spark in his piercing blue eyes.

The man placed him between Cora and Valent then finished getting everything on the table for breakfast.

"Who's that?" he asked.

"Koan Omb –– a butler, so just ignore him," Mackenzie answered as he sat down opposite Jayden.

Jayden frowned. Ignoring someone based on their job was not okay.

When Koan came back into the dining room, he made a point to meet the man's gaze and sat thanks for helping him to the table and for the food. Koan gave him a smile and a small bow.

"Breakfast is served," Koan announced before leaving the room.

He watched the man leave. He was tempted to follow and join Koan in the kitchen,

"Jay, we need to talk," Leeran said.

He grimaced and tensed. He sat in silence as Leeran left a full plate of food in front of him.

"It's ... Well, you need to stop ignoring your brother and cease this passive aggressive behavior towards your mother and me," Taylin said.

Jayden glanced from Leeran to Taylin to Mackenzie, feeling his anger rising.

"We share DNA, that's all. You and Leeran didn't raise me, and he killed my brother, mom, and dad," Jayden shot back.

"He did those things under the control of the Council of 8. It's been almost nine years and Mackenzie has changed. So it's time for you to move on," Taylin insisted.

Jayden had to swallow his initial reaction to fling his knife at the man.

"What did he say to explain his actions ..." Jayden thought for a moment. "Oh, right! Mackenzie said he was jealous of what I had so apparently that meant he had every right to murder innocent people. And it doesn't matter how long it's been for you or anyone else. He still did what he did and I will never let it go!" Jayden snapped.

"Jay, I'm really sorry. I've been spending every day trying to atone for what I did back then. I even visit and put flowers at the graves, and I ask the Lugians for forgiveness," Mackenzie explained.

Hearing that had Jayden blinded with rage. "You *what*? How dare you! Stay away from me and my family."

He pushed away from the table and stepped away from his chair.

"Breakfast isn't finished and neither is this conversation," Leeran said.

"You can shove your breakfast up your —-"

"Jayden Laiyfe-Rain, do not speak to your mother like that," scolded Taylin.

"That's not my name!" Jayden shouted.

The glasses on the table shattered. Jayden immediately clamped down on his Abilities and swayed a little on his feet. Glaring, he wiped his nose, ignored the blood on his hand, and hobbled away.

By the time he made it to the hallway, he regretted leaving the wheelchair behind. He was dizzy with pain and almost ready to collapse. He slumped against the wall and closed his eyes.

"Jayden?"

He opened his eyes, ready for another fight, but it was a relief to see Koan standing there with his wheelchair.

"I'll take you to your room," Koan said.

"Thanks," he murmured.

Jayden pushed away from the wall and eased himself down onto the chair. As he was taken back to his room, he lightly massaged his thigh. His knee was on fire and the agony had him on the verge of tears.

Once he was in his bedroom, Koan helped Jayden into bed and even went as far as to prop his knee up with pillows underneath it. The man disappeared for a moment and came back with a heat pack and a glass of water. Jayden muttered a thanks as Koan handed over the cup and retrieved the painkillers from a bedside table drawer.

He washed down a couple of tablets, ready for the relief they would provide, and dropped his head back.

"Sir, may I?" Koan asked.

"May what?'

"Give you some advice," Koan specified.

He shifted his focus to the man and nodded, "Ahh, sure."

"It is best to ignore those three as much as possible otherwise you'll be the one worse for wear," Koan advised.

Jayden sighed and stared at his hands in his lap. "I know, I know. Mom used to tell me to step away from those without good intentions. She'd be disappointed with how I reacted."

"She sounds like a wise woman," Koan smiled.

"She was," Jayden agreed. "I'm sorry for the mess I created."

"It's fine. Try to get some rest. I'll bring you some food and some books to help pass the time," Koan said.

Jayden nodded. "Thank you."

When he was alone, he slumped against his pillow and sighed. Leeran and Taylin had seemed nice when he had first met them but as soon as Theresa and Ron had died, they had been quick to step into the role of mother and father. There was no time to get to know each other. There wasn't even time for Jayden to mourn his loss.

Koan briefly came back in and dropped off a pile of books and a plate of scrambled eggs. He told Jayden that he would check in every now and then with him to see how he was going and if he needed anything else.

Jayden took a book from the pile and made an attempt to read while he ate. By the time he was half way through his eggs, he was drifting off to sleep.

- **Chapter Two** -

A knock on the door snapped him awake. He wiped his face tiredly and glanced around his room. The plate of eggs sitting beside him had gone cold and the book he had been reading was resting on his stomach. Despite the initial shock awake, he was still groggy and ready to go back to sleep.

"Yes?" Jayden answered.

Iris came into the room, followed by his other grandparents.

"How are you feeling?" Cora asked as Aster set her chair beside the mattress.

"Painkillers are working," he answered.

"I'm sorry, Jayden. I didn't expect them to ambush you on the matter this morning," Iris apologized.

He glanced between his grandparents, gnawing on his bottom lip.

"My name is Jayden Lugian. I'm not … I can't …"

Iris sat on the edge of the mattress and took his bandaged hand gently.

"We know and we don't expect you to be anyone else."

He struggled to hold back his emotions. Grandparents he barely knew were more understanding than he could have hoped for but that begged the question — why did his grandparents understand his position better than his birth parents?

"There's something going on with our children. We're not sure what, and we've struggled to find out," Iris said.

Jayden frowned as something tugged on his memories. "Does this … Is this why you told me not to trust them when we first met?"

He had met his grandparents before the final fight with the remaining members of the Council of 8. Aster had hugged him and during the embrace, had whispered something that had confused him. He hadn't understood why he was being told not to trust his birthparents, but he was beginning to see why.

There was something wrong with Leeran and Taylin. There was coldness in their gaze and they refused to let Jayden be.

"Yes." Aster nodded. "I wanted to explain more but with them around and the urgency of war, it was hard."

"How did you know back then?" he asked.

"You learn to be able to judge someone's intentions by how their Abilities feel. Leeran had a kind nature, very nurturing, while Taylin had a more protective sense to him. When we all met up at The Balgaire back then, what we felt … it was synthetic and wrong," Aster explained.

"I see …" Jayden mumbled.

"We have noticed over time how much their personalities have changed. One could say it was to be expected after being on the run for so long, but something else has happened to them," Cora added.

Jayden nodded in understanding.

"I can't live here with him," he blurted out.

His grandparents shared a look and nodded in agreement.

"We know," Valent said.

"I can … I can see if I can stay at The Balgaire. If I had a phone, I could ask …" Jayden trailed off.

"We will help you as much as we can but you need to focus on healing first," Iris said.

"Why can't I leave now?"

"The rooms there are on the second floor and with your knee the way it is now, getting up to the rooms without aggravating the injury would be problematic if you don't wish to use your Abilities or allow a Healing Ward to be used," Iris explained.

He stared at his propped up knee covered with a heat pack and sighed in defeat.

"Right."

There were still two and a half weeks to go before his next appointment in order to see how he was healing up. Compared to how he had been while in the hospital, he could now put some weight on his knee but not enough and not for long enough to matter.

"When we knew you had survived, we went ahead and changed our wills. You are our sole beneficiary. We've arranged for you to have access to the family funds. Our money is your money," Aster said.

Jayden stilled, unsure if he had heard correctly.

"I don't understand."

"Our families have always strived to protect others above all else," Aster explained.

"Humans *and* Szaephian," Valent clarified.

"To you, there is no difference between the two races. That's why you were able to call our old friends for help," Aster continued.

"Old friends?"

Iris turned his arm over and ran a finger over the bandages. The glow of a Ward barely came through.

"Ignatius Halium and Thaddeus Eclipse," Jayden murmured.

Cora and Valent nodded in confirmation.

"Whenever you need help, they are still there to answer your call," Cora said.

"For now, focus on healing and we will help you get into a better living arrangement," Aster compromised.

"Okay," Jayden agreed. "I can … I can be civil until then."

Two weeks dragged on agonizingly slowly. He found it hard to bite his tongue every time Leeran, Taylin, or Mackenzie tested his patience. Thankfully, the three of them seemed to have things going on between breakfast and dinner so in the end, there wasn't much time spent with them, forced or otherwise. Plus, whenever they got too much for him to deal with, he was able to escape to his room under the pretense of needing to rest.

Once his appointment came round, Koan had volunteered to take him. He had actually insisted on it when Leeran and Taylin had said that one of them would take him. Jayden was thankful for the man being there to help out.

It was a relief when the cast and bandages came off. He lightly stretched both arms out and was happy when there was no pain. His knee was poked and prodded but he was still experiencing too much pain and tenderness so he was instructed to do a few physiotherapy exercises and to make sure not to push it too much. Lastly, stitches were taken out and then he was free to go.

Dinner that night was harder to get through. He chose to help Koan set up the table, and as soon as Mackenzie saw them he made a remark about Jayden becoming a part of the help.

Jayden clenched his jaw tightly to stop himself from retorting.

"Knowing how to care for one's self is a quality of independence and something every adult should know how to do – should they be capable of learning how," Koan said.

"Excuse me?" Mackenzie said.

Koan raised an eyebrow and said, "Dinner is ready."

An amused smile was shared between Koan and Jayden.

As usual for their family meals, he sat between Cora and Valent. He helped his grandparents out by filling their plates and sat back down to enjoy the food as much as possible.

"Have the doctors given you a clean bill of health?" Taylin asked.

Jayden played with a bean for a second before answering. "Close enough."

"Good. I'd like you to start thinking about attending classes in order to learn how to use your Abilities," Taylin said.

Jayden frowned. "No, thanks."

"You need to learn in order to be able to live here," Leeran said.

"Then I'll go back to the Human Plane," Jayden said with a shrug.

"There are expectations that you must meet as not only a Harbinon but as a Laiyfe-Rain as well. You *need* to go to school," Leeran pushed.

He glanced over to his grandparents for help. He didn't know how to get Leeran and Taylin to listen and he had promised to be civil.

"Leeran and Taylin, Jayden is allowed to decide for himself what he'd like to do when he has more strength. For now, let's focus on eating this meal," Cora suggested.

Silence reigned over dinner and his appetite had disappeared.

"Can I be excused?" he asked.

"Dinner hasn't fin –-"

"Yes," Aster interrupted, giving Leeran and Taylin a pointed look.

He smiled gratefully and left the dining table. Instead of going back to his room, he went to the little nook off to the side of the kitchen and knocked.

"Do you mind if I join you?" Jayden asked.

Koan glanced up, moved several thick books off the table, and gestured for him to sit down.

"Can I get you anything?" Koan asked.

Jayden shook his head. "No, it's fine. I couldn't sit and have dinner with them. I can leave if you wanted some peace to read and eat."

The butler looked over to his books and smiled. "No, it's fine. I was only rereading something."

"You sure?" Jayden checked.

"Yes," Koan confirmed.

He glanced around, suddenly feeling awkward for interrupting the man's meal time. The room was pretty bare. There was a table big enough for two people propped up against one wall, a small two door cabinet opposite the table with a vase of flowers he didn't recognize, and a door leading towards the kitchen.

"Here. Eat."

Koan slid a plate in front of him with a small portion of what had been cooked for dinner.

"But —"

"That's leftovers. Don't worry, just eat and enjoy," Koan instructed.

Jayden nodded and dug in. The food was delicious as always but with Koan watching him, he struggled to concentrate on his meal.

"Why are you watching me?" Jayden asked after he finished chewing.

Koan smiled and shook his head.

"What?"

"You're different," Koan noted.

"Thanks? I grew up with an ordinary, human family. Or did you miss that part?" Jayden huffed.

"That's not what I meant," Koan said.

"Oh." Jayden grimaced. "Sorry."

Silence settled between them as they finished eating. Koan took their empty plates and stacked them in the dishwasher.

"What happened in the dining room?" Koan asked.

Instead of answering right away, he focused on his finger drawing circles along the table.

"Leeran and Taylin want me to go to school to learn how to use my Abilities but I said no and they wouldn't listen," Jayden explained.

"What's your objection to learning?" Koan asked.

"I like learning and I was eager to learn about Wards and how to use my Abilities back when I first found out about everything. But I don't want to use them anymore. Just because I have powers, doesn't mean I want or need them."

"But you do need to know how to control them," Koan pointed out.

Jayden sighed and nodded.

"I know but …"

"How about instead of dismissing the idea completely, you think about it? Even if you learn through one-on-one tutoring or with a friend, at least it's something. Learning doesn't always need to happen in a traditional setting," Koan said.

Jayden scratched his head and conceded defeat. "Yeah, okay."

"After I've finished with what I need to do tonight, I will bring you a couple more books. One is on the history of Szantium, and the other on Ward theory. Okay?" Koan said.

"Okay, thanks," Jayden said, standing up. "I'm going to duck outside before any of them try to find me."

Chapter Three

Pamphlets for a training school had been left on his bed while he had been out for a small walk around the garden. His first reaction was anger, and as he was about to tear them apart, Jayden hesitated. Koan telling him to not completely reject the idea echoed in his mind. Instead, he took a deep, calming breath as he sat down, and went through the pamphlets.

All of them had photos of the same massive arena. Photos had been taken at different angles of raised chairs surrounding a green field, locker rooms, meeting rooms, a cafeteria, and an indoor gym area. There was information about the different classes and levels each school provided, and trainer pictures with a snippet of who they were.

After going through, he tore them up and put the remnants in the bin. He was not interested in signing up to some expensive school. Jayden had a teacher; although Kalarney was currently missing, he still had a teacher.

"No good?" Koan asked.

He glanced up from the bin to find Koan standing there with a couple of books in hand and a frown.

"No," Jayden answered.

"I can give you my recommendations," Koan offered.

"No, it's fine. I already have a teacher," he said, shaking his head.

"Oh."

"Are those the books you were telling me about?" Jayden asked, nodding to the books.

"Yes," Koan answered, handing them over.

The books were old hardcovers that were clearly well taken care of. Jayden flicked through one of them, stopping every now and then when a passage caught his attention, and when he looked up to thank Koan, he found the man studying him.

"You keep staring at me," Jayden pointed out.

"Yes," Koan agreed.

"Why?" he asked.

"I'm learning," Koan answered.

"Koan, don't you have work to tend to?" Leeran interrupted.

Jayden jumped at the intruding voice while Koan stepped back and shrouded his expression. Watching the change in the man set him on edge and he sent a glare at the woman standing by the doorway.

"I'm finished for the night," Koan responded.

"A butler's job is never done. I doubt you could offer Jayden anything of value other than cleaning advice. So leave," Leeran demanded.

"Don't be rude!" Jayden snapped.

Leeran raised an eyebrow at him, which shifted to a patient smile.

"Did you find the pamphlets I left for you, Jay?" Leeran asked.

"It's *Jayden* and the pamphlets are in the bin. In pieces," Jayden replied.

"You need to go to school. No matter how much you suck up to our parents, you *will* be going," Leeran growled before leaving.

His fists shook with heated anger. He wanted to punch something or throw his Abilities at the woman.

"If you need any clarification with anything you read in those, please don't hesitate to ask. Despite what certain people seem to think, I am well educated," Koan said.

Jayden grimaced. "I know. Thank you."

He waited until Koan had left before settling in bed with the books. He glanced through the tome on Ward theory but decided to put that aside and focus on the ones that were on history. It was interesting learning a different side to events that had been happening in the human world and discovering just how thin the lines between the two versions were. Each community had crisscrossed, and on occasion, clashed.

Flicking through the contents and acknowledgment pages, he found a note that said, *'Jay, I think you might be interested in pages 50 to 75, and 234 to 236. Do make sure to read the whole book but I ask that you focus on these sections as they may help with future tasks.'*

The note was signed by someone named Jimin Park.

Jayden stared at the name. He didn't know anyone by that name and he wondered why Koan would give him a book with a note from someone else.

After making a mental note to ask Koan in the morning about it, he settled in with the book.

Once again, he woke to find himself struggling out of another nightmare. This time, he had been running through a foggy battlefield. Wards were shooting past from all directions, and he could hear others struggling in the fight. He wanted to stop and help but something was chasing after him. When he did finally stop to catch his breath, the sky exploded in a river of blue and green.

Waking up, Jayden was left panting and covered in a sheen of sweat. His heard pounded against his chest and it took a moment to remember that he was safe. Taking a shaky deep breath, he sat up and dug the palms of his hands against his eyes as he focused on slowing his breathing.

He got out of bed and quietly made his way outside. The night air was cool on his bare skin and caused the hair on his arms to stand on end. The sky was littered with bright stars and the moon was barely a sliver. The lack of familiarity in his everyday life and the exhaustion from broken sleep highlighted how much he missed his life prior to being sent to the Anchor with his friends.

When the ground began shaking, he scrambled away from the house and watched in confused horror. A sharp jolt knocked his legs out from underneath him painfully. He held on to his knee while he attempted to scramble out of the way of falling roof tiles.

"Jayden!" Koan called out.

"H-here!" Jayden shouted.

Koan held on to the doorframe as he searched for Jayden. He raised an arm to show where he was and Koan stepped back inside. A moment later, he came out with Iris and Cora. Behind them, Mackenzie was helping Aster out, and Taylin was with Valent.

Koan eased Iris on to a nearby bench and went over to help Jayden to his feet.

"You okay?" Koan asked.

"Yeah," he answered.

He tried to put pressure on his knee, but sharp pain made him recoil his foot back up. Jayden cursed his luck. He hoped he hadn't ruined all the progress he had made with his knee.

"Again?" Mackenzie huffed, watching the old mansion sway a little.

"It appears like it," Leeran answered.

That caught his attention. "This has happened before?"

Leeran nodded. "Mackenzie, go see if there's anyone that needs help."

Mackenzie ran off, stumbling a little with the sway of the earth.

Jayden wanted to ask again about it all but before he could get the words sorted in his head, Leeran was turning to them and speaking.

"It looks like the earthquake has finally stopped," Leeran noted. "Let's get —-"

Koan helped Jayden to his feet and slowly back inside with Iris pushing Cora along with them. Every time his foot hit the ground, it send shockwaves of agony through his knee.

"How can there be an earthquake?" Jayden asked.

He was eased down on the chair by Cora's bed. He massaged his thigh, being careful not to touch his knee too much. Koan helped Cora to bed and glanced back towards the door. Jayden followed his gaze but no one was there.

"What's going on?" he asked.

"It's …" Iris trailed off.

"Complicated? Nothing to worry about? Sure, right. I'm going back to bed," Jayden huffed.

Clenching his jaw, he pushed himself out of the chair and bit his bottom lip as he limped towards the door. He almost let out a whimper when Koan asked him to wait.

With a frustrated sigh, Jayden looked back at the three.

"People I know are working on it but it's slow going. The only thing we can currently say is to take a walk through the forest and see what's happening in there when your knee allows it," Koan advised.

"Why can't any of you tell me now?" Jayden asked.

"The current government doesn't want to announce anything until they have solid answers to the inevitable questions. As Iris and I are a part of The Elders, we are sworn to silence as to what's going on," Cora explained.

"But —"

"Go into the forest and you'll understand," Koan emphasized.

Jayden rolled his eyes.

As Koan helped him to his room, they walked past Leeran and Taylin who were engaged in hushed whispers by the door. They stopped talking when they realized they had an audience and told him to go to bed.

"Change into a pair of shorts so I can help put your knee brace on," Koan instructed.

He nodded and did as told with Koan's help. While he sat on the bed, Koan strapped Jayden's knee and retrieved some painkillers.

"I'm not going to be able to get back to sleep," Jayden muttered.

"I know but you need to rest that knee of yours," Koan said.

"In a moment," he sighed.

He eased himself off the bed and limped to the bathroom. As he washed and dried his face, he kept his gaze down. Every time he had a chance to see his reflection, he had shied away, scared of what might be looking back at him. It hadn't been all that difficult to do when he could barely stand or leave the bed.

Taking a deep breath, he raised his eyes and stared into the mirror. He didn't know what he had been expecting but what he saw was how he remembered himself to be. His skin was still pale, though he had dark circles under his eyes. His black hair was still a mess and sticking out at odd angles from sleep, but it was longer and draped in front of his dark eyes.

He still looked like his tired sixteen year old self.

Jayden blinked and frowned. Almost nine years had passed so by his calculations, he should be twenty-four years old.

It made him wonder whether or not what ever happened to him in the nine years since he went missing had caused his time to freeze.

"Koan, what date is it?" Jayden asked as he limped back into his bedroom.

Koan was no longer in his room.

Jayden contemplated what to do. He had so many questions and barely any idea were to go to find answers. However, the way his knee was going, he wouldn't be walking out of the house unassisted tonight.

Giving up for the evening, he settled down in bed with pillows propping his knee and stared at the ceiling. When he grew bored of that, Jayden pulled over the history book he had been reading.

- Chapter Four -

"Koan, how far is The Balgaire from here?"

Koan stopped plating up breakfast to look over to him.

"Good morning to you, too," Koan greeted. "You'd have to walk half an hour to get there unless a Teleportation Ward is used."

Jayden glanced down at his wrapped knee. He was not ready for a walk that long.

"Looking for a meal out?" Koan asked.

"No. Balthezier and Roderick are there and I wanted to catch up with them since they haven't visited," Jayden explained.

"Have you tried calling them?" Koan suggested.

"Don't have a phone and even if I did, I don't know their numbers," Jayden pointed out.

Koan glanced to the door with a frown. "They didn't …"

Jayden tilted his head, wondering what was going on.

"I'll get you a phone, don't worry about that," Koan eventually said.

"I can get it. It's fine," Jayden objected. "I just want to get out for a bit and see other people."

Koan held up a finger and peeked out through the door, making sure no one else was around. When he was satisfied with what he saw, Koan came back and quickly put together an egg toasted sandwich, shoved it in a bag and pulled out a small bottle of juice. Jayden watched on in confusion, which grew even further when Koan bagged both with some painkillers and handed it over.

"Breakfast and dinner are a must but only on the insistence of Leeran and Taylin. I thought a takeout breakfast would be best for today so that you can walk through the forest. If you want to go see the city, just head west to go out of the forest," Koan instructed.

Jayden stood still, blinking as he soaked in what Koan had said. Slowly, a grateful smile grew.

"Thank you."

Koan fished out a wallet and phone from his pocket and held them out to him.

"Take these. The phone is mine so if you need help getting back, just call either of your grandparents to get in touch with me," Koan explained.

"I can't take either of these," he objected.

"I'll be here all day. If anyone calls, just let it go to voicemail and I'll worry about it later. The wallet is yours with a card to access family funds and an ID. There's a piece of paper inside with the bank card pin number. Your grandparents had organized all of this but it took a bit for everything to arrive without raising suspicion," Koan added.

Seeing his hesitation, Koan opened the wallet and showed him the cards.

"See?"

He read the name on both of them and couldn't believe it.

"Jayden Lugian …" he read aloud.

He was overwhelmed and full of emotion. He hadn't thought that he'd ever see the Lugian name tucked in behind his first name again, not if Leeran and Taylin had any say in the matter.

"How was all this done?"

"Go. Have a morning off from this madhouse and make sure you go through the forest," Koan insisted.

The butler ushered him out through the side door in the kitchen.

"You're not really a butler are you?" Jayden asked.

"What makes you say that?" Koan replied.

Jayden shrugged. "Just a hunch."

Koan chuckled and shooed Jayden away. "Go."

Jayden studied the man for a second longer before slowly walking into the forest. With trees surrounding him, he glanced back at the mansion.

He didn't know who Koan was beyond the talks they'd had but Jayden was already sensing there was something more beyond what the man presented to them.

Turning his attention back to the forest, he headed further in, taking in every sound and stopping every now and then to take in the sights around him. It reminded him of the forest back on the Anchor.

Thinking of the Anchor caused him to stop walking. Would anyone have visited Babyloneous while he had been gone? Had anyone looked for Kalarney? Did anyone else know or care that she was missing? Where was Dusk?

The only one who would have those answers would be Balthezier, and after the first week of being hospitalized, Jayden hadn't seen nor heard from the man.

He walked until he came across a fallen tree where he took a seat and hungrily dug into the toasted egg sandwich.

Halfway through his food, something caught his attention. He bagged the rest of the sandwich and approached cautiously. To his surprise, he had found a cliff's edge. When he looked down, a wave of vertigo sent him staggering back. Swimming below was the same river of blue and green light that haunted his nightmares.

He glanced left to right and walked in each direction of the fallen tree he had taken a seat on. He had found the edge of Szantium. Is that what Koan had wanted him to see?

Almost as if to answer his question, the ground shook and to his horror, he saw the edge crumble away.

"What the …" Jayden murmured.

This was troubling. This was *very* troubling.

Jayden turned away from the disappearing edge and headed in what he hoped was the direction of the city.

Along the way, he needed to stop and take the supplied painkillers. He spent a few minutes resting in a bid to stop the pain from worsening before he continued on his way.

There was a bustle of activity in the streets of the city. People were making their way to work, appointments, early classes, or completing a bit of shopping. No one seemed concerned at all about what was happening.

Biting his bottom lip, he wandered a little, trying to figure out where to go.

"Jayden!"

He tensed at the voice. He glanced around, trying to find a way to hide but Taylin was pushing through the crowd towards him with a smile and he knew there was no escape.

"There you are! Walk with me, son. There are a few things that I need to explain before your meeting with The Elders this morning," Taylin said.

"What meeting and with who?" Jayden asked.

Taylin ignored his question and gestured for them to get moving. Jayden tried to hide how much pain he was in as he walked with Taylin but he couldn't stop the increasing limp. He hoped that wherever Taylin was leading him, it wasn't too far.

"In almost nine years, a lot has changed. Without the Council of 8 holding us back, we were able to progress and catch up with humans in terms of technology and the overall quality of life in the city. Szantium owes you a lot for what you did."

Taylin stopped in front of a large stone pillar and frowned as he stared at it.

"The memorial was erected for those lost in the battles against the Council of 8. They will never be forgotten."

The stone was a clear bright blue on the surface that deepened in color towards the core. Names and symbols had been carved out across the stone. When he brushed a hand over a name, a face appeared and smiled at him. Jayden stepped back in shock and the hologram disappeared. Gray stone surrounded the memorial with different symbols for 'Rest', 'Calm', and 'Home' written across the surface.

Jayden wondered if his name was somewhere on the blue stone.

"Not long after everything happened, a temporary government made up of the elderly women from each of the remaining Original 8 families was put in place while we worked on creating something more permanent. It took quite a few years but now we have a stable government that everyone is happy with."

"Now, as a community, we've decided to keep measures in place to prevent any more Harbinons from being created. New and improved solutions to keep offspring's Abilities from rising too high are currently being tested with willing expecting parents. However, if another Harbinon is born, we will treat them like a Level Eight and not in the barbaric way you were briefly exposed to."

It was good to know that Szaephians had rebuilt their society from the ground up in order to accommodate fairer ruling, promote progress, and accept those who are different.

Squealing laughter caught his attention. A young boy was wrestling and running around with an animal Jayden wasn't familiar with. Every now and then a little girl with the same curly brown hair would waddle over with her arms out, wanting to join in on the fun. However, the boy kept picking her up and taking her back to who he assumed were their parents. Each time he did so, the girl grew more and more upset.

Halfway back to their parents again, the boy stopped and put his squirming sister down and stepped back. He drew something in the air and golden tendrils lazily circled away from his finger until they formed butterflies.

Tears turned into giggles, and the two siblings and their animal companion played around with the golden butterflies.

"If those kids had been born during the reign of the Council of 8, they would have been punished for playing around with Wards like that," Taylin explained. "Even now, people are still trying to remember that they now have the freedom to use their Abilities in a way that makes it unique to them."

Taylin continued to explain the new way Szaephians lived, making it impossible for Jayden to say anything.

"Jayden?"

He looked over to the man and wondered if he had missed any instruction or question.

"The Elders are inside. From here, you'll go in alone but remember not to embarrass yourself or your family, and do not reject anything they request from you. I'll wait out here," Taylin instructed.

Jayden rolled his eyes and stared at the building they had stopped in front of. It was giant stone pantheon, a step away from the modern structures surrounding it. Trees and follower bushes had been planted in the grass lining along the bottom of the raised stone floor leading into the building.

- Chapter Five -

Footsteps echoed around the wide open space. The furniture inside was a row of intricately detailed wooden chairs with royal red cushions. Behind them, the wall had been hollowed out and barricaded with red rope.

Statues of men and women in various poses lined the stone walls in shallow alcoves. Jayden stared up at one of the women holding a spear with battle worn confidence and wondered who she was.

There was a sense of loneliness and emptiness lingering in the building that often came from neglect. However, now there was life seeping into the corners

Shuffling noises reached his ears, and when he glanced around, six elderly women were slowly assisted past the rope barrier by six women in fitted suits and masks. Once five took a seat and Cora was stationed beside Iris, the younger women quickly left. Aside from his two grandparents, he could barely remember who the others were.

Silently, he limped away from the statue and stood before them.

"It is great to finally have this meeting with you, Jayden. I'm Abigail Quiroz. To my left is May Bixlar, Lily Wyka, and June Gaede," Abigail introduced. "And of course, you know Cora and Iris. Welcome to the Temple of 8. This is the place where our leaders have and will find their final rest, a place where the young can learn from them, and where our people can be led."

Abigail Quiroz reminded him of Charly. She had the olive skin, soft brown eyes, and wavy short hair that was mostly silver with some dark streaks through it.

Beside her was May Bixlar, a short woman with a cane beside her chair. Her long, dark gray hair was tied up in a plait that hung over her shoulder. Her dark hair and dark olive skin made her bright green eyes stand out.

Lily Wyka stared at him with a stern look. Her teal eyes didn't hold any warmth and made him feel like he was under a microscope. Her almost white hair was cut into a bob that sat along her jaw with a slight wave.

June Gaede was an older version of Octavia and Artemis. Her aged grey-blue eyes smiled kindly at him and her face was lined by a light grey fringe and hair that cascaded down her chest. Jayden couldn't help but smile and he wanted to talk to her to see how Octavia and Artemis were doing.

All of the women were wearing blue and green robes edged in silver with giant hoods lining their shoulders and the back of their necks.

"We wanted to thank you for sacrificing yourself for our freedom and the safety of the humans," Iris said.

Jayden frowned. "All I wanted to do was to protect my family and friends."

"And yet you accomplished so much more. Is there anything that you wish for?" Cora asked.

He shook his head. There was nothing he wanted that anyone could ever give him.

"Surely there is something?" she pushed.

When they received nothing in response, the six women spared a moment to glance at each other and the air around them changed.

"Jayden, you have shown us what great potential you carry but also what dangers lurk within your heart. We ask for one thing and in return, you will be given a place amongst the First Circle," May said.

"The what? I don't want —"

"Child, we are old. There is only so much sway we have now and the new government will not wait much longer for our final say," Abigail explained.

"Find someone else," Jayden huffed.

June smiled gently. "You're smart and observant so I imagine by now that you've noticed our land is shrinking. The new government needs to lead our people into the warmth of the real sun again. You were raised by humans so you have experience in knowing what they do and do not fear.”

“There are Szaephians living in the Human Plane. They should know as well,” Jayden pointed out, annoyed.

“Just because we live amongst them and protect them from our world, it doesn’t mean we understand them,” Lily rebutted.

He scrunched his fists tightly and clenched his jaw. He didn’t like this, and he had a niggling feeling that they weren’t telling him everything. The last thing he wanted or needed was to be someone’s puppet. He’d be having words with Cora and Iris back at home about it all.

“Training will begin in two days. You are required to show the Examiners what your skill level is and from there, they will determine what lessons to start you with. This is our gift to you,” Lily instructed.

He glared at The Elders. Didn’t anyone listen to him? Cora and Iris knew he was against going to any school Szantium had to offer.

“I don’t want any part of this! You should be more concerned about Szantium disappearing,” Jayden snapped.

“The decision is final,” Lily declared. “Report to the Examiners or face the consequences.”

Growling in frustration, he stormed out of the building.

“Jayden?” Taylin called out.

“Leave me alone!”

“Jayden Laiyfe-Rain, stop and talk to me,” growled Taylin.

Jayden’s step faltered and his fists shook.

“That’s not my name,” Jayden snapped as he continued on.

Balthezier was waiting for him when Jayden limped away from the group he had arrived with on the train platform in the Human Plane. Jayden took a few seconds to glance over his friend before walking off without a word. He pocketed his hands as he took the escalator up to the concourse and made his way out of the station.

Humans ignored the small crowd coming up from the platform barricaded off with the construction tape. It amazed him how often regular people ignored the ways the Szaephian world bled into theirs.

“Hello to you, too, Jay. How have you been? I’ve been okay, thanks. I see you’ve taken advantage of the transport docks they set up instead of using your own Abilities. What have I been doing all this time you ask? Well, my dear friend, for the last, oh nine years, I have been going about the seemingly impossible task of trying to find Kalarney," Balthezier said sarcastically.

Jayden stopped in his tracks and stared at him with wide eyes.

Balthezier now wore his sandy blond hair in a small ponytail but the sides and back were still shaved. He wore three-quarter cargos that ended with cuffs around his calves, worn black boots, and a brown shirt with a thick looking black parka. His skin was slightly darker, but he still had the same playful smile, dark blue eyes, and calming air around him.

Balthezier smirked and said, "That got your attention, huh?"

"Have you found her?" Jayden asked.

Balthezier grimaced, shaking his head. "I can't even find any hints of where she might've been."

He sighed and nodded.

"I'll help," Jayden volunteered.

"No. I've got it. You have training to attend to soon," Balthezier said, clapping him on the back.

"How do you know that?"

Balthezier tapped his nose with a twinkle in his eye. "I know a lot of things."

"I'm not doing it," Jayden rolled his eyes.

"Jay —-"

"No," he interrupted. "I need answers to too many questions and I don't want to use my Abilities."

"Okay, here's what's going to happen. You *are* going to attend training. You *are* going to show the Examiners what skill level you're currently at, and you *are* going to shut up about it. Only idiots refuse training," Balthezier growled.

"But —-"

"I've got a few contacts keeping an eye out. If I hear anything then I'll come find you and we look into it together. But until then, stop fighting us at every opportunity. We're only trying to help," Balthezier interrupted.

"An eye out for what? You've never even met Kalarney."

"No, but you did send me a picture of her nine years ago. Though my phone was destroyed in the fight against the Council of 8 so that didn't matter. However, unlike someone I know, I use my Abilities. The earth on the Anchor carried memories of her so I was able to use it to get an image.

You can't get out of training. I won't let you waste this chance," Balthezier answered.

The teasing and lightheartedness Balthezier usually presented was gone. He was completely serious.

Jayden didn't want to fight with his friend on the matter anymore so instead, he sighed and said, "You need to catch me up on everything that's happened and answer my questions."

Wrapping an arm around Jayden's shoulders, Balthezier led him down the street with a smirk.

Coming out of his room in the early morning, he was barely surprised to see Balthezier inviting himself into the mansion.

"Morning, sunshine," Balthezier greeted with a huge smile.

Unable to muster anything more than a tired eye roll, Jayden continued on towards the kitchen. Koan greeted him as he walked past on the way to the dining table full with plates of food. He snagged a piece of toast and made his way to the front door.

"What about breakfast?" Balthezier asked, pouting.

Jayden waved the piece of toast around and slipped into a jacket.

"Breakfast, Jayden! I need breakfast and you need to learn how to eat better. We're sitting down and having a proper meal," Balthezier told him.

Ignoring his friend, he continued to try to slip outside unnoticed by any of the Laiyfe-Rain's.

"Hello, Balthezier. Breakfast is ready. Jayden, you know the rules. You've already skipped a family meal this week so don't you dare think about doing that again," Leeran warned.

He hunched his shoulders and held back the torrent he wanted to unleash. Hands steered him away from the door and back to the dining room table.

Before he could get another piece of toast, Balthezier slapped his hand away and stared heaping food on to two plates.

"Liz," Jayden warned.

Balthezier smirked as he handed over the packed plate.

"Finish that," the blond ordered.

He eyed the plate with disdain. It had been a while since he had eaten a large amount of food. The last time would have been with the Lugians.

Normally, he'd make sure to have as little as possible on his plate in the morning so that he wouldn't have to stick around the table for long.

Thankfully, Koan replaced the heaping plate with a piece of toast covered with an egg and slice of bacon.

"Thanks," Jayden said and smiled gratefully.

"Excuse me, and who are you?" Balthezier asked, raising an eyebrow.

"Koan Omb."

"That's just the butler. Ignore him, Balthezier. He's been favoring Jayden a little too much," Leeran sneered.

"Well, nothing wrong with that. Jay is new to our world and anyone willing to be his friend and help him out is okay in my book," Balthezier countered with a shrug.

Jayden glanced between Koan and Balthezier. The two were staring at each other. There was something between them that he couldn't quite read or understand.

"Do we know each other?" Balthezier asked.

"No. Enjoy your breakfast," Koan said and went back into the kitchen.

He was tempted to follow Koan and keep him company for breakfast but he knew Leeran and Taylin were keeping an eye on him.

"Jay, eat. We need to go soon," Balthezier urged.

He nodded and focused on eating his breakfast.

"It's good to hear that you're finally getting some much needed training," Taylin noted.

He hummed, tired of having the same argument.

"Jay, before you go, Iris and I would like to speak with you. We've gotten you a new knee brace that should make training easier while ensuring your knee has the optimal support," Cora said.

Jayden glanced over to his grandmothers and nodded. He hadn't spoken to them since the meeting with The Elders. The whole affair had left him thinking that maybe they weren't as understanding as he had been led to believe.

"Mom, Jay needs to focus and go to school. You two can talk to him afterwards," Leeran objected.

"It's Jayden," he corrected.

Cora waved her hand, dismissing Leeran's words. "Nonsense. Jay can spare a few moments while he puts on the knee brace."

"You're not going to correct Cora, *Jay*?" Mackenzie asked.

"No," Jayden answered.

"Why not?" Mackenzie pushed.

He contemplated whether or not he should keep silent but he was exhausted and not in a patient mood.

"You killed my entire family, and Leeran and Taylin refuse to listen to me and like to pretend the Lugian's never existed," Jayden explained.

"I've been making up for it every day and I've been trying to show you. You've done nothing but be antagonistic towards us since you've been back. Our grandparents and Koan coddle you and let you get away with a lot. You can't keep treating us like the enemy when we're not," Mackenzie argued.

Before Jayden could release his anger, Cora took his hand and squeezed it.

He knew then that he shouldn't have taken the bait. His grandparents had requested that he'd remain civil until he was able to leave and he just shoved that request in the bin. All he was doing was creating problems.

"Mackenzie, Leeran, and Taylin — you three need to leave or you'll be late," Aster spoke up.

His tone didn't leave any room for argument.

The three quickly finished their breakfast and left the dining room, shooting glares sharp as daggers at Jayden.

He slumped in his seat and sighed. Just once he would like to have a meal without being targeted for something.

"I'm sorry," Jayden said. "I didn't mean to bring all that up but Mackenzie …"

"I take it that's been building up all this time?" Balthezier asked.

Jayden nodded. "I'm sorry."

"It may have been unreasonable for us to have asked you to be civil when they keep pushing and baiting you," Valent apologized.

"No. It was completely reasonable. I tried, but they keep forgetting what happened nine years ago for them, is my yesterday," Jayden said.

Iris checked her watched and grimaced. "You don't have much time before they expect you at the training grounds. Cora and I wanted to apologize for what happened the other day. We were both outnumbered in the decision and didn't have time to forewarn you."

He looked between the two elderly women and nodded, regretting previous thoughts he'd had about the whole situation.

"It's fine. I should've expected that living with everyone would mean I would need to show I can remain in control," Jayden said in defeat.

Cora took out a small box from a pocket on the side of the wheelchair and slid it in front of him.

"It's one of the latest phones. Our numbers and Koan's have all been added already for your convenience. And here's the new knee brace. Go put on some shorts and the new brace, then run along," Cora instructed.

"Thank you," Jayden murmured, taking both items.

He quickly changed and slipped the knee brace on, bending his knee a few times to get a feel of how it moved, and met Balthezier by the front door.

His friend clapped him on the shoulder and they left the mansion.

The walk down the street was silent and Jayden barely paid attention to their surroundings. Thoughts tossed and turned, not one lingering long enough for him to focus on. His hands absently fiddled with the new phone he had slipped in his jacket pocket.

"What's going on in that head of yours?" Balthezier asked.

"Do you know Jimin Park is?" Jayden asked.

There was a moment of hesitation before Balthezier answered, "Nope. Why?"

"I … Do you know where I was all that time?" Jayden chose to ask instead.

"No one's explained it to you?" Balthezier asked.

Jayden shook his head. "They were more concerned about me healing."

"Well, when you and the remaining Council members clashed at the end, it caused a rip to appear from the sky to the ground, showing the In Between. I assumed that's where you were dragged into since you were nowhere to be seen," Balthezier explained.

"Is that why I still look sixteen?" Jayden asked.

"That's a good question," Balthezier noted. "I'm not sure. We can check with dad."

Jayden licked his bottom lip nervously at the mention of Roderick.

"Do you think … I can live at The Balgaire?" Jayden asked. "I wanted to try and get to know Leeran and Taylin better but …"

"What happened at breakfast isn't the first time things have blown up like that?" Balthezier asked.

"No. They push and push my patience and refuse to understand where I'm coming from every single day. I can never forgive Mackenzie for what he did, no matter how many times he insists he's been trying to make up for it. He still murdered my family."

"Well," Balthezier said. "You technically still have a room there and I'm sure dad wouldn't mind having you stay with us again. You could work to earn your keep and have spending money. We can help you get your GED and help with your Szaephian training."

It was a much better option compared to what he currently had.

"My GED?" Jayden frowned.

"I did get that right, right?" Balthezier checked.

"Yes, but how did you know about it?" Jayden asked.

Balthezier shrugged. "I completed mine a few years ago out of boredom. I decided to experience more of the human world that you loved so much."

He stared at his friend in amazement before ducking his head with a smile and small blush.

- **Chapter Six -**

Sensing followers behind them caused Jayden to tense up. Were these people friend or foe? Did they mean to attack or pass them by? The possibilities of what could or would happen ran through his head and he clenched his fists.

"Looks like you'll have an audience," Balthezier remarked.

Jayden sighed in annoyance and murmured, "Great."

He ran a hand down his face. He needed to stop overthinking everything.

"Get used to it, buddy. They're the ones The Elders want you to be in the First Circle with."

"How do you know all this? What's the First Circle?"

"I told you — I know things," Balthezier smirked.

He rolled his eyes and chuckled under his breath.

"The government is broken up into eight different levels they call 'Circles'. The First Circle consists of our generation of the Original 8 families. The Second Circle are a bunch of nominated nobles with sticks up their butts. The Third Circle is for the Academics, who value information and are a rather secretive bunch so no one outside of their group know much about them. The Fourth is for the Hunters who take care of Shadows. The Fifth is for the medics. The Sixth is for teachers and trainers. The Seventh Circle is for a union called Architects, who are comprised of traders, bakers, mechanics, and such. And finally, the Eighth Circle is dedicated to the lower to middle classes who aren't represented in the Seventh Circle," Balthezier explained. "Everyone gets a say now."

Jayden was rather impressed with how inclusive the new government was. It was a step up from having a government of just eight, power hungry people.

"I don't want to govern anything with anyone," Jayden huffed.

"Too bad. The tribe has spoken," Balthezier told him, clapping him on the shoulder.

"The tribe sucks," Jayden grunted.

Mackenzie was amongst the milling crowd, sitting on a stone garden hedge in mid-conversation with someone Jayden didn't recognize. Those following eventually passed by and a guy with hair dyed ash white that faded to a dark gray-red along the ends, dressed in fitted dark jeans, a dark blue shirt, and a gray jacket threw him an unimpressed look.

There were too many people waiting around and watching for Jayden to be comfortable with.

"Crap," Balthezier muttered. "Your Examiners are Heran and Tahnee, and they're not known for their leniency or patience."

"Your confidence in this is overwhelming," Jayden commented dryly.

Balthezier laughed and shoved him aside playfully. Before he could retaliate, a brunette man in a button up maroon tunic and dark pants tucked into calf length boots cleared his throat and everyone fell silent.

"Thank you for finally joining us. We are your Examiners. This is Examiner Tahnee and I am Examiner Heran. For the next few hours you will undergo a series of trials to test your Abilities and fighting capabilities."

"I still have healing injuries," Jayden told them, gesturing to his knee.

The woman beside Heran narrowed her eyes at Jayden. He shifted nervously. She had her mousy blonde hair tied back in a tight ponytail and wore clothing similar to Heran, however her tunic was a dark green.

"This time is to test your Abilities, not your physical abilities," Heran said.

Jayden grumbled and murmured, "This is a waste of time."

"What *is* a waste of time, Jayden Laiyfe-Rain, is coming here to test a boy when he should already be more than capable of fulfilling his duties to the community. You were raised by humans and you are a

Harbinon, and in this society, that makes you a liability. It is our job to ensure you receive the correct training, and *maybe* there will be hope for you," snapped Heran.

By the end of the degrading speech, his hands ached from nails digging in harshly as he tried to keep his expression as neutral as possible. He didn't want them to know how much those words got to him.

It appeared the Examiners had already made a decision about him and no matter what he would do, that decision wouldn't change.

"In the arena," Tahnee instructed.

Jayden gave Balthezier his new phone and silently went through the door Tahnee indicated. A permanent stench of musty sweat wafted in the air that no amount of cleaning would ever be able to save the hallway from.

Rows of seats encircled the arena. The ground was packed tightly with light brown gravel along the fence line and green grass in the middle. On the other end was another entryway and he could make out people moving in and out of view, indicating there was more to the arena then initially seen.

The crowd took a seat in the stands and the two Examiners stood in the center of the field, waiting with two large black boxes rattling behind them.

He approached with caution.

"Inside these boxes are Shadows of various levels. They will be your opponents in the second half of the examination. For now, we need to make sure you are even able to handle a Level One Shadow," Heran explained.

Tahnee stepped forward. "For now, I am your opponent. Attack and deflect."

The woman barely wasted a second before she sent a wave of vines towards him. Jayden didn't have time to react. A vine wrapped around his ankle and flung him away. The air was knocked out of him as his body crashed into the arena's fence.

All he had time to do was shake his head clear before clambering back to his feet.

Each time an attack came, he only focused on dodging. As every chance to attack passed and he only ran or used his arms to defend himself, the Examiners grew more and more frustrated.

By the time Tahnee stopped, he was dripping with sweat, panting heavily, and covered in red marks and cuts. His knee throbbed and he knew he was going to have trouble with it if they didn't stop this nonsense now.

"The goal of this is to determine where you are lacking with your control and knowledge in regards to your Abilities. There is no room for refusal!" Heran shouted.

"My knee —-"

"Keep going," Heran interrupted.

Tahnee kept going after him until he couldn't get back on to his feet. His knee refused to support his weight.

"Enough! Leave," Heran demanded.

Jayden wiped sweat from his forehead and used the arena's wall to help ease himself back on to his feet. The first step towards the exit caused him to sway from dizziness and overwhelming agony but he forced himself to keep going.

"Wait up!" Balthezier shouted, jogging up to him. "What the hell are you thinking?"

With a sigh, he sat down on the bench outside of the arena, stretching out his leg.

"I told you that I didn't want any part of this," Jayden said.

"And I told you to take this chance to learn, you idiot. You have a chance to actually learn something from qualified teachers instead of winging things on the fly, and you're blowing it up!" Balthezier growled. "I thought you were going to give this a shot."

Jayden looked away. Yes, he understood his position and he reluctantly agreed to go along with everything but for whatever reason, when the time came, he couldn't do it.

"I —-"

"Ladies and gentleman, the Laiyfe-Rain legacy —- one mass murderer pointlessly seeking redemption, and someone as useless as a Ricornon."

The same guy who had followed him to the arena stood there with his arms crossed over his chest. There were a few sniggering guys hanging behind him, all dressed as lavishly as their leader.

Jayden rolled his eyes. He knew that if Kalarney were here, she'd show everyone just how useless a Ricornon was until they cried for mercy.

"Jayden and any Ricornon are ten times more useful than you'll ever be, Reid," Balthezier bit back.

Amongst the group of people milling around, a young brunette woman caught his attention and had him standing up and limping around the two arguing men.

"Artemis?" Jayden asked, waving to her.

Artemis smiled widely and hugged him tightly.

Before he could figure out how to ask how she'd been, Balthezier wrapped his arms around both of their shoulders.

"I think it's time for some good café styled food," Balthezier declared as he awkwardly moved his hands around in order to sign to her.

Jayden glanced back at Reid. The young man was clawing at his throat as he silently screamed.

Frowning, he looked to his friend for an explanation, who only smirked and winked.

- Chapter Seven -

The move to The Balgaire was met with a lot of resistance from Leeran and Taylin. He tried to explain they hadn't made him feel welcomed and maybe the space would be good for them. They'd be able to slowly get to know each other and figure things out as they came. However, that only caused Mackenzie to blow up as well. Jayden was labeled as selfish and the only one who hadn't been making an effort already.

Thankfully, Roderick pushed his way through to collect Jayden's meager belongings out of the mansion with the help of Koan.

"Consider this your last act as butler in this house," Taylin said.

"You have no say in his employment, Taylin," Valent growled.

"Dad, Koan has been brainwashing our child into thinking we're not suitable parents. Jayden needs to live with us," Taylin argued.

Jayden raised his eyebrows in disbelief. Where had that idea come from?

Valent glared at his son and blocked Jayden from Taylin's view.

"Enough! Jayden is not your child. You and Leeran gave up those rights when he was an infant. He has been patient enough with the both of you and neither of you have given him time to adjust. Right now, Roderick and Balthezier are more of a family to him than any of us," Valent boomed.

"Don't you think it's about time you two moved out as well?" Aster added.

"Dad, this is our home and he's our son," Leeran moaned.

"Jay?"

He glanced down as Cora reached out to take his hands.

"I'm okay," he told her.

Cora gave him a knowing look and squeezed his hands reassuringly.

"Do stay in touch," she requested.

"I will," Jayden agreed.

He hugged his grandparents and stood back with a bag slung over his shoulders.

"Thanks for your help," Jayden said.

"You're our grandson. We'll always help. Make sure to let us know if there's anything you need," Iris requested.

With a smile, he nodded.

While Balthezier dragged him around with an arm slung over his shoulders, Koan and Roderick carried what little belongings he had, as well as a few things his grandparents had gotten him for the move.

At The Balgaire, Roderick showed them upstairs to a room. It had a single bed in the middle of the room with two bedside tables, a desk against one wall, a single wardrobe, a chest of drawers, and a small cushioned nook by the window.

"Thank you, Roderick," Jayden said.

"Not a problem, kiddo. It's good to have you back. Get settled in and come downstairs for something to eat," Roderick instructed.

Roderick pulled his son out of the room, leaving Jayden and Koan alone.

"Thanks for helping me, Koan," Jayden said. "Sorry about … well everything."

"No need to be sorry. I packed a couple of books that may interest you. Some will help you with the theory side of your studies. Do contact me if you need help with anything," Koan told him.

He opened his mouth to say something but he couldn't think of anything. Instead, he stood there silently as Koan squeezed his shoulder before he walked out. Alone, Jayden turned back to the boxes and bags, and focused on sorting through his things.

Jayden closed his book with a frown. There was something niggling at him, something he couldn't remember if he had asked before but knew he should have.

"Why the number eight?" Jayden asked Roderick as he walked past.

The older man glanced at him with a confused frown before continuing on to the table he had been serving drinks to.

"Give me five minutes. Someone is slacking off on their shift," Roderick grunted.

Both Jayden and Roderick turned to look at Balthezier leaning against the counter, deep in conversation with a black haired woman dressed in denim overalls, a baggy white shirt underneath, a red flannel shirt tied around her waist, and black and white shoes.

He couldn't help but be curious about who Balthezier was talking to. A strange power faintly radiating from her tugged on his mind. It was distracting.

"Always slacking off," Roderick huffed. "Balthezier! Get us some drinks and pay more attention to the rest of our customers. It's nice to see you again, Jet."

"Plain water, coming right up," Balthezier shouted back.

Jet raised a hand to wave to Roderick but hesitated when she caught Jayden staring. There was a knowing twinkle in those brown eyes and he couldn't help but sit up straighter.

He wanted to go after her. He wanted to ask what was drawing him to her. He got as far as standing up from his seat.

"It's not just a number," Roderick said.

Jayden snapped his attention over to the man, startled. He had forgotten Roderick was there.

"What?" he asked dumbly.

His attention wandered back to Jet. She stopped by the door and stared at him for a few more seconds. She turned back to Balthezier and said something Jayden couldn't hear and finally left The Balgaire.

"Are you going to listen or can I go back to my customers?" Roderick huffed.

"What? Right, yes. Sorry," Jayden stammered.

"The eight is not just a number," Roderick repeated. "It's the motion. No matter which way it travels, it'll always be continuous."

"It's an infinity thing?" Jayden asked.

"No. Well, yes, but think more *yin-yang*. It's balance."

"What do you mean? What does it extend to?" Jayden asked.

"Everything, including our fair city. There are eight Compass Points to protect Szantium, eight leading families, eight levels of Abilities, etc. What's with all the questions that could have been answered if you hadn't skipped school? Again," Roderick said.

Jayden frowned and dismissed the mention of school.

"But there are more than eight levels of Abilities. There's Ricornon and Harbinon," he pointed out.

"Don't take this the wrong way, but they weren't classified as Ability levels. They were more of a subspecies of Szaephian," Roderick clarified.

Jayden rolled his eyes.

"Let's go back to your trainers. Come on," Balthezier said, sliding in on the seat next to him.

"I'll pass, thanks. I need to go see my grandparents and I wanted to have a look in the library today," Jayden said.

"Tough luck," Balthezier argued. "You're going. Someone has to stop you from being an idiot."

Balthezier pulled him to his feet and nudged him out to the streets of the city.

The reasons why he kept skipping training no longer boiled down to not wanting to go or not wanting to use his Abilities. His body ached and his mind was constantly on edge from dizziness. The days he did go, he kept refusing to use his Abilities and his trainers pushed harder and harder to get him to cooperate.

When they finally arrived, another class was in the process of leaving the training grounds and his trainers were busy with chatting to someone near the other door.

He spotted Artemis, Mackenzie, and a few others waiting in the stands. Artemis waved a little when she caught his attention and he waved back. He watched as Balthezier took a seat with her. There was a pang of wanting to be there with them instead of being the one to provide everyone's entertainment.

"It's nice of you to show up."

Keith Brennan and Seeley Mason were reasonable and patient trainers. However, Jayden tested their patience every time he refused to use his Abilities or show up. He thoroughly enjoyed the theory lessons with them and both men took as much time as he needed to understand what they were teaching. They would recommend books for him to read and encouraged his questions. The fact that the three of them got along as teacher and student made him feel guilty for being uncooperative the rest of the time.

"Today you'll have a sparring partner. His main objective will be to force you into showcasing something for our guests today –– Examiners Heran and Tahnee. We would *appreciate* it if you would stop wasting our time and do as instructed. Begin," Seeley informed Jayden.

There was barely a second between the trainer's instructions and Reid darting in close to him with a fist full of black electricity. He barely managed to stumble away and avoid any serious injury.

Reid didn't waste a single moment. He twisted around and went after Jayden.

He ran the length of the field, weaving around in a bid to avoid being hit. The air heated up from the electrical attack.

It didn't take long for exhaustion and dizziness to slow him down. His body worked against him every second he pushed it to move. However, Reid was becoming more and more destructive. The guy was determined to force Jayden into a position where he had no choice but to use his Abilities and he was enjoying it.

A blast of wind slammed against his arm, causing him to propel forward and trip.

Jayden rolled on to his back and groaned. Sitting up caused him to hiss in pain. His arm felt like it was on fire and when he tried to move it, the pain blew up to unbearable levels.

Using his other arm, he hoisted himself back to his feet. He could barely touch his arm without the pain worsening.

Jayden clenched his teeth and growled.

When he looked up from his arm, Reid was nowhere to be seen. He frantically looked around until he saw Balthezier on his feet, shouting and pointing above him.

Reid was bearing down on him with a sword covered in red and black electricity. He was trapped. All he could do was use his Abilities to create a shield over his head. As the sword slammed against the force field, a large explosion sent Reid hurtling into the stands and caved the ground beneath his feet.

The ground rippled and power slammed into the fence line. Seating was ripped up and the audience, Examiners, and trainers had to raise shields to protect themselves. The thick walls enclosing the arena shook and groaned with the pressure before cracking in multiple places.

When the dust settled, white static bounced off and arched around Jayden. He stood with his head down and body loose. Thoughts were a mess and he couldn't move.

"Jayden?"

Blood dripped from his nose as he slowly looked up. He couldn't recognize anyone in front of him. Faces blurred and voices became background noise.

"Give them our gift, Jayden."

He could see the power building around him. The air became heavy with it and the ground trembled.

"Stop him!"

"Wait, don't attack!"

A man with ash white and red hair threw himself at Jayden. The power coming off the man was laughable and when it tried to touch him, it was no more than an annoying itch. While he was preoccupied, another power source attempted to sneak up behind him. Jayden didn't even need to take his eyes away from the man in front of him in order to deal with the new playmate.

Whoever was behind him, was sent hurtling back into the stands.

Jayden laughed in glee. This was too much fun.

The arena erupted in a soft green light. He glanced around, confused. There were wispy lights floating upwards all around them and a soothing warmth spread through the air.

His Abilities were reined in and he was left disorientated and drained.

The world around him exploded in panicked sound. He couldn't understand what he was seeing or hearing. The training grounds had been shredding. People were staring at him with a mixture of fear and caution. He had become a threat.

However, he barely had a chance to understand what was going on before his head jerked forward from a coughing fit and blood spattered past his lips.

- Chapter Eight -

Jayden stared up at the ceiling and sighed into the breathing mask strapped over his mouth and nose. He had been dragged to the hospital and whisked away by doctors. They had cleaned him and tried to ease him through the panic. Their attempts barely had any effect, and in the end, a nurse used a Calming Ward on him and coaxed Jayden into slowing his breathing down.

With him calm, relaxed, and barely able to keep his eyes open, a doctor was finally able to get whatever tests and scans they wanted completed.

After he was left alone, all he had the energy for was to stare listlessly at the ceiling.

"Hey, you okay?"

He shifted his gaze at the sound of Balthezier's voice. Artemis, Leeran, Taylin, and Mackenzie were all crowding around his bed with his blond friend.

"Peachy. Can I go home now?" Jayden asked, taking off the breathing mask.

"Not until the doctors come back with your test results," Leeran answered.

He growled in tired annoyance. They were all wasting their time. Everything was happening because his Abilities were acting out from lack of use. There was also the chance the In Between had some sort of influence after spending so much time inside of it. Any number of reasons could explain what had happened.

Sick and tired of laying around, he tried to get out of bed.

"What do you think you're doing? You're not leaving until we get those test results," Balthezier growled. "Apart from healing injuries, you've been healthy and fine since you got out of the hospital so don't tell me you lost control and coughed up blood because of exertion."

Jayden rolled his eyes. "How would you know? You left while I was stuck in here the first time so don't talk to me about how I've been. Reid could have hit any number of spots to have caused this. He did break my arm."

"You know exactly why I was gone! And you know why using Reid as an excuse doesn't add up? Because when the doctor initially looked you over, he couldn't find anything wrong. Even your arm had healed by the time I got you here," Balthezier shouted. "Now. Lay. Back. Down!"

Jayden huffed and still chose to keep trying to leave until Doctor Gray stepped into the room, alarmed, with another doctor currently tapping away at a tablet.

"What's going on in here?" Doctor Gray asked.

"I'm leaving," Jayden stated.

The doctor raised an eyebrow. "No, you're not. Not without us speaking to you first. Anyone who isn't Jayden or a doctor, please leave."

Balthezier and Artemis left with a concerned glance back at him. Leeran, Taylin, and Mackenzie, however, stayed.

"I'm not leaving my son," Leeran objected.

"Considering that Mr. Lugian is almost twenty-five years old and has not listed any of the Laiyfe-Rain's as emergency contacts, none of you are entitled to participate in this conversation," the other doctor said as he pocketed his device.

"Jayden is not almost twenty-five. Look at him! He's still a teenager and any emergency contact he would have is dead," Taylin argued.

"Actually, the Adlers have been listed. If you don't leave now, you will be forced to leave," the doctor said curtly.

The Laiyfe-Rain's stared at Jayden in disbelief. He blinked and looked at the unknown doctor. He couldn't remember listing anyone as his emergency contact but he was glad the Adlers had been. The last thing he wanted was for Leeran and Taylin to be able to make any more decisions on his behalf.

"Leave," the doctor reiterated.

Mackenzie gave Jayden a look of disappointment before he followed his parents out.

"It's good to see you again, Jayden," Doctor Gray said once they were alone. "This is my colleague, Doctor Misha Turner."

Jayden nodded and watched as Doctor Turner closed the blinds to hide them away from prying eyes.

"How have you been?" Doctor Gray asked.

"Okay, I guess," he shrugged.

"Adjusting well?"

"Most of the time," he answered.

"To be expected. Almost nine years is a long time to be gone. A lot of changes occur in a blink of an eye when you think about it, and the rest of us take it all for granted. Have you been using your Abilities at all since you've been back?" Doctor Turner asked.

He shook his head. "There's been no point."

Doctor Turner combed his fingers through his light brown hair and wrote down notes on his tablet. When he looked up again, Jayden was startled to see curiosity in those green eyes behind a set of glasses. It was unsettling and made him feel like he was a scientist's specimen.

"Do you remember what happened when you came back?" he asked.

Jayden frowned. "What? Um … no. Why?"

Doctor Turner added to his notes instead of answering.

"What about during your training session with Mr. Wyka?"

"Yes, why? What's with these questions?" Jayden asked, turning to Doctor Gray.

"Enlighten us, please," she urged.

"The trainers decided to use Reid as a sparring partner in order to force me to use my Abilities so the Examiners could grade me. At one point, my arm broke and while I was distracted with that, Reid attacked me from above. I didn't have time to do anything else so I threw up a shield. I guess I got it wrong because there was an explosion. Liz said I went out of control and coughed up blood," Jayden explained.

Doctor Turner sighed. "I had instructed them not to say anything to you. Did he say that that we were running tests?"

"Yeah," Jayden nodded.

"We checked your heart and lungs, we even checked to see if there were any scrapes in your mouth. Everything indicated that you are a healthy male. So I ordered blood tests," Doctor Turner explained. "Your Abilities are attacking you on a cellular level and it's causing an unknown illness to spread through your body via your blood."

Jayden blinked at the doctors, unsure if he was hearing correctly. "What?"

"If left unchecked, this could be fatal," Doctor Turner added.

His mouth went dry and his chest constricted. The words were crushing. After everything he had gone through, after all the fighting and the chaos, it was his body that would kill him.

When Doctor Gray grabbed his shoulder, the world snapped back into place.

"Hey, are you okay?" Doctor Gray asked.

He managed a jerky nod.

"Getting the right medication for this will be trial and error," Doctor Turner said.

"In the meantime, I'm presenting your case to a colleague of mine who specializes in the treatment of blood-borne illnesses. She'll help get to the bottom of what we're facing," Doctor Gray said.

Swallowing the lump in his throat, he asked, "What … what are my chances of …"

"At this point in time, we can't say for certain. From what we can see, both problems were caught in the early stages, so theoretically, you have a higher chance of surviving. This, of course, rests on if we can find the appropriate treatment quickly enough. There has never been a case of Abilities attacking the user and there is still so much we don't know about Harbinons. Trust me when I tell you that we will do *everything* in our power to make sure you pull through," Doctor Gray explained.

"If … if it comes to the point where this … whatever this is … is winning, promise me you'll tell me without hesitation. There are some people I'd like to be able to say goodbye to before …" Jayden gradually managed to get out.

Doctor Gray hesitated before nodding.

"Just as long as you promise me that you'll talk to someone who isn't a doctor about this. It's better if you've got support."

"Okay," he agreed.

"See you in a week," Doctor Turner said as he turned and left.

"We *will* fight this," Doctor Gray reassured him before leaving him alone.

Balthezier pushed his way past everyone milling outside and stood in front of him. The others weren't far behind with questioning looks.

"What did they say?" Taylin asked.

"I'm free to go," Jayden replied, pushing past to get to the bag of clothes on the bedside table.

"The test results!" Balthezier exclaimed impatiently.

"Came back as nothing but I've got to come back for another check-up in a week to make sure that everything is still okay," Jayden lied.

"Charlotte wouldn't have told us to leave if it was nothing," Leeran pointed out.

Jayden ignored them as he took off the hospital gown and slipped into normal clothes.

"Jay!" Leeran pushed.

"It's Jayden and drop it!" Jayden growled. "I'm fine and it's none of your damn business what's going on in my life."

"Hey! Stop talking to mom like that. We're your family," Mackenzie butted in.

Without missing a beat, Jayden said, "You killed mine."

Mackenzie flinched and glanced away.

Leeran stepped forward and without warning, slapped Jayden across the cheek.

"Your brother had no choice. He was a pawn for the Council of 8, as were a lot of people. Every single one of them is doing everything in their power for redemption, including your brother," Leeran growled.

Jayden stood frozen, unable to believe what had just happened. Not even Theresa had raised a hand at him.

Balthezier stepped in front of him, blocking him from the Laiyfe-Rain's.

"Get out."

"This is none of your business," Leeran retorted.

"It is when you're hurting my friend," Balthezier said.

Turning to Jayden, Balthezier added, "Let's go home."

"I think it's best if he came back to live with us, his *real* family, until we know for certain that he's okay," Taylin pressed.

"I am going home to my family," Jayden said.

He stepped around Balthezier and approached his twin with a carefully blank expression.

"You will *never* be forgiven for taking them away from me," he hissed.

Artemis took hold of his hand and led him out with Balthezier taking up the rear. All he wanted to do was hide away and shut the world out for a while.

- **Chapter Nine -**

Peace at The Balgaire lasted until the next morning. As Jayden sat down to eat his scrambled eggs, Balthezier came storming downstairs.

"That's it!" Balthezier slammed his hands down on the table. "You talk or I'm going down to break into the hospital and find your file."

Roderick wiped his face tiredly with an exasperated sigh but before he could rein in his son, Jayden spoke up.

"I'll tell you, okay? Just give me another day to think everything over."

"One more day is more than enough," Roderick agreed, shooting his son a look.

Before Balthezier could argue, Jayden gave up pretending that he had an appetite, dumped his uneaten food in the bin, and left to go upstairs.

As soon as the bedroom door was closed, he leaned against it and closed his eyes. He focused on the act of breathing and the loudness of his constricting heart. The doctor's words kept echoing in his head.

He was sick. He was sick and possibly dying and there was nothing that he could do. There was no family left to tell him that it was going to be okay and they would figure it out. He was alone.

Tears spilled down his cheeks and he was overwhelmed with rage. It wasn't fair! How could he go through all those sleepless nights and terrifying life and death moments, and end up dying because his body was fighting against itself?

Growling, he grabbed the nightstand by its legs and threw it against the wall. He grabbed books and ripped them apart before tossing them aside. Drawers were yanked out of the dressing table and slammed against the bedposts. Conjuring up the first Ward that came to mind, Jayden hurtled his Abilities around his room.

Pieces of wood and fabric flew everywhere and walls caved in. His belongings and furniture were reduced to shards flying through the air. The Balgaire trembled and the old foundations groaned in protest.

"Jayden!"

Arms wrapped around him and a calming effect pressed into his back.

"Easy, easy. Just relax."

He forcefully took a deep breath and slowly exhaled. He did it over and over again until he was left with exhaustion.

Running his fingers through his hair, he stepped away and looked at the mess he had caused.

"Jay, you're bleeding," Balthezier said.

His friend drew a Ward in the air and in a matter of seconds, the room was clean and whole again.

"Sit," Balthezier instructed.

Wordlessly, he did as told. Balthezier knelt in front of him and gently wiped a tissue under his nose, the corners of his eyes, and ears. Not once did he demand an explanation, even though Jayden could see he wanted to.

Roderick leaned against the doorframe, arms folded against his chest, looking like he was seconds away from asking.

Looking at the two Adler men, he realized he had never been alone. Even though the Lugians were dead, he still had people he could call family.

He knew he couldn't wait another day to explain what was going on.

"My Abilities …" Jayden tried to start. "My Abilities are attacking me and … and it's making me sick."

"Jay —"

"Are you going to tell the Laiyfe-Rain's?" Roderick asked, interrupting his son.

"My grandparents, yes," Jayden answered.

"Leeran and Taylin?" Roderick checked.

"No. Why would I?"

"Because they're family," Roderick said.

Jayden gently pushed away Balthezier's helping hand.

"They share DNA. That doesn't make them family," Jayden growled.

Roderick raised his hands in apology. "Okay, okay. Just making sure we're on the same page. What can we do to help?"

"I'm not sure," Jayden shrugged.

"Okay. Well until you have that follow up appointment, you're to take it easy. The only thing I want you to do is rest and concentrate on your theory studies," Roderick instructed.

"We can work on your GED studies," Balthezier offered.

Jayden nodded.

"For now, rest. You've overexerted your body so don't give me that nonsense about feeling fine. You're not," Roderick said.

He ran a hand over his face, too exhausted to argue.

"Can I get some books that don't involve studying?" Jayden asked.

"Not a problem. There's a couple of things I want you to read up on. It'll help," Roderick said.

"Help with what?" Jayden asked as Roderick left.

He turned to Balthezier for answers but instead, he got a shrug.

"I think I know what will help you relax," Balthezier said.

The blond opened the window, stuck his head out, and whistled loudly. A howl echoed through in response and within seconds, a rush of black came through the window.

Jayden sat up straighter, eyes wide.

In front of him was a wolf that stood at waist level with black fur and forest green eyes. It flickered to a skeletal form before settling on flesh.

"Dusk?"

The Linstonate snapped his eyes to Jayden and when there was no recognition, his heart broke.

"It's me, Dusk," he tried.

He stood up and slowly approached with his hand held out.

When Dusk recognized his scent, his eyes lit up, his tail wagged frantically, and he whimpered. Dusk rubbed himself up against Jayden's leg, circled around, and jumped up, pushing him down to the ground.

He couldn't help but laugh as his animal companion climbed all over him, whimpering and licking him. He wrapped his arms around Dusk and took a deep breath. Tears welled up and Jayden felt himself finally relax.

"Missed you, too," Jayden murmured.

He kept his hold on Dusk, even after the Linstonate had calmed down.

"He's been helping me search for Kalarney," Balthezier spoke up.

"Thank you," Jayden whispered.

"Get some rest and I'll tell you more," Balthezier said.

He nodded and crawled into bed. Dusk curled up against him, burying his nose against Jayden's neck.

Three days into the week of rest and Jayden was going insane. He needed to be busy and do something. Luckily, the afternoon influx of customers at The Balgaire meant that Balthezier and Roderick were distracted enough to not notice him sneaking off with Dusk and a bag full of books.

Walking through the city, he took a deep breath and finally felt like the walls weren't closing in on him. He wanted to go to the Human Plane and visit his family's graves, however, he didn't have the energy to go too far, even with the aid of the Transport Docks. If he used The Balgaire's connect to the Human Plane, he risked getting caught by either of the Adler's.

Jayden checked the time on his phone. There were still a few hours left until the work day was done, which would give him time to visit his grandparents without running into his birth parents.

Once he and Dusk arrived at the mansion, he wasn't sure whether or not he should knock or let himself in. Choosing to be polite, he knocked on the front door.

"Jayden? Hi," Koan greeted.

The butler stepped aside to let him in.

"Who's your friend?" Koan asked.

Jayden ruffled Dusk's fur between his ears. "This is Dusk. Are my grandparents here?"

"They're this way. How have you been?" Koan asked.

He faltered and wondered if they had heard about the explosion he caused at the training grounds.

Instead of answering, he dug out the books from his bag and held them out for Koan.

"I've finished reading them. Thanks," Jayden said.

Koan smiled and took the books. "I'll get you some more if you'd like."

Jayden nodded. "Sure."

"Jayden, are you okay?" Cora greeted.

He glanced over to his grandmother and tried to give her a reassuring smile.

"It's … uh, complicated," he tried.

Cora grimaced before turning to Koan. "Please bring some tea to the library."

Koan bowed slightly and left. Jayden watched him go, noting that the man moved with stiffness.

"Is he okay?" Jayden asked.

"We've all been worried and his other duties took a turn," Cora explained.

"I'll go help him."

Before his grandmother could say otherwise, he darted off after the butler. He leant against the kitchen doorway, spending a moment to just watch the man.

"Are you okay?" Jayden asked.

"Yes," Koan answered.

Jayden frowned but instead of pointing out the obvious lie, he stepped forward and placed a hand in between Koan's shoulder blades. He felt the older man tense ever so slightly and it made him step back, hand falling down beside him.

"Don't worry about the tea. Let's go to where my grandparents are waiting and I'll tell you all what's happening," Jayden said.

"Cora has req —-"

"Never mind that," Jayden interrupted.

Koan didn't move for a second but when he did, he wrapped Jayden up in a tight hug. He froze, unsure of what was happening or why. The man had always been professional, even when it's just been the two of them.

"It's okay. I already know," Koan whispered.

When Koan released him, Jayden struggled to look him in the eye.

"Y-you do?" he checked.

"Yes." Koan bent down a little so that he was sure Jayden could see his face. "You're not alone in this. We'll do whatever it take to help you get through this, okay?"

Jayden nodded as he gnawed on his bottom lip.

"Go talk to your grandparents," Koan said.

Letting out a shaky breath, he shuffled to the library. He sat down next to Valent and stared at his hands. It had taken him by surprise to hear that Koan already knew and that he was already working on trying to help. He wondered how he found out.

"Jay?" Iris said gently.

He swallowed the lump in his throat and took a deep breath.

"You guys heard about what happened at the training arena, right?" Jayden checked.

"Yes," Valent confirmed.

"It turns out my Abilities are attacking me and it's caused a sickness in my blood," Jayden shakily admitted.

Jayden clenched his fists and stared at the floor. He didn't want to see the pity or sadness. He didn't want to deal with any of it.

"If there is anything we can do to help, we're here for you," Aster said.

"Thanks," Jayden murmured.

Valent wrapped an arm around his shoulders and squeezed a little.

Feeling a tightness in his chest, Jayden abruptly stood up.

"We should go. I don't want them to know what's going on so … I'll see you guys later," Jayden said.

He hunched his shoulders as he quickly left the mansion. He ignored Koan calling out for him and ignored Dusk trying to get his attention.

Wanting some time away from people, he turned into the forest and froze. The hairs on the back of his neck stood up and he spun around, eyes wide and searching. Dusk wrapped around his legs, growling.

Something was following them into the trees.

He bolted through the trees and didn't stop until he had a thick trunk pressed against his back and Dusk didn't look like he was ready to attack.

"We're okay," he said to Dusk, scratching between his ears.

They walked further into the forest, enjoying the peace and quiet. The Linstonate sniffed around but didn't wander too far away.

Eventually, he steered in the direction he thought the borderline would be. When he found it, the edge was still slowly crumbling away. It was slow going but Jayden couldn't believe it. The forest was silently disappearing, and once that was gone, the city would fall.

"The earthquakes must be an after effect," Jayden murmured.

Tiny cries of distress snatched his attention. He and Dusk rushed over to the noise and found two pudgy creatures close to the edge. Brown wings were curled up against their gray and white fur, and wide blue and green eyes were full of fear and searching.

He pressed a finger to his lips to tell Dusk to be silent and gestured for him to follow. They searched around the area for any signs of their parents. However, after only finding birds and a rabbit-lizard hybrid, Jayden went back to the pups and tried to think of what to do.

Glancing back to the city, he bit his bottom lip with uncertainty. He couldn't leave the two pups alone, especially close to an edge that was disappearing. Once they were safe, he would spend more time searching for their family.

Decision made, he stepped into the clearing, alerting the pups to his presence. The bigger of the two stood defensively in front of the other and growled. When the Linstonate made an appearance, the pups scrambled back, growling in fear.

"Easy, easy," he tried to coax, holding out a hand for them to sniff.

Neither of them stepped an inch closer.

When the ground started trembling, the little pup cried in confusion and fear, and he watched as the crumbling edge closed in on them faster.

"Dusk!"

Acting quickly, he scooped up one pup while Dusk picked up the other and ran through the forest. He was glad he had Dusk with him. The Linstonate guided him back to The Balgaire and neither of them stopped until they were in Jayden's room.

Both pups were deposited on the bed and Jayden stepped back.

"Jay?" Balthezier poked his head in. "Hey, where … Why do you have a couple of growling animals on your bed?"

"I found them at the border," Jayden said.

"And? They have parents out there. You can't just bring wildlife home," Balthezier pointed out.

He shook his head. "I couldn't find anything other than birds and rodents. The edge of the border was breaking away and I had to make a decision quickly so we took them in. I was going to look for their parents once they were safe."

They watched as the two pups made uncertain attempts at trying to get off the bed. Dusk stood at the mattress and nudged them a little.

"Let's get those scratches patched up then we'll go take them to a keeper." Balthezier nodded towards Jayden's arms.

Jayden glanced down at the scratches and red marks covering his arms.

"I'll look after them," Jayden said.

"You sure? They'll need exercise, and even in this city, they're unusual," Balthezier said.

"Is my Anchor still around?" he asked.

Balthezier looked sheepish as he scratched the back of his head. "I may have taken over the Anchor and changed the security system a little. I mean, when I got to it, it was starting to disappear. It's still there, and Dusk has been living there with that giant serpent in the valley."

Jayden shook his head in amusement.

"Do you know what they are?" Jayden asked.

Both of them watched as Dusk placed his two front paws on the mattress and made rumbly sounds in the back of his throat in response to the brave one's growls and tiny barks.

A thin pupil was encased in blue and green coloring. Their wings were a tawny brown with flecks of white, and they had big paws, indicating that they were possibly going to be as big as Dusk.

"No idea," Balthezier answered.

"We can ask Roderick later," Jayden said and shrugged.

"Are you sure you want to keep them?" Balthezier checked.

"Yes," Jayden answered.

Dusk pushed away from the bed and licked his hand. With a smile, he ran a hand over the animal's head.

"What are you going to name them?" Balthezier asked.

"Don't know."

"Fair enough. You'll need to focus on getting them to trust you before they maul your face off while you sleep," Balthezier suggested.

Jayden nodded with a sigh.

He knew that even with Dusk's help, getting the trust of both twins would be a challenge.

Chapter Ten

Sitting in the corner of the waiting room for a bunch of specialists with rooms in the hospital had Jayden on edge. Roderick sat next to him, engrossed in a book and seemingly unaware of Jayden's growing anxiety. There were a few others in the waiting room with them. Most were either on their phones or flicking through magazines.

"Jayden Lugian?"

He snapped his attention over to where the voice came from. Doctor Turner stood there in his lab coat, white button-up shirt, and loose black tie, already tapping away on his tablet.

"If you'll follow me we'll start the tests. Mr. Adler, please wait here. He will need assistance afterwards," Doctor Turner advised.

"Didn't plan on leaving without him," Roderick murmured, not even bothering to look up from his book.

"Very well. This way, Jayden."

He followed the doctor down a hallway, past the specialist rooms, and stopped in front of a door labeled 'Testing'.

"In here."

Jayden bit his bottom lip as he stepped into the large room. A single desk with two chairs had been placed along the wall closest to the door and an examination chair wasn't that far away. The rest of the room was bare. Not even a poster or sign had been hung on the walls.

"Take a seat and I'll explain what's going to happen," Doctor Turner instructed.

He did as told and squeezed his shaking hands together.

"I'm going to check your blood pressure and pulse, listen to your heart, and take a blood test to get a base of what your body is like prior to anything else. Once that's all done, you'll perform Wards with varying degrees of strength behind a clear wall on the other side of the room. A second blood test will be taken halfway through the Ability test, and a third will be taken when we're finished. This is going to be uncomfortable and if I think you're struggling or can no longer proceed, I'll stop the tests. Understand?"

Jayden swallowed the lump in his throat and nodded.

Doctor Turner grabbed his arm and began checking his pulse and blood pressure. He could see his eyes stop briefly at the Band-Aids and patches covering his skin.

"The bandages?" he asked.

"I adopted a couple of pups," Jayden answered.

"What breed?"

He shrugged. It may have been an innocent question to ask, however it made him uneasy.

Doctor Turner hummed and proceeded to listen to Jayden's chest. Satisfied, the results were jotted into the tablet and retrieved the equipment for blood tests.

Jayden focused on trying to keep calm. Every time he thought about what was happening, anxiety worsened and he could feel himself beginning to shut everything out. If he had a panic attack during this time, the whole session would become counterproductive and might even cause harm.

"Easy part is done. Stand behind the clear wall and take off your shirt," Doctor Turner said.

His thoughts were derailed and he was forced to refocus on the doctor. He blinked a couple of times and nodded. As he moved behind the clear wall, he discarded his shirt, revealing a defined pale torso covered in cuts and fading bruises.

The doctor didn't bat an eye at the sight as he attached little circular patches on Jayden's chest, abdomen, spine, and temples. Once done, Doctor Turner stepped behind the clear wall and pulled out his tablet from one of his lab coat pockets.

There was a moment where the doctor tapped away at his device and Jayden was left feeling awkward standing there without his shirt.

"Use the Ward for air and create a light breeze," Doctor Turner instructed.

Jayden nodded and tried to remember the right symbol. Doctor Turner sighed and drew the Ward impatiently for him.

With the Ward in mind, his Abilities flared to life and a light breeze swept around him. The relief he felt after his pent up Abilities were allowed to stretch out was short lived as he quickly became lightheaded.

"Use the Ward to create a small piece of earth, followed by a small flame, a bubble of water, and a small glowing orb."

After each Ward, the feeling of relief was less and less and he began to dread using his Abilities.

Not once did Doctor Turner look up from his tablet. It made him wonder what exactly the physician was seeing on the device that he couldn't see happening right in front of him.

"What did you feel after each Ward and how do you feel now?" Doctor Turner asked.

"Relief for a moment but more lightheaded," Jayden answered.

Doctor Turner nodded as he tapped away on his tablet.

"Relief from what?"

"Not using my Abilities," Jayden replied.

"Okay. Now, let's move on to something stronger. Remember to keep it contained."

He nodded, the corners of his lips tugging down with uncertainty. He hadn't tried to contain a Ward before.

Taking a deep breath, he readied himself for the first Ward the doctor wanted to see. The moment he pushed his Abilities to work a little more, feeling lightheaded wasn't the worst thing that happened. The room shifted at nauseating levels, causing him to stumble back.

"Do you need a moment?" Doctor Turner asked after the second Ward.

Jayden leaned against the wall and closed his eyes. "Yeah."

While he focused on breathing, he watched as the doctor spent a quiet moment writing down notes.

Eventually, he felt good enough to step away from the wall and stand back in position. Doctor Turner finished up with his tablet and the look he gave caused Jayden to shift uncomfortably.

It quickly became obvious what his limits were. The stronger the Ward, the more he felt his control slip, and the more his body struggled. Blood dripped out of his ears and nose, and his body swayed as black spots edged around his vision.

Before he could understand what was happening, his Abilities tore apart the remnants of his control. His Abilities slammed into the clear wall and a spider web of cracks snapped across it until the pressure against it grew too unbearable and it exploded.

Doctor Turner sighed and thick shards of plastic froze in midair before they reached him.

"Stop."

The order was simple and yet was weighed down with so much power that he could feel his Abilities obey.

"Interesting data but I suggest you keep everything under wraps for a moment. We don't want anyone upsetting our plans now," Doctor Turner told him. "I will work on easing the side effects, but for now, it's time to sleep, pet."

Two days after the hospital visit, he still felt lethargic and his memory about what had happened was hazy. He had woken up slumped against Roderick's back on the way home, feeling like he had been hit by a truck.

Since then, the Adler's had taken turns keeping a close eye on him, and for once, he hadn't minded. It was a reassurance that there was someone nearby to make sure nothing happened while he was able to sort himself out.

When Mackenzie stormed into The Balgaire with fury causing static to arch along his shoulders, Jayden barely had seconds to react. Mackenzie strode right up to him, ignored the threatening growls from Dusk, and shoved him back.

"You want to live here, fine. You're apparently old enough to live where you want. But why is it that we had to find out from someone else that you're sick and having your Abilities tested by a doctor? We keep trying to fit you into our lives but all you can focus on are dead humans!" Mackenzie shouted.

"That's —"

Dusk jumped onto a nearby table and snapped his teeth in warning, body angrily flicking between flesh and skeletal.

He was shoved back again and he stumbled into a wall. His twin stepped closer, hand raised, and he flinched.

"Jay, no!"

The air between the twins exploded. Jayden was pushed back against the wall until it caved in, and Mackenzie was throw across the room and tumbled over a table.

For a moment, everything was still and quiet. Those who had been having a meal were on their feet, waiting to see if they would need to step in to help, stop a fight, or leave.

Jayden pushed away from the wall, leaning his forehead in the palm of his hand. His knees buckled as he broke out into a coughing fit. Panic engulfed him when he saw blood spattered on his hand.

A pulse of power rippled through the floor, causing others to cautiously step back. The pups whined and hid behind Roderick and Balthezier. Dusk leapt from table to table in order to get to Jayden. The Linstonate nudged and pushed in a bid to distract him. However, it wasn't enough.

Black electricity danced around his back and hands as he struggled to catch his breath and regain control.

"Control yourself!" Mackenzie shouted.

Jayden managed to glare over at Mackenzie, blood welling up in his eyes like tears before pain caused him to fold over and another pulse of power swept through the floor.

"What in the world is wrong with him? Why can't he control himself?" Mackenzie demanded.

"Liz? What's going on?" another asked.

Balthezier didn't answer. Instead, he reached out a hand and a green glowing symbol grew out. The black electricity shattered the symbol and the ground shook. Other Abilities shot out towards him but they barely came close to touching him.

The shaking grew worse and people were knocked around with tables and chairs.

He cried out as another wave of his Abilities shot out of him.

Balthezier picked him up but was stopped from going anywhere by Mackenzie.

"What's wrong with him?" Mackenzie asked.

Dusk snapped his teeth at Mackenzie to force him to back off. Sharp teeth narrowly avoided piercing flesh. As the blond carried Jayden upstairs, the Linstonate stayed at the base of the staircase, growling.

"You. Get out of my place!" Roderick growled.

Jayden caught a glimpse of Roderick with a few patrons forcing Mackenzie towards the front door.

"I've got you, Jay. Just rest now," his friend said as he lowered him on the bed.

This time when Balthezier used the Calming Ward, there was no resistance. As he struggled to keep his eyes open, he wanted to say thank you.

A coppery taste lingered in his mouth and labored breathing eventually evened out.

When Doctor Gray was the first person he saw after waking up, he groaned.

"What happened to resting, Jayden?" Doctor Gray asked.

"Sorry. I didn't …" Jayden croaked.

"Mackenzie came over and started pushing him," Balthezier helpfully supplied.

The doctor grimaced. "I see. Instinct or otherwise, to you, Mackenzie is still a threat and so your Abilities must have reacted accordingly."

"He'll always be a threat. What are you doing here?" Jayden huffed.

"I came to eat lunch with my wife and found the place in a shambles. Roderick asked me to check on you. As I understand it, Doctor Turner is currently looking into ways to relieve at least some of the effects you're feeling, but in the meantime here's the contact information of the specialist I mentioned to you at the hospital. She's had a look at some of your samples and would like to speak with you soon. Doctor Zero is human but she knows about our world and has helped before," Doctor Gray said, handing Jayden a business card.

"Thanks," Jayden said.

The morning that he felt better, he pulled on his jacket and shoes with the intent of leaving and getting a dose of much needed fresh air. He was more determined than ever to lead a normal life and if that included going to the one place he had wanted to avoid before, then so be it.

"Are you sure you want to go? You didn't want to before," Balthezier pointed out.

Jayden raised his eyebrows and smirked, "And to think all it took was house arrest."

"That's not funny! You're sick," Balthezier whined.

He sighed. At this rate, he was going to miss the time allocated to him for training.

"Look, if it makes you feel any better, why don't you tag along and watch me not use my Abilities like I did before and Dusk can look after the pups while we're gone," Jayden offered. "I'm probably going to be doing theory today anyway."

Balthezier let out an overdramatic sigh.

"Fine, but I will cart your sorry behind back home if you push yourself too hard."

Jayden rolled his eyes as he finally stepped outside. "Yeah, yeah. Let's go, otherwise you'll make me late."

Walking through the streets, Jayden took a deep breath and found himself enjoying the time. Balthezier chuckled and wrapped an arm around his shoulders. He playfully pushed his friend away, a small smile showing.

Once at the training grounds, he wasn't sure what was going on. The place was busier than usual and his trainers were occupied instructing a couple of kids on the other side of the field.

Frowning, Jayden ventured inside, passed the locker rooms and trainer offices, and went straight to the schedule board. Every session was completely booked out and he couldn't find his name listed anywhere. However, he did find his name on a piece of paper attached to a clipboard.

"Medical leave?" Jayden murmured.

Before Balthezier could catch on to what was going on, Jayden stormed back to the field and over to his trainers.

"I'm not on medical leave! I'm … Hey! Don't ignore me," Jayden shouted as he quickened his pace until he was ahead of his trainers.

Seeley shook his head and stepped around him to continue the lesson.

"Mr. Keith, what's going on?" Jayden asked.

"You'll have to bring it up with your parents. They've pulled you out of any future lessons, citing medical issues that'll prevent you from training," Keith explained.

"My parents … The Elders are the ones who put me in here. Leeran and Taylin have nothing to do with this," Jayden argued.

Keith gave him an apologetic. "Sorry, kid. You can check out books from the library and if you have any questions, I can help out but other than that, my hands are tied."

When the trainer left, Jayden was left with seething anger.

"Well, at least you got what you've been wanting from the start," Balthezier unhelpfully supplied.

He shot his friend a dirty look and left the arena. Leeran and Taylin were still trying to force their way into his life and control every aspect of it. No matter what Mackenzie thought was going on, none of them were respecting his wishes or privacy.

"Hey, Jay? Where are you going?" Balthezier asked.

He ignored him and continued on to the mansion. At the front steps, the ground shifted and rocked. Cracks snapped along the ground in front of the building and he couldn't help but glance over to the forest as he held on to a pillar.

Leeran and Taylin came running out of the house as roof tiles smashed into the ground.

"Jayden? Are you okay?" Leeran asked.

Concern about the quake was shoved aside by anger and it took everything for him to remember to keep a firm enough grasp on his Abilities.

"You … both of you! Neither of you have any right to decide what happens in my life!" Jayden growled.

"Excuse me? As we keep telling you, we're your parents and unlike Mr. Adler, we actually care about your welfare," Taylin retorted.

Jayden clenched his fists as he saw red but before he acted, Balthezier stood in front of him. Despite the relaxed and casual look, he could feel the tension running through his friend.

"It's nice seeing you again, Mr. and Mrs. Laiyfe-Rain," Balthezier smiled. "I'll ask my father to forward on any bills we've received from the hospital as well as an invoice for any money spent so far on Jayden's everyday expenses. After all, I wouldn't want my father to financially worry about someone he doesn't care about."

"Excuse me?" Leeran frowned.

"You two are the only ones who care about his welfare, right? Family pays medical bills, food, accommodation when kids are involved, and so forth. Coming from an old wealthy family with a nice house, that won't be a problem, will it?" Balthezier asked.

"Listen here. We know exactly what it involves, both the good and the bad. Jayden is our son and he's our respon —-"

"Do you? Because from an outsider's point of view, you're treating him like you own him, not like an adult," Balthezier interrupted.

"Jayden is not an adult! He's sixteen years old," Leeran argued.

"Let's go home, Jay," Balthezier said.

Balthezier grabbed his arm and pulled him away from the mansion. The blond fumed with rage all the way to The Balgaire.

"Liz?"

When Balthezier didn't answer, Jayden pulled hard on his arm. When that didn't work, he punched his friend on the shoulder.

"Ow!" Balthezier hissed.

"You lied," Jayden pointed out.

"Huh?"

"We haven't been charged for anything and I'm working at The Balgaire," Jayden said.

Balthezier chuckled sheepishly. "Guess I forgot that part."

"Why did you bring money into it anyway?"

"Didn't you ever wonder why they're still with their parents even after having nine years of freedom? They don't have jobs and their connections are only through their parents. Neither of them has really done anything to stand out or to support themselves," Balthezier explained. "They just … do their own thing. Not exactly sure what."

Jayden frowned and tilted his head. He wondered what Leeran and Taylin could be getting up to every day if they didn't have jobs that would expose them to the public.

"They don't have access to the family fortune. Neither does Mackenzie, though he did manage to get a job in the city," Balthezier said.

"I know," Jayden said. "My grandparents said I'm the only one in their will and I've got access to the family fortune."

"You do? Why didn't you say anything?" Balthezier asked.

He shrugged. "I haven't actually used the card they gave me and I'd rather work than rely on money that could be used in an emergency or something."

"How responsible of you," Balthezier teased.

Jayden rolled his eyes.

"Come on. I'm hungry," Balthezier said.

- Chapter Eleven -

Despite it being lunch hour, The Balgaire was fairly quiet. Jayden sighed as he finished wiping down tables after the last lot of customers had left.

Once the cloth was back in the sink, he turned his attention to the pups and Dusk. He had been working with his friend to gain the pups' trust and teach them a few things like sit and stay. It was hard work but with Dusk around, he was slowly able to get through to them.

"Jayden, there's a visitor for you," Balthezier called out.

He glanced from his friend and over to the door. Doctor Gray made her way to one of the booths and gestured for him to join her. At that point, he wanted to disappear upstairs but he knew from glancing at Balthezier, it wasn't an option.

Grudgingly, he went over and plopped down in the seat in front of the doctor.

"I'd like to talk to you about a couple of things," Doctor Gray said by way of a greeting.

Jayden nodded and gave Roderick a small grateful smile as the man placed plates with chicken and salad sandwiches, and hot chips in front of him and the doctor.

"You're looking better compared to the last time I saw you," Doctor Gray noted.

He hummed around a chip, not wanting to be a part of this conversation.

"Have you booked an appointment in to see Doctor Zero yet?"
Doctor Gray.

"Who?" Jayden frowned.

"Doctor Madeline Zero –– the specialist that I told you to contact,"
she clarified.

Jayden shook his head.

"Thought so. I invited her here for lunch with us."

He fidgeted with his fork. He no longer had any sort of appetite.

"Sorry to keep you waiting. I kept getting lost," a woman said as
she took a seat beside Doctor Gray.

Doctor Gray smiled warmly at the newcomer. She had wavy
blonde hair that cascaded past her shoulders and light blue eyes filled with
love. She was dressed in a long woolen coat with a rayon blouse and pencil
skirt.

"You have a terrible sense of direction, Maddy. You do remember
we've been here multiple times over the years?"

"I know, I know. I'm sorry. Hi. You must be Jayden. I'm Madeline
Zero, the specialist Charlotte should have told you about."

"Hi," Jayden greeted meekly.

"So, where are we at? Lunch or serious talking time?" Doctor Zero
asked.

"Lunch. I've already ordered for you," Doctor Gray said.

"Thanks," Doctor Zero smiled.

Jayden played around with his food and glanced over to Balthezier.

"Charlotte gave me the results from every one of your blood tests,"
Doctor Zero said.

"Maddy, how about we enjoy lunch first?" Doctor Gray suggested.

"Jayden has barely touched his food and I doubt he will while
we're here with him. And you, Charlotte, will be stealing from my plate
instead of eating from yours," Doctor Zero pointed out.

Doctor Gray shrugged with a smirk. "Yours always tastes better."

"Then why don't you order the same thing?" Doctor Zero asked.

Roderick gave Doctor Zero a plate of shelled pasta covered in
white sauce with mushrooms, and as he walked off, squeezed Jayden's
shoulder encouragingly.

Before Doctor Zero could even pick up her fork, Doctor gray was
already helping herself to the pasta.

"Hey!" she objected.

Doctor Gray chuckled but she didn't take another helping.

"Try eating something, Jayden. You need the strength," Doctor Gray encouraged.

"I'm not hungry," he murmured.

"Don't eat for hunger. Eat for strength," she advised.

He stared at his food. He couldn't convince himself to eat. The little food he had already eaten was threatening to make its way back up.

Shaking his head, he lied, "I ate not too long ago."

Doctor Gray flicked her gaze over to the pub counter where Balthezier was still watching them and didn't press Jayden any further.

"Okay, then let's get this conversation over with," Doctor Zero said. "The lab is running through every test possible so hopefully we'll have results soon. Tell me, what have you been experiencing since you've been back?"

He shrugged. "I'm not too sure. I've put certain things like being tired, a bit of weight loss, and waking up in a … um … in a cold sweat down to what I've been through. I'm not … I …"

Jayden rubbed his head in frustration. It was hard getting the words out when thinking about what was happening to him caused his mind to stall.

"It's okay, Jayden. Take a deep breath in and slowly let it out. There you go. Nice and slow," Doctor Gray coaxed.

He gulped down air with desperation to make it all stop. Dusk whined a little and leaned against his hip. Having his companion there beside him helped. He hugged the Linstonate until he was ready to face the doctors again.

"You okay?" Doctor Gray asked.

He nodded and shakily sipped his water.

"Understanding what your body is going through when you've got a life-altering diagnosis is hard. I'll be working closely with Doctor Turner to work out appropriate medications," Doctor Zero said.

"And you, Doctor Gray?"

"My expertise is in surgery. I'm here mostly because you seem to trust me enough to actually talk about what's going on," Doctor Gray explained.

The first memory he had after coming back was being in the hospital surrounded by doctors and nurses trying to hold him down and deal with his injuries. However, he hadn't felt safe and he struggled in a bid to leave. Looking back on it now, he wondered just how many times he had struggled against medical staff while in a blind panic.

"Everyone else … they don't listen. And it's not just doctors or nurses. It's everyone. They expect me to bow down and accept something I don't want or need. No one will let me live my life the way I want to," Jayden ranted.

When he finally stopped, he took a deep breath and buried his face in his hands.

"Jayden, you need to find someone to talk to about all of this. You can't keep all of this pent up. There are quite a few humans in the known that ca —-"

"No! It's fine. I'm fine," Jayden objected.

A phone buzzing on the table broke the conversation and he took the chance to take a deep breath and pushed back his anger and frustration.

"Sorry, excuse me," Doctor Zero said as she took her phone and left the table.

"I'll talk to someone. I just need to get to their place so just … stop. Please," Jayden begged.

Doctor Gray nodded. "I'm sorry for overstepping. I really am. I'm just trying to help make things a bit easier for you so you can concentrate on other things."

"I know and I'm sorry for snapping," Jayden said.

When Doctor Zero returned, she was hesitant and the seriousness had him on edge.

"That was the lab. Is there somewhere we can talk in private?" Doctor Zero asked.

"Tell me," Jayden said.

"I think it's best if we do this out of the public eye."

"Tell me!" Jayden growled.

Doctor Zero glanced at the woman beside her with a grimace.

"My team is struggling to identify what's happening and they need more samples in order to make a final report. What they have gotten so far is a bit of a mess. No matter how many times they've checked and have gotten others to check, one moment there are cancerous cells, and the next there aren't. Your white blood cell and red blood cell counts are all over the place. All they can confirm is that there is an abundance of cells that aren't considered normal and they've been absorbing or destroying normal cells. We're going to have to —-"

"Maddy!"

Jayden felt his heart constrict and black dots edged around his vision. He needed to get out. Feet stumbled around as he tried to remember how to breathe. How could he be in such a mess that multiple tests couldn't confirm anything? What was going on?

The two doctors rushed over. Hands kept him steady and ushered back to his seat. He was gently coaxed forward, head down, and a voice kept urging him to breathe.

Muffled words wafted around and Balthezier knelt in front of him, radiating calm.

"Jay, slow and steady. You can do it," Balthezier encouraged.

Jayden shook his head.

"Yes, you can. Hold on to Dusk," Balthezier said.

Balthezier moved out of sight and a black mass pushed its way against Jayden. He wrapped his arm the creature and held on tightly.

"I'm sorry, Jayden. This is very difficult and I should have done this in a more private place," Doctor Zero apologized.

Pushing away, he left and shut himself in his room with Dusk and the pups. He slumped against the door and took a moment to breathe. He couldn't think about any of this.

Once he wasn't so shaky, he sat by the window to read. Dusk curled up against his legs, head in his lap.

He wasn't left alone for long before there was a tap on his door and Doctor Gray poked her head in.

"Are you okay?" she asked.

"If you intend to suggest that I go talk to someone again, then you can buzz off right now," Jayden warned.

The doctor stepped in and closed the door.

"Maddy and I … We've seen what life changing news can do to someone. It'll be exhausting, both mentally and physically. If you don't want to talk to a professional, then please seek out a person that you can confide in."

"I know. I will," Jayden sighed, shutting his book.

The brunette woman took a seat on the edge of the bed. "Tell me one thing that has gotten you on edge. Something that wasn't a part of the rant downstairs and we'll leave it for today, okay?"

He swallowed the lump in his throat and thought for a moment.

"I keep wishing my parents were here. They would know what to do and …"

Doctor Gray leaned forward and placed a gentle hand over his heart, her eyes softening with shared pain.

"This is going to sound cliché, but it helped me when I lost my mom. She may not be with me physically anymore but she'll always remain in my heart. Your memories of your family will keep them alive. Their love for you will last until your reunion in the Stream of Life. All you have to do is close your eyes and remember," Doctor Gray told him.

Jayden bit his bottom lip and focused on Dusk in an effort to stop the tears from falling.

"You're not alone, Jayden. Remember that, okay?"

- Chapter Twelve -

Between the day the test results were revealed and Doctor Zero visiting The Balgaire the following afternoon, Jayden hadn't left his bedroom. He'd spent the time staring at the pages of a book, not taking anything in, and not engaging with Roderick and Balthezier whenever they popped in to make sure he was okay.

Doctor Zero moved the desk chair to sit in front of him by the window.

"How are you?" she asked.

Jayden shrugged. "Fine."

Doctor Zero grimaced. "Sorry. We want to get you in for more tests in order to determine what's going on so I've booked you in to come see me in a week. I don't want to put you on any medication until we have a solid confirmation of diagnosis."

Doctor Zero placed an orange pill bottle in front of him and he couldn't stop staring at it.

"This is from Doctor Turner. He said to take one once a day, and it's best to be taken with food. It'll hopefully suppress your Abilities and keep them from causing you any further damage," she explained.

"Thanks," he struggled to say.

"If there is anything you need, just call or pop into my office. Otherwise, I'll see you in a week. I'll give the details to Roderick," Doctor Zero offered.

He picked up his book and made another attempt at distracting himself from his problems.

When he finally put the book down, he was alone and the evening sun was bathing his room. Jayden took out a tablet from the container and finally ventured downstairs. Balthezier gave him a serving of chips and a glass of water with a supportive smile.

He managed to eat a little and wash down the tablet while barely thinking about it too much. Once he was finished, he sighed and leaned against his friend.

"Do you know where Kelly is these days?" Jayden asked.

"Yeah. Want me to ask her to come by?" Balthezier checked.

"No, it's okay. I want to go and visit," Jayden replied.

"Sure. Got an idea on the when?"

Jayden hummed and answered, "Soon. Before everything becomes a bigger mess."

"We'll go tomorrow," Balthezier told him. "Have you read those books dad gave you yet?"

"Not yet. It's been hard to concentrate on anything," Jayden said.

"Read the books," Balthezier said.

"Why?"

"It'll help with certain things."

"I don't like it when you're being cryptic," he said with a frown.

Balthezier chuckled. "Go. I'll get in touch with Kelly."

Jayden went back upstairs and took a book over to his window seat. The twin pups were attempting to rip apart one of his pillows. He had no energy left to try and get them to stop.

Buzzing stole his attention away from his book. Pulling his phone from his pocket, he frowned at the unknown number called.

"Hello?"

"I swear this better not be a joke. Is this really Jayden Lugian?"

He blinked in confusion. "Who is this?"

"Kelly Ozmat … well, Mane now? Is this really Jayden Lugian?" Kelly pressed.

"Yes. How'd you get my number?" Jayden asked.

"Balthezier. I thought you … They told me you were dead," Kelly said.

"I wasn't, just missing. I don't understand how but … Are you free to meet up? I want to talk to you about something," Jayden asked.

"I won't be free until the weekend. Did you want to go to Café 8 or meet at The Balgaire?" Kelly asked.

"Café 8 will be fine. Message me a time that works and I'll ask Balthezier to help me get there."

"Help you get there? Jay, are you okay?" Kelly asked.

He could hear the worry in her voice. It was tempting to spill the beans over the phone but it would be better to see her in person.

"I'll talk to you later. Bye, Kelly," he said before hanging up.

Waking up in the late morning on Friday, he knew something was wrong. His mind was cloudy and his joints ached. He could feel his Abilities sluggishly trying to reach out for him. It was a struggle to get out of bed and after ten minutes, he gave up and faded back into sleep until Roderick came to check on him.

"Hey, kiddo. You okay?" he asked, sitting on the edge of the mattress.

"Tired," Jayden mumbled.

Dusk whined and nuzzled against his neck to try and coax him up.

Roderick nodded. "Okay. I'll have some soup brought up for you."

Jayden couldn't help but fall asleep instead of responding.

When he woke up again, the pups were gnawing on his fingers. Despite still feeling exhausted, he was sure that if he didn't get up now, he wouldn't be able to all weekend.

He waved his hand around until he managed to turn on his lamp. Dusk eased Jayden up and out of bed. It was a reassurance when the Linstonate pressed against his leg and kept him steady as they made their way to the bathroom.

A hot shower helped washed away some of the exhaustion, however, as he stepped out and wrapped a towel around his waist, he winced from pain clinging to sluggish limbs.

Stepping out of the bathroom, he was met with curious stares from the pups. He wondered if they were able to smell or sense in some way that something was wrong.

Artemis was sitting with Balthezier when he eventually made it downstairs.

"Look who's risen from the dead," Balthezier joked.

Jayden took a seat and slumped against him.

"You okay?" Balthezier asked.

"Tired," Jayden answered.

Artemis reached over and brushed some hair away from his face, flashing him a concerned smile.

"We were thinking about seeing if you would be up to going out for dinner but …" Balthezier trailed off.

"We?" Jayden asked.

"You remember Artemis's mother, Octavia?" Balthezier nodded towards the older brunette woman joining them.

"I remember. Can we go out?"

"You sure?" Octavia checked.

It was like looking at an older version of Artemis. While both women had kind grey-blue eyes, Octavia had crow's feet lining hers. Her brown hair was tied up in a ponytail and a fringe was swept to the left.

Jayden nodded. "I need to get out and start moving around."

Balthezier looked like he was going to argue but Jayden stood up and gave him an expectant look.

"Dusk, please look after the pups," Jayden instructed the Linstonate.

Dusk rubbed his head against Jayden's leg gently and went upstairs.

Octavia led them through the streets of Szantium, going as fast as Jayden was able to move. Along the way, he couldn't shake the feeling they were being followed, but when he glanced back, the only thing even remotely out of place was the few stares directed at them and the whispering. It was starting to make him feel paranoid.

"Are we nearly there?" Jayden asked.

"Yes, sorry, we are," Octavia answered.

They entered a restaurant tucked away in a side street. The lights were soft and the lively hum of music and chatter filled the air. The foyer was packed with people waiting for tables in the dining area to free up.

They milled about for half an hour and by the time they were seated, he was ready to go back to sleep. Balthezier and Artemis took a seat on either side of him at the booth. He rubbed his eyes and rested his head on Balthezier's shoulder.

A waitress came over and flicked her eyes over to Jayden before addressing the group.

"Hi! My name is Kate and I'll be your waitress this evening. Here are your menus. Would you like me to go over tonight's specials?" she asked.

"No, thank you," Octavia answered.

"Very well. Please let me know if you have any questions. I'll be back in a few minutes to take your orders," she said.

Jayden pushed himself upright and flicked through the menu, struggling to take in the words he was seeing. Artemis helpfully pointed to a few dishes. He read through the recommendations and was able to decide quickly what he wanted. After telling Octavia his order, he went back to leaning against his friend, yawning.

"I'll get you some juice. Maybe the sugar will help," Octavia said.

"Thanks," Jayden mumbled.

The next thing he knew, Balthezier was nudging him awake and there was a plate of vegetables and a couple of chicken Kievs in front of him.

Jayden wiped his face tiredly as he sat up and slowly nibbled away at his meal. It was rather nice, however, he was barely able to stay awake long enough to properly enjoy it.

"Okay, that's it. I'm calling your doctors," Balthezier growled.

"I'm okay," Jayden mumbled.

"I'll get everything put into containers and we'll leave," Octavia said.

"Sounds good," Balthezier agreed.

Once the bill was sorted and Octavia was given the containers of food, the group quickly left. However, shortly after, Balthezier ended up giving him a piggyback.

"I'm sorry," Jayden yawned as he laid down on his bed.

"Don't worry," Balthezier, taking off Jayden's shoes. "Get some rest."

Jayden hummed as Artemis leaned over and kissed his forehead.

He watched as Doctor Turner tapped away on his tablet and he was tempted to ask what was so captivating on the device.

"How are you feeling?" Doctor Turner asked.

"Tired," he answered.

"So I've heard," the doctor said. "What tablets are you taking?"

He waved his arm over to the pill bottle on the bedside table. The doctor took a look and hummed.

"I'll take these back and adjust the dosage. Try to avoid situations where your Abilities will be triggered in the meantime," Doctor Turner said, pocketing the bottle. "I'll take a blood test to see what other effects the tablets are having. How have your Abilities been?"

"Okay, I guess. I lost control once before I was given the tablets," Jayden answered.

Doctor Turner nodded and added to the notes on his device before leaning over to clean Jayden's arm and take the blood sample.

"I'll see you within the week," he said.

As he left, Doctors Gray and Zero stepped in.

"How are you feeling?" Doctor Gray checked.

"Tired," Jayden sighed.

He was getting annoyed at having to repeat himself.

"Doctor Turner is going to adjust the tablets to help," Jayden added.

Both doctors nodded.

"I need to take a blood sample for my lab, but first I need to see your chest," Doctor Zero said.

Jayden groaned but sat up and did as he was told. Despite being overly tired, he didn't miss the grimace the doctors shared. He followed their gazes and saw bruises and faded signs of a rash along his stomach.

"What?" Jayden asked.

"How long have you had these for?" Doctor Zero asked.

He shrugged. "The scratches are from those little terrors. Not sure about the bruises but they're probably from them as well."

The two doctors glanced at the pups poking their heads over Dusk's fluffy tail.

"Have you experienced any shortness of breath, itchiness, sore joints, or abdominal pain?" Doctor Zero asked.

As Doctor Zero talked, his attention was stolen by whining. He watched as the gentler of the two pups climbed over Dusk and on to his leg. Jayden didn't want to move in case he startled the pup but as the little guy settled, he ran a hand over his back.

"Jayden, are you okay?" Doctor Zero checked.

He hummed, eyes closing.

"Jayden?"

"Sorry," he murmured.

"Don't be. We'll be as quick as possible so you can lay back down," Doctor Gray said.

Before she could take the blood sample, Jayden started listing to the side. A body pressed against his to keep him steady. A rosy pink spread across his cheeks and breathing became labored. Doctor Zero held a hand to his forehead and grimaced.

"Charlotte, his temperature has spiked," Doctor Zero said.

His clothes stuck to his skin as sweat soaked through. His arms felt like lead and he was too tired to move.

Doctor Gray's words were muddled. It took too long for his sluggish and overheated mind to understand what was being asked.

He was gently eased down to his pillow. One of the animals whimpered and nudged his cheek. He wanted to reassure his companions that he was okay but he didn't have any energy to.

Jayden sniffed and a coppery taste oozed into his mouth. When the sniffing didn't help, he wiped his nose and blood smeared the back of his hand.

"Okay, that's it. Maddy, help me get him to the bathroom," Doctor Gray said.

Dusk helped both doctors. The shower was turned on and he was placed on the floor underneath the cold spray. The freezing water snapped him awake as it stung his heated skin enough to make him try to crawl away.

"Stay, Jayden. We need to get you cooled down," Doctor Zero said, reaching in to make sure he stayed.

He groaned as he started to drift off again.

"No, stay awake," Doctor Zero urged.

"—'m tired," he mumbled.

"I know but try to stay awake," she pushed. "Charlotte, get Roderick. We're taking him to the hospital."

Jayden tried to use the last of his strength to stay awake but the overwhelming heat dragged him into the black void of sleep.

- **Chapter Thirteen -**

A thundering boom startled Jayden upright. Glancing around, he struggled to understand what was happening around him. Hands pushed him back down and he watched as the ceiling passed by. There was a nurse on either side of him, pushing the bed along with an air of urgency.

"What's —-"

"There was a quake," the nurse to the left explained.

Ceiling gave way to blinding light. His bed was wheeled further away from the hospital and under a tent. He was left alone, which gave him time to debate whether or not he'd bother trying to get out of bed.

"Hey," Balthezier greeted, popping into view.

"What's going on?" Jayden asked.

"Hang on."

The head of the bed was eased up and Jayden was able to see the mess. A wide crack ran through the ground, causing a part of the hospital to splinter and sink partially into the ground.

"I didn't think the quakes were strong enough yet," Jayden noted.

"They weren't until now," Balthezier said.

"Was anyone …" Jayden trailed off, slowly moving his legs off the bed.

"Hey, hey! Stay in bed. No one has been hurt. It's all just structural damage. Patients are being taken to human hospitals the administration has partnerships with," Balthezier explained.

Jayden nodded and regretted it as a wave of dizziness washed over him. Rubbing his temples, he closed his eyes and slumped back against his pillow.

"How are you?" Balthezier asked.

"I'm not as tired as before," Jayden answered.

"That's good. The doctors couldn't get your temperature to stop rising but when Doctor Turner stepped in to help, they were able to gradually get it down," Balthezier explained.

"When can I go home?" Jayden asked.

"Once your temperature is back to normal," Doctor Gray answered as she approached.

She stuck a thermometer into his mouth, grabbed his wrist, and stared at her watch. Jayden sat there in silence, watching the activity around him. He wanted to get out of bed and help.

When the thermometer beeped, Doctor Gray took it out and hummed at the results.

"Your temperature is still up but it's not as bad as it had been," she said.

He nodded. "How long was I out for?"

"A day and a half. Try to get a bit more rest."

Any arguments he had were muffled by a yawn.

Breathing came in sharp, painful bursts as he kept pushing cramped legs into motion. The moment he glanced back, he crashed into a concrete wall and landed with a splash. When he looked at his hands, they were covered in thick red liquid.

Wide-eyed, Jayden scrambled back to his feet and tried to wipe blood off his hands. He froze when a chilling roar shook the walls. Not wanting to find out what it belonged to, he bolted.

Hungry growls echoed around the maze of corridors. He didn't know how far away the beast was. All he knew was that he had to keep moving.

Until he stumbled into a crossroads.

He wasted precious seconds trying to decide which way to go. However, the thing chasing him was getting closer and that knowledge forced him to decide.

Choosing to go left, he ran until the corridor in front was shrouded in darkness. Going into an area where he couldn't see was too much of a risk and using his Abilities to create a light source would only attract the thing chasing him.

Jayden frowned.

How did he know that?

Before he could figure out what to do, a warm brush of foul smelling air hit the back of his neck. Eyes widened in fear, he slowly turned around. Within inches of his face, was a creature of nightmares.

A crooked mouth full of razor sharp teeth smiled at him. The eyes were sewn shut but he knew the creature would be compensating with its hearing and sense of smell. Its arms hung stiffly in front with joints dislocated at sickening angles. It was bone thin and towered above Jayden as it stretched out to its full height.

He stepped back, a scream in the back of his throat threatening to rip through time and space itself.

Jayden flung himself out of bed and frantically glanced around. Panting, he struggled to remember why he had the sense of urgency to run.

"Jay, are you okay?" Balthezier asked.

Everyone in the makeshift hospital was staring at him in concerned confusion.

"Jay?" Balthezier asked, gently squeezing his shoulder.

"I'm … I'm okay," Jayden said as he leaned back against the pillows.

He took a deep breath and focused on his friend.

"What are you dreaming about?" Balthezier asked.

The more he thought about the nightmare, the less he could remember.

"I … I don't know," he answered. "I can't remember."

A bad feeling settled in the pit of his stomach.

"You okay?" Balthezier checked again.

Jayden nodded distractedly. The disappearance of his dream left him with a sense that he was forgetting something rather important.

"I'll find the doctor," Balthezier said, pointing off to the side.

"Mr. Lugian?"

He blinked, refocusing on what was happening around him. Doctor Turner smiled when he had Jayden's attention. It was an unsettling look. The smile didn't reach his eyes.

"The tablets I gave you appear to not have been strong enough to completely block your Abilities. Unfortunately, as your Abilities still weren't controlled enough, they fought back against the tablets and that was the cause of the fever and fatigue," Doctor Turner explained.

"I see," Jayden mumbled.

Of course, his Abilities wouldn't make this easy. He wiped his face tiredly. What would he do if nothing ended up working?

"I'll get a nurse to take your temperature and if they're happy with the results, they can discharge you," Doctor Turner told him before leaving.

"Okay."

"He's an odd man," Balthezier said, appearing beside Jayden, watching the doctor.

Doctor Turner weaved his way through the crowd, barely looking up from his tablet.

Jayden nodded. He couldn't get a read on the doctor, no matter how often they met.

Once a nurse was heading their way, he sat up straighter, earning a snicker from his friend.

"Shh," Jayden hushed.

That elicited an amused snort from his friend.

"Okay, Mr. Lugian. Let's see how your temperature is so you can be on your way," the nurse said.

"Thanks."

A thermometer was stuck underneath his tongue and fingers held the inside of his wrist. While the nurse checked him over, he took to watching what was happening around him. Portable curtains were being erected and a group of people were setting up a temporary transport deck.

"Okay, looks like you're finally in the all clear. I'll fill out the discharge papers," the nurse said.

"Thanks."

Balthezier plopped a bag of clothes on the bed as the nurse left.

"I'll give you some privacy to get dressed," Balthezier said.

The blond used his Abilities to erect a circular wall around Jayden.

He slipped out of the hospital gown and into his own clothes. With a frown, he pulled his shirt away from his chest. His clothes felt bigger than normal.

"Are these yours?" Jayden asked.

"Nope, yours. Why?" Balthezier answered.

"I'm done," Jayden called out.

Balthezier waved the Ward away as Jayden finished tying his shoelaces.

"I need a shower," Jayden said.

"Yeah, you do," Balthezier agreed.

Jayden rolled his eyes.

Three people he hadn't expected to see at the makeshift hospital caught his eye. Iris was in a wheelchair with a sick bag in hand and Aster was standing beside her. Koan said something to the two of them and walked off.

"I'll be back," Jayden murmured.

He made his way through the crowd towards his grandparents.

"Are you two okay?" Jayden greeted.

"Jayden? It's good to see you up and about," Aster smiled. "Iris has a bout of food poisoning. Nothing to worry about too much."

"But Koan cooks everything, right?" Jayden checked.

"Normally, yes. But he got caught up with a few things and Leeran ended up getting us all take-out," Aster explained.

"Is there anything I can do to help?" Jayden asked.

"You need to rest," Iris said.

"But …"

Iris took his hand. "You need to focus on your health and try to gain back some weight. Don't worry about us. Koan is getting some help so this won't happen again."

"It's good to see you again, Jayden," Koan greeted, coming to stand beside him. "A nurse will be here shortly."

"Thank you. Please take Jayden back to his bed," Iris instructed.

Koan nodded and gestured for Jayden to lead the way. He hesitated for a second as he didn't want to leave his grandparents.

"Go," Iris urged.

Sighing, Jayden quickly hugged both of them and walked back to Balthezier with Koan.

"Jayden, we will talk soon," Koan said.

"About what?"

"Everything," Koan answered.

Chapter Fourteen

Jayden mindlessly finished stacking the breakfast dishes in the dishwasher and yawned. Not too far away, the pups were chomping down their breakfast under the watchful gaze of Dusk.

"Have you finished?" Roderick asked.

"Almost. I just need to turn the dishwasher on and wipe down the bench," Jayden answered.

"Leave that for Balthezier. Come with me," Roderick replied.

He washed and dried his hands before following Roderick down into the basement. The last time he had been down there had been when Leeran and Taylin had attempted to teach him control by using Kelly and her Halium heritage.

To Jayden's surprise, the basement had been renovated. It was no longer open space. Now, it had a short corridor that ended with a metal door.

"Look, kid. Balthezier isn't always going to be around to help you out if you lose control. I know sometimes you can sense when it's about to happen so in the hope that you do and can get here in time, I want you to use this room," Roderick explained.

Roderick opened the door and beckoned him in. Jayden didn't know how to react. It was a perfectly normal looking room, however, the air was laced with the warmth of the Calming Ward Balthezier always used on him.

"The Calming Ward is ingrained into the walls and floor so not even Mackenzie will be able to provoke you in here. There's a mini fridge over in the corner, a bathroom on the other side of that door on the far right, and I've placed a few of your belongings and new books inside to keep you occupied when your mind is back," Roderick listed.

Jayden struggled to understand what he was seeing and hearing.

"Why did you … I don't understand," Jayden said.

"This is your home, kiddo. And I want to help you in any way, shape, or form that I can," Roderick said.

He rubbed the back of his neck as he turned away. He was overwhelmed by the continuous support from the Adlers.

He walked around the room, taking everything in. There were cushions piled on top of the bed lining the wall. Beside it sat a bedside table with a lamp and a small clock. Along the opposite wall was a shelving unit that stood at waist height and stacked with books, and the mini fridge was not that far away from it in the corner.

"I … thank you so much, Roderick," Jayden eventually said.

"Jayden, there's a couple of guests here for you!" Balthezier shouted from the top of the stairs.

"This is your space. Neither of us will step inside unless you invite us in," Roderick said.

"Thank you," Jayden said and smiled.

The door to the room was closed and both climbed back upstairs.

"Liz?"

"Thanks is not necessary," Balthezier smirked.

"Okay, but can you move, please?" Jayden asked, raising an eyebrow.

Balthezier blinked a few times before it dawned on him that he was in the middle of the doorway.

Out on the pub floor, Doctors Gray and Zero were at one table, and another were Kelly and Spencer. Both options set him on edge. After the last few days, he didn't have the energy to face either conversation.

Swallowing the lump in his throat, Jayden forced his legs to take him to the two doctors.

"Hi," he greeted. "Is everything okay?"

"Yes, sorry. Take a seat. We wanted to let you know that we're being sent overseas for a bit," Doctor Gray explained.

"Oh," Jayden murmured.

"While we're gone, I'd like you to touch base with a colleague of mine — Doctor Fox. He'll be in contact with the lab and will be the one to decide if we need to put you on a course of tablets," Doctor Zero said.

"We also wanted to let you know that Leeran and Taylin have been rather vocal about you being unwell and they have been caught trying to get into —"

The building rattled and swayed. Glasses and plates danced off tables and smashed on the ground. Customers were on their feet, glancing around nervously. Some stumbled over to pillars and held on, clenching their eyes shut in fear.

"The border," Jayden gasped.

Thankfully, the quake didn't gain strength and barely lasted half a minute.

"Are you two alright?" Doctor Gray asked.

"Yeah," Jayden answered distractedly.

"I'm okay," Doctor Zero confirmed.

"We've got to go and finish packing. Please don't hesitate to call us if you need anything, even if it's just to talk, okay?" Doctor Gray said.

He nodded. "Have a safe trip."

After the mess from the quake was cleaned up, he sat down and buried his face in his hands. Something had to be done about the instability of Szantium. He'd have to venture out soon to see how much land had been lost.

The flare of heated Abilities told Jayden Kelly was nearby by and he tensed sharply. The anger and urge to unleash his Abilities destructively was almost overwhelming. It took everything he had to keep his powers under control.

Glancing over to Balthezier and Roderick talking to customers, he stood up.

"Not to be rude but can we have this conversation downstairs?"

Kelly nodded. "Sure."

Silently, he led her down to the room Roderick had given him. The Calming Ward immediately banished the effects of the Halium bloodline, making it easier for him to concentrate.

"You really are back," Kelly stated.

Jayden nodded.

"And you're sick. How bad?"

"You heard, huh?" Jayden sighed, sitting on the bed. "It's bad. My Abilities are attacking me and it's making me sick. The doctors are still trying to figure out why though."

"Jay —-"

He shook his head and sighed.

Kelly had grown up and he could see much of the anger she had carried as a teen had simmered down. There was a gentleness in her eyes that hadn't been there before. Her brown hair had been cut to shoulder length, and sports clothes had been replaced with a dark pair of jean legs, a V-neck top, and a long cardigan.

"My doctors keep telling me that I need to talk to someone to help me cope and the last thing I want to do is to talk to a shrink," Jayden admitted.

"Why me?" Kelly asked.

"Roderick and Liz are the obvious choices, right? I do talk to them, but at this point, I rely on them too much and that'll only increase as I get worse. You were there to help me before. When I found out I was a dead man walking, I wanted to see someone from my life before all of this."

Kelly nudged him gently as she sat down beside him. "I know we weren't really close. That was Nicholas. But I was really happy when I found out that you were alive. Whatever you need, Jay, you can count on me."

Jayden flashed her a grateful smile.

"Tell me what's happened over the last nine years," Jayden requested.

"Balthezier, can you take me to my Anchor, please?" Jayden asked.

"Yeah, sure. Give me five minutes," Balthezier replied.

Jayden grimaced and glanced over to where Roderick was in a heated argument with Leeran and Taylin.

"They're back, huh?" Balthezier remarked.

"Second time today and still demanding I go back so they can look after me," Jayden said.

For days now, Leeran and Taylin had been storming into The Balgaire and demanding Jayden go back to the Laiyfe-Rain mansion. Roderick always stopped them from getting too far into the establishment to find him but seeing the man having to deal with his birth parents made him feel terrible.

"Meet me upstairs," Balthezier said.

Jayden ushered the pups and Dusk to his room and waited.

"Okay, dad has gotten them out of here but those two need a walk anyway," Balthezier said, coming into the room.

"Thanks," Jayden said.

The moment they appeared in the valley, his animal companions ran off.

He took a deep breath and slowly exhaled. It was great to be back. It was peaceful amongst the trees and he walked until his shoes were brushed by water.

'Welcome back, Jayden Lugian,' Babyloneous greeted.

He turned around and smiled up at the serpent. Babyloneous looked exactly like he had the last time Jayden saw him. Light blue and green scales glistened in the sun. A tuft of sea green hair fell between two pointed ears and cream tendrils fell down on either side of his snout.

"Sorry, it's been a while," Jayden said.

'I have had the company of Dusk and Balthezier, even if they cannot hear my words,' Babyloneous said.

The serpent nuzzled Jayden, who wrapped his arms around his snout in a hug.

'I can smell the sickness,' Babyloneous said as he pulled away.

"Oh," Jayden murmured. "The doctors don't know what exactly is happening, only that my Abilities have a mind of their own."

Babyloneous leaned in closer. *'May I?'*

"Ahh, okay?" Jayden said, frowning.

Babyloneous ran his forked tongue over him and inhaled deeply. It was tense waiting for the serpent to conclude his search. Jayden couldn't stop his body from shaking in anticipation.

"What's wrong with me?" Jayden asked in desperation.

'Someone has tampered with the core of who you are. This change has caused a major imbalance and conflict within. Your Abilities are trying to help but what has happened to you is far too much for even someone of your strength. The resulting conflict is the reason why your body is failing,' Babyloneous intoned.

Jayden couldn't breathe. Did he change because of his exposure to the In Between? He shook his head. Babyloneous said some*one*, not some*thing*. Had it been the Council of 8? He couldn't think of anyone who would have done this or when they would have had the chance to mess around with him like that.

The pups came to a skidding halt against the back of his legs. One took up a growling stance between Jayden and Babyloneous. However, Jayden could barely understand what was going on beyond the whirlwind of thoughts.

Sensing the incoming panic attack, Dusk knocked him down and crowded in to lick his face.

He took a sharp, shaky breath and hugged the Linstonate.

Babyloneous lowered his head and inspected the defensive winged pup. He flashed large fangs and chuckled when the pup continued to growl.

'Where did you find these little ones?' Babyloneous asked.

"N-near the edge of Szantium," Jayden answered.

'Keep them close. They contain old power that will aid you in your tasks ahead,' Babyloneous advised.

"Tasks?" Jayden asked.

'You will be sent off to find eight important pieces of Szantium,' Babyloneous said before disappearing amongst the trees.

Jayden stood up, ruffling Dusk between the ears, eyes watching the serpent leave. Balthezier popped in next to him. The blond glanced from Jayden to the trees and leaned in closer in order to follow his gaze.

"What are you looking at?" Balthezier asked.

"Trees," Jayden answered.

Balthezier gave him an unimpressed look.

"Ha. Ha. It's time to go home."

The pups were gathered close with Dusk putting a paw on one to get them to stay and with a squeeze of Jayden's shoulder, Balthezier took them all back home.

"Jayden! Just who we were wanting to see."

He glanced over to the counter and saw Octavia and Artemis with Roderick.

"Artemis and I would like to take you out for lunch," Octavia said.

Jayden glanced over to the Adlers. He wanted to tell them what he had learnt from Babyloneous but he was scared they wouldn't believe him.

"Okay," Jayden said. "Roderick, can we talk later, please?"

"Sure."

He followed the two Gaede women to Café 8.

Artemis sat beside him at a corner booth and smiled. She gave him a pen and paper with a note asking if he was okay. He wrote back that he was fine and asked if she was okay as well.

They traded notes back and forth until Octavia came back with a table number.

"I've ordered everyone something to eat," Octavia said.

"How much do I owe you?" Jayden asked, getting out his wallet.

"Don't worry about it. My treat," Octavia dismissed.

"Are you sure?" he checked.

Artemis quickly scribbled down on their notepaper and passed it to him.

'Don't worry about it. Promise. You can treat us to a meal another time, okay?'

He wrote back, *'Sure?'*

Artemis smiled and nodded.

"We actually brought you out for lunch so that we can teach you sign language," Octavia told him.

"Oh. Thanks," Jayden said.

"If you're serious about being Artemis's friend, that is," Octavia tacked on.

He frowned in confusion. "Excuse me? Artemis has been there for me through a lot. I'm not going to ditch her because I have to learn a new way to communicate with her."

The older woman studied him before turning to Artemis and signing to her.

In the meantime, their food and drinks were delivered. Jayden watched the activity going on in the café. There were a few customers around and he could feel that there was a mixture of human and Szaephian. It was a peaceful atmosphere and he found himself relaxing.

A soft touch on his arm brought his attention back to his companions.

"Eat up and we'll begin lessons," Octavia said.

He nodded and ate as much as possible.

Once they were all finished eating, plates were taken away and cups refilled, they started on the basics of sign language. It was a little difficult to remember where he needed to put fingers and his floundering attempts had both women giggling, which lead to a smile tugging on his lips. Despite the slow progress, he was having fun.

- **Chapter Fifteen -**

Jayden, Balthezier, and Artemis were walking across the grass in the city square with the intent of sitting underneath a shady tree to work on Jayden's sign language lessons when the quake hit.

They were knocked to the ground, and around them buildings wobbled on their foundations before cracking and giving way. Screams were muffled as thundering crashing echoed through the city.

Jayden watched in horror as the ground split open in the direction of the border and into the city square, stopping mere meters in front of the trio.

When the shaking finally stopped, he helped Artemis to her feet and cautiously approached the splintered earth. The In Between sloshed against the earthy walls. Feeling a bout of vertigo, he took a step back and let out a shaky breath.

"Lugian! Emergency meeting, now! Bring Artemis."

He looked over to the well-dressed man who had called out.

"Go," Balthezier urged. "I'm going to see how my dad and The Balgaire are."

After Balthezier signed to Artemis what was going on, she nodded and dragged Jayden by the hand through the streets. He wanted to stop and help those they passed but she kept a firm hand on him.

He was taken into the Temple of 8, past the knocked over barrier ropes, and down a long spiral staircase. They came out into a well-lit cone shaped room. Eight seats and benches wrapped around eight levels that were broken up by two staircases. The air was full of panic. Jayden wondered if now they'd listen to reason and vacate the city before it was too late.

Without stopping, Artemis led him straight to the bottom where four young adults were waiting.

"If everyone could take a seat, we'll start the meeting."

Jayden took a seat beside Artemis and glanced around the room in confusion. Was this the Council he had been forced to join?

Artemis nudged him and nodded down to the note she held.

'It's the new Council.'

He made a silent 'oh' with his lips.

"Szantium is breaking apart. The lives of everyone in this city are at risk. We must decide here and now what we are going to do."

He tilted his head. It was the man who had called out to them and it was niggling in the back of his mind where he had previously seen the man.

'Emmerson Judge,' Artemis wrote.

He remembered Emmerson Judge had led one of the groups in the last fight against the Council of 8. The man donned an expensive fitted black suit.

As ideas on what to do were thrown around, Jayden tried his best to write as quickly as possible for Artemis. Once or twice he had tried to sign but he didn't know enough to be of any help.

Thankfully, the person sitting on Artemis's other side leaned over and said, "I got this, man."

He watched as the guy flawlessly translated for her.

"Thanks," he mumbled.

Artemis linked her hand with his and squeezed reassuringly.

"We need to abandon the city. There's plenty of land in the Human Plane left unclaimed we can rebuild on," a person from the top said.

"Abandon the city? Are you series? After everything we've gone through, the last thing anyone would want is to abandon their home," objected a man dressed in an expensive looking suit.

"Enough!" Emmerson's voice boomed over everyone else's. "Bookman will address the Council."

A boy, no older than ten years old with dark hair and tanned skin stood up and stared down at the First Circle. Jayden swept his gaze over the rest of the Council in confusion. There was no way someone that young could be a part of the Council and command so much attention.

"There is an old tale about how Szantium was taken out of the Human Plane and into its own reality. As we know, the Original 8 created eight Compass Points in order to keep Szantium stable outside of the normal parameters. If the Compass Points were found, we would be able to put Szantium back," Bookman said.

"Even if they existed, no one knows what they look like or even where to locate them," someone from the fifth level stated.

"That's even more absurd than abandoning the city," shouted the same suited man from before.

"Let's not dismiss that idea just yet. Strong Abilities have kept Szantium safe and everyone knows the stories of what the Original 8 did to save our people back then. The Compass Points need to be found. Can anyone else here suggest another way to save our city?" one of Bookman's companions asked.

"Who in their right mind would leave now in order to find those mythical things? Szantium doesn't have time for a wild goose chase. We need to act now!"

Arguments became louder and more heated. The longer it went on, the more people weren't willing to budge or suggest anything else outside of abandoning the city or looking for something most didn't believe existed anymore.

Jayden rubbed his forehead in annoyance and sighed.

"I'll go," he announced.

The chamber fell silent and every pair of eyes stared at him in disbelief.

Next to him, Artemis signed to her translator and raised her hand.

"Artemis Gaede volunteers to go as well," announced the translator.

The stunned bubble popped and all at once objections rang out loudly around them. He glanced at his friend. The arguments were as clear as day. No one wanted two people they thought were unreliable to search for something even if they didn't believe it existed.

He turned his attention away from the arguments and realized Bookman was staring intently at him.

With a raise of his hand, Bookman commanded the entire room into silence.

"We do not have time for arguments. By our research, we have a month and a half to try and save the city or abandon it to save our people. If Mr. Lugian and Miss Gaede are willing to volunteer for our cause then how about the entirety of the First Circle take care of searching for the Compass Points while the rest of the Council work on giving them enough time to carry out their search. If they come back unsuccessful, then we can put the option to the people."

"Wait a minute! No," objected Reid.

"We, the Architects, agree with Bookman," a muscled man in overalls announced.

One by one, the different sections of the Council agreed.

"The First Circle will depart in four days. I suggest the six of you use the time to gather as much information as possible. You will be given four weeks to search for all eight Compass Points. At that point, the Council will decide what to do," Bookman declared.

With a course of action finally decided and agreed upon, everyone started filing out.

Jayden stood up to leave but as Reid stormed past, he shoved Jayden back and glared at Artemis. Rolling his eyes, he stayed until only Artemis, Mackenzie, Artemis's translator, and one other remained.

"I hope you know what you're doing."

He raised an eyebrow at Artemis's translator. The guy had olive skin, dark brown eyes, and floppy brown hair. He was dressed in a blue, red, and purple plaid shirt that covered a black shirt, slim fit grey chinos, and a pair of sneakers.

"Easy, easy. I'm with you on this. I'm just stating what we're all thinking. I'm Van Bixlar," the brunette said.

"I'm Sera Quiroz," a young woman with a friendly smile said.

Sera had a slightly darker tone of olive skin compared to Van but she had lighter brown eyes. Her brown hair was braided around the back of her head with strands framing her face. She was dressed in a loose button up white shirt barely tucked into black jeans, and heeled boots.

"And I can't believe what you're doing! You're sick. You can't be gallivanting across the world searching for things that don't exist anymore," Mackenzie snapped.

Jayden barely glanced over at his twin.

"We should go talk to Octavia and Roderick," Jayden suggested as he fumbled with his hands to sign to Artemis.

She beamed with pride and took his hand.

"Hey! Don't ignore me," Mackenzie yelled.

When he went to grab Jayden, Artemis turned around and conjured up a Ward quicker than their eyes could track, and forced Mackenzie to back off by throwing him into the level above him.

Satisfied there weren't going to be any more problems, Artemis led Jayden, Van, and Sera off to The Balgaire and Café 8.

- Chapter Sixteen -

Jayden, Artemis, Van, and Sera spent the first day leading up to the departure buried in books at the Great Library. No matter how many books they went through, they could barely find anything related to the Compass Points beyond the rare and brief mentions.

It was a disheartening first day.

There were no clues as to how the Original 8 had created them, no mention of how exactly they worked, or even what they looked like. The little information they did find stated that the Compass Points were the pillars of Szantium and without any one of them or something called The Heart, Szantium would fall.

Sighing, he ran a hand through his hair.

"I'm heading home. I've got to talk to Roderick anyway," Jayden said.

He glanced over to Van. The guy had fallen asleep about an hour ago while flipping through a large old book.

"Don't stay too much longer," Jayden said.

"Don't worry about Van. He got a bit excited about research so he went through his family's library instead of sleeping. He's just staying around because I promised food. We'll be leaving soon anyway," Sera said.

Jayden carefully signed a goodbye to Artemis and left the library. He had spent the night before with Balthezier and going through online videos practicing sign language. It was slow going but the time he had spent was paying off as he was able to communicate a little better with her outside of pen and paper.

An intersection away from the Great Library and the sense of being followed flared up to new heights. He glanced around frantically.

Nestled in the shadows was a black, disfigured creature. Jayden swallowed the lump in his throat as it snapped its attention towards him. It had a mouth full of razor sharp teeth and when it stepped out into the light, he could see its eyes had been sewn shut. Gangly thin arms hung around in front of it at sickening angles.

Fear pounded against Jayden and it paralyzed him.

Jostling reminded him of where he was. A crowd had formed around him. There was a rise of power in the air and people were either backing away or preparing to fight. He could barely pay attention to anyone else. There was a voice shouting at him to run.

In an effort to back away, he collided with numerous people. Ignoring angry words and looks, Jayden ran as fast as he could until he was inside The Balgaire.

"Jay, are you okay?" Roderick asked.

He panted as he leaned against the door. His head spun and his legs felt like jelly. Dusk approached and rubbed against him. Taking a deep breath, Jayden made his way upstairs to his room with Roderick and Dusk following behind.

"What happened?" Roderick asked.

"I don't know. I saw this … this *thing* after I left the Great Library and I panicked," Jayden answered, sitting down on his bed.

"What thing?" Roderick asked.

"I don't know! It had sharp teeth, no eyes, and it looked kind of disfigured," Jayden tried to explain.

Roderick frowned. "Doesn't sound familiar. I'll get you some water."

Jayden nodded and focused on trying to catch his breath. He couldn't pause his frenzied mind. The scary thing was, he was pretty certain he had seen the creature before … somewhere.

Frustrated, he buried his face in his hands and growled.

He couldn't think of where or when. There was a mental block stopping him from remembering.

"Here."

Accepting the glass of water the older man held out for him, he sipped while he thought things over. There was no time for this nonsense.

"Jayden, you need to read those books I gave you," Roderick said.

Jayden raised an eyebrow. "I have more pressing matters."

"Read them," Roderick pressed.

"Not until you tell me why," Jayden stubbornly argued.

Roderick took the books from the desk and sat down on the edge of the mattress.

"There are certain things in these books that will help in your search for the Compass Points. I'm forbidden from talking about the exact nature as these books were supposed to have been destroyed many years ago. We have kept these hidden until those who only sought to help Szantium were looking for the Compass Points," Roderick explained.

"You do know that only leaves more questions, right?" Jayden pointed out.

"Just read them," Roderick urged before leaving Jayden with the books.

Breathing came in sharp, painful bursts as he kept pushing cramped legs into motion. The moment he glanced back, he crashed into a concrete wall and landed with a splash. When he looked at his hands, they were covered in thick red liquid.

Wide eyed, Jayden scrambled back to his feet and tried to wipe blood off his hands. He froze when a chilling roar shook the walls. Not wanting to find out what it belonged to, he bolted.

Hungry growls echoed around the maze of corridors. He didn't know how far the beast was. All he knew was that he had to keep moving.

Until he stumbled into a crossroads.

He wasted precious seconds trying to decide which way to go. However, the thing chasing him was getting closer and that knowledge forced him to decide.

Choosing to go left, he ran until the corridor in front was shrouded in darkness. Going into an area where he couldn't see was too much of a risk and using his Abilities to create a light source would only attract the thing that was chasing him.

Jayden frowned.

How did he know that?

Before he could figure out what to do, a warm brush of foul smelling air hit the back of his neck. Eyes widened in fear, he slowly turned around. Within inches of his face, was a creature of nightmares.

A crooked mouth full of razor sharp teeth smiled at him. The eyes were sewn shut but he knew the creature would be compensating with its hearing and sense of smell. Its arms hung stiffly in front with joints dislocated at sickening angles. It was bone thin and towered over Jayden as it stretched out to its full height.

He stepped back, a scream in the back of his throat threatening to rip through time and space itself.

He woke up covered in sweat and struggling to breathe. His legs were twisted in the thin blanket and it took a moment to remember where he was. There were whines coming from the left side of the room. Before he could see what was going on, there was a loud crash around him, causing him to jump.

Pushing himself up with shaky arms, he reached out for his lamp to see what was going on. However, he was met with open air. Moving his legs off the mattress felt like moving through mud.

Slowly, he inched along the wall until he found the light switch.

Furniture was splayed everywhere. All except his bed had toppled over. Fearing his Abilities had a mind of their own while he had been asleep, he checked for blood on his face. Nothing came back on his fingers before he could see his pillow and sheets were streaked with dried stains.

With panic on the verge of taking over, he quickly yanked off the covers from his bed. He needed to clean up before someone came in to see what happened.

As adrenaline disappeared, dizziness took over.

"I've got you," Balthezier said, taking hold of his shoulders.

Jayden tried to push him off but Balthezier maneuvered him over to the seat by the window. Without a word, the blond stripped off the bed, disposing of stained sheets in the washing basket and replacing them with fresh ones. Once he was finished, he knelt down in front of Jayden and gently wiped the dried blood off with a wet cloth.

"You're having more and more nightmares," Balthezier pointed out.

Jayden hummed.

"What's going on?" Balthezier asked.

"Nothing. Everyone is entitled to their nightmares," Jayden replied. "Get out so I can go back to sleep."

"You and I both know that won't happen, Mr. Cranky Pants," Balthezier said.

"Then just leave," Jayden huffed.

Balthezier stared with a frown but he thankfully didn't push the matter any further.

Alone, he ran a hand through his hair and closed his eyes. Dusk sat next to him, resting his head on Jayden's shoulder. The timid pup slowly approached with ears flat against his head and sat in his lap. The other took his time joining them and curled up in between Dusk's paws.

"I should come up with names for both of you. It's been long enough," he murmured.

A head tilted in his lap and there was huff next to his leg.

"I have to call you something," he pointed out.

He leaned against Dusk and sighed. He was tired.

"Liz?" Jayden called out, coming downstairs.

"Sit, eat, and talk," Balthezier said.

He sat at a table with Dusk and the twins by his feet. Balthezier brought over two bowls of freshly chopped fruit and yoghurt, placed them on the table, and went back to the counter to get the bowls of food for the animals.

"Thank you," Jayden said as he dug in.

"Not a problem. I'm just glad you're eating after last night. Hurry up and finish so we can go to your appointment."

"I cancelled it."

Balthezier looked at him with raised eyebrows. "Excuse me? Why?"

"I haven't had the chance to really say anything yet but Babyloneous checked me over and he told me that I'm sick because someone has changed who I was and my Abilities are trying to help but they're losing. So doctors, especially human medicine, can't really help," Jayden explained.

"Dad, get in here!" Balthezier shouted.

"Hold on!"

"Now. Jayden needs to tell you something," Balthezier said.

"Liz, please. Don't make a big deal out of this," Jayden begged.

Roderick came over, huffing, and glared at his son.

"Some of us are busy trying to get this place ready for the day," Roderick growled.

"Jayden, explain," Balthezier demanded.

He sighed and went over what he had told Balthezier. Roderick went from being impatient with his son to frowning in thought.

"Has this Babyloneous ever been wrong?" Roderick asked.

"No," Jayden answered.

Roderick nodded. "Okay. We will need to try and figure out what has actually happened to you while also making sure you don't get any worse. If you do, then we're bringing your doctors back into it. Got it?"

"Okay," Jayden agreed.

"You'll need to tell your doctors," Roderick said.

Jayden almost slumped over from relief. He was glad both Adlers believed him.

"I'll give Doctor Zero a call," Jayden said.

"When you leave, make sure you check in every now and then. We know you'll get help when you need it so make sure you don't wait until you're struggling to do anything. Okay?" Roderick said.

"I'll try," Jayden agreed. "If we're done with this conversation, can I be sent to my Anchor for an hour please?"

"What for? Aren't you meeting Artemis soon?" Balthezier asked.

"I want to see if Babyloneous knows anything about the Compass Points," Jayden explained.

"Have you read the books yet?" Balthezier asked.

Jayden gave him an unimpressed look. "I tried last night but I couldn't concentrate. I'll try again when I'm not so tired."

The blond folded his arms across his chest and hummed.

"Fine," he huffed.

There was a look on Balthezier's face that he couldn't quite understand. It felt like the blond was scared and worried about the whole thing. Before he could ask about the look, his friend transported him and his animal companions to the Anchor.

Jayden was glad they had arrived by the river. While he took off his shoes, Dusk and the pups ran off to burn some energy. He rolled up his pants to his knees and walked into the river. The water felt nice against his skin and he sighed as he took a moment to relax.

When he heard something large approach from behind, he turned and waited on shore for the serpent.

'Hello, Jayden Lugian,' Babyloneous greeted.

"You told me last time that I'd be searching for important pieces of Szantium. Was that about the Compass Points?"

Babyloneous nodded and curled his body up. Jayden gathered his shoes and socks and took a seat in front of the serpent.

'Shortly after they were created, the Compass Points were placed across the three different levels of existence –- the Human Plane, the Szaephian Plane, and the In Between. They were created as living entities with power and free will.'

"Do you know what they look like or where they went?"

'They're not called Compass Points simply for the sake of it. Each of these eight pieces are in charge of a specific direction –- North, North-East, East, South-East, South, South-West, West, and North-West. Each of these is connected by a single point,' Babyloneous answered.

He had heard this before.

"The Heart, right? I remember Kalarney telling me something about it all before. She said that without The Heart, the Compass Points didn't communicate at first and it had caused Szantium to destabilize … which is what's happening now."

Babyloneous nodded.

"But why now? Has The Heart disappeared or is it because something is wrong with the Compass Points?" Jayden asked.

'The Heart has been damaged.'

Jayden rubbed his eyes in frustration. That wasn't good.

"How will I know if I've found one?"

'If they wish to show themselves to you, they will carry old power. It is the only way to tell them apart from others.'

Jayden frowned and glanced towards where Dusk and the pups were playing.

Old power …

'Jayden, be aware of what's happening around you. Some will seek you out in order to help and some will hinder you on your journey. Friends can turn out to be enemies and those who you thought were enemies could be your greatest allies. It has been a pleasure being your friend. Thank you, Jayden Lugian,' Babyloneous said.

The serpent nuzzled him affectionately, rubbing his snout along both of Jayden's cheeks.

Jayden pursed his lips in confusion. He wanted to ask what he meant but the giant serpent was already heading back into the trees.

Chapter Seventeen

The horrible creature was waiting for him when he stepped outside in the morning. No matter where he ran or hid, it was always in the corner of his eye. By the time Jayden made it to the Great Library, his heart felt like it was going to explode.

Shaking his head, he tried to forget the creature in order to focus on researching. He walked through the aisles, surrounded by books on each side of him. Every now and then, he took out a book and flipped through its pages. A few patrons suggested titles when he asked for recommendations on the history of Szantium and its people.

He was focused reading a passage as he sat down at the table Artemis, Van, and Sera had occupied. A deep frown was set across his brow. What he was reading, didn't make sense.

"I'm reading conflicting information," Jayden noted.

He rubbed his forehead in frustration.

"What's conflicting?" Sera said.

"It's just … Take this book for example. This detailed the relationship between Szaephian and Humans prior to the whole living in a different plane of existence thing. This book indicates there was no relationship. Szaephians stuck to themselves and if found out, humans killed them," Jayden said.

"Yeah. That's common knowledge, dude," Sera said. "I believe humans called it a witch hunt."

The brunette rolled her eyes and stretched out her arms and back.

"The thing is though, another book I read stated that prior to the witch hunts the humans documented, Szaephian and humans lived together peacefully. They had a mutually beneficial relationship. There was no animosity, no us against them, at least not until religious fear mongering happened," Jayden added.

"Where'd you read that?" Van checked.

Jayden stretched to his full height and folded his arms across his chest.

"Koan has been giving me books to read and I … really like learning the history of this place," Jayden said, blushing a little.

He barely caught the thoughtful look Van wore.

"It isn't just this that I've found to have conflicting information. There's actually surprisingly a lot. Who would know which version is true or not?" he asked.

Artemis tapped him on the arm and slowly signed, 'The Academics should know.'

'I don't know anyone in the Academics,' Jayden replied.

He slumped down in a chair and growled in frustration. He wondered whether or not there were books in the library that would confirm or deny the true version of events. However, that might not be the case considering he knew the Council of 8 had guarded the library before.

"Of course …" Jayden sighed.

He sat up in his chair and ran a hand over his face.

"Of course what?" Sera asked.

"Was anyone allowed in here while the Council of 8 was in power?" Jayden asked.

"Only those who had proven to be loyal," Sera answered.

"In the past amongst humans, leaders would change, ban, or destroy certain books. Sometimes it was to erase history of those who came before them, other times it was to make history be on their side," Jayden explained.

"And you think the Council did this?" Sera checked.

"If only their loyal followers were allowed in here, who's to say what they hid or changed. Whatever was taught in school would have had to be approved by the government in charge otherwise who's to say how many uprisings or challenges to their power there would have been," Jayden said.

'So we might not even find anything about the Compass Points here?' Artemis asked.

Sera dropped her forehead against the table after Van translated the sign language and groaned.

"How about lunch and then let's see if I can sneak everyone into the family library," Van suggested.

After packing up their books and making sure they weren't leaving anything behind, all four of them went to Café 8 for lunch. Along the way, Jayden spotted the distorted creature following them in the shadows. He couldn't help but tense. Why was it following him around the city? Every time the others turned to look at what had him on edge, the thing disappeared.

To make matters worse, they ran into Mackenzie along the street. As soon as the guy saw them, he tried to get Jayden to talk to him. When Artemis stepped in to help, Mackenzie resorted to insulting both of them. Before he could respond, Van and Sera were shoving Mackenzie away and ushering them into the café.

Danielle and Tatum greeted them warmly but when his twin tried to step in to follow them, both adults ordered Mackenzie out, telling him to never think about stepping into their establishment again.

After lunch, Van escorted them to his parents' house however, there were too many people hanging around and it was decided they couldn't risk sneaking into a library outsiders weren't allowed in. The four ended up back at the Great Library, unsure of what to do.

Leeran and Taylin were waiting for him outside the library when he stepped out in the evening.

Huffing in tired frustration, he tried to ignore them.

"Jayden, wait. You have to talk to us," Leeran insisted.

"No, I don't. Leave me alone," Jayden said.

"We're your parents. Your brother is upset you're ignoring him and we have a doctor ready to help you," Taylin objected.

"Excuse —-"

Jayden froze. The creature was crawling down a wall on the building across the path from the library.

Leeran followed his gaze as the creature dropped into a bush.

"Jay?"

"What? It's Jayden. Leave me alone," Jayden said distractedly.

He rushed back to The Balgaire and wiped his face. He had no energy left to waste on hyper-vigilance.

It wasn't a surprise when a Council meeting was called by Mackenzie with Leeran and Taylin the day before the First Circle were due to leave.

Jayden arrived with Artemis, books in hand, dreading to find out what trouble they were stirring now.

"Do you know what's going on?" Sera asked, standing beside him.

"Trouble," he answered.

"As if we didn't have enough on our plates," she groaned.

"Why have you called the Council and brought outsiders into the Chambers, Mackenzie?" Emmerson asked, silencing everyone.

"Jayden Laiyfe-Rain is not fit to leave the city and search for something as important as the Compass Points," Mackenzie declared.

Jayden took a step towards him, fists shaking with fury. How dare they?

Before he could do or say anything, Artemis grabbed his hand and shook her head when he glanced back at her.

Emmerson sighed impatiently. "You —"

"He's sick and losing his mind. We've seen him running around the city like a madman being chased," Mackenzie interrupted.

Bookman stood up with a stack of papers. "In my hands are multiple reports from witnesses stating a creature of unknown origins has been hanging around in the shadows over the last week. Seven of which came to my attention yesterday after witnesses saw the creature chasing Mr. Lugian multiple times throughout the day. So, not only have you wasted the Council's time but you've wasted your fellow First Circle's limited and valuable time. Unless you have anything that's useful to share, then I suggest all three of you keep your noses out of things that don't concern you."

"Jayden will only —"

"Taylin and Leeran, I suggest you keep your opinions to yourself while you are in the Council Chambers. Neither of you are a part of the new council and nor have we, as a collective, invited you here to speak. As such, your voices are not recognized. If you speak again, you will be escorted out of here," Bookman warned.

"He's only going to slow us down!" Mackenzie exclaimed. "He can't even stay in control."

"What's slowing us down, are your constant petty interruptions," Sera stated.

"Jayden is getting sicker and sicker. He has to focus on his health," Taylin said.

"I warned you both. Hunter Reagan, Hunter Morgan, please escort Leeran and Taylin out of the Chamber," Bookman ordered.

The two Hunters made their way down to the First Circle level and grabbed Leeran and Taylin. Jayden watched as they struggled and disappeared out of the Chambers. It was tiring dealing with those two and he felt guilty their obsession was causing problems for others.

"Look, man, what's your problem? Jayden has done more in the last three days than you or your parents have *ever* done. If you're so keen to point fingers as to who's dragging us down or holding us back, it's you," Van said.

"Actually, Mackenzie has a point," Reid spoke up. "So what if Jayden is great at being a bookworm? We've all seen him in action. If he's not coughing up blood, then he's losing control or being chased around by monsters. Just how useful would someone like that be out in the field?"

"Reid, shut up," Van growled.

"Enough!" shouted Bookman. "Jayden Lugian will be a part of this search. You'll be split into three teams for efficiency. The teams will be —- Mackenzie and Van, Sera and Artemis, and Jayden with Reid. Council is dismissed."

Before anyone in the First Circle could argue any further, the rest of the Council stood up and shuffled out.

"Jayden Lugian?" Bookman called out through the crowd. "I would like a moment of your time if you would be so kind."

Jayden looked over to Artemis and signed that he'd meet her outside in a moment. She nodded with a smile and left with Van and Sera.

He waited for the little kid to push through the crowd and proceeded to wait until they were the only ones left in the Chamber.

Bookman walked around him, looking up and down. Uncomfortable, Jayden shifted around.

"If all you wanted to do was look at me, could you do this some other time? I've got things to do and people to see," Jayden huffed.

"Does my appearance make you uncomfortable?" Bookman asked.

"You're a kid that looks like someone I … You're a kid," Jayden shook his head.

"I'm twenty-six years old, and taller than you," Bookman informed him.

Jayden raised his eyebrows at the boy. Bookman smirked as he stepped back. He rolled up a sleeve and ran a finger across a black tattoo on his forearm. The markings glowed blue and Bookman grew and aged.

In adult form, Bookman had dyed gray hair shaved along the sides and styled so that it was fluffed up and pushed back. The purple contacts made his eyes pop against his tanned skin. Underneath a semi-casual black jacket, was a green V-neck shirt loosely tucked into black skinny jeans.

Light pink tinged Jayden's cheeks when he was caught staring. Bookman tilted his head, stepped closer, and sniffed.

He leaned back, frowning. "Whoa! What are you doing?"

"Academics can see the truth in a lot of things. We search for knowledge and guard it against those who wish to erase it," Bookman explained, straightening up. "You, on the other hand, remain a mystery to us. What's your truth?"

"Excuse me?"

Bookman took his hand and held it up with his, palm to fingertips pressed together. Warmth spread between their hands and stretched down Jayden's arm before dispersing through the rest of his body. He watched in confused curiosity, earning a gentle smile from the man in front of him.

"I'm taking a peek into your condition. This isn't the most accurate way for me to do this but the other way is a little inappropriate," Bookman explained.

"The other way?" Jayden asked.

"Kissing."

Jayden nodded, feeling the heat grow in his cheeks.

"How old am I?" Jayden asked.

Bookman didn't answer. He was concentrating on their hands, and looked more and more concerned. The warmth between them grew until it became unbearable. Hissing, he yanked his hand away, shaking it in pain.

"My apologies. It seems there is a power blocking my attempts at seeing anything," Bookman told him.

"That'd be right," Jayden murmured. "Did you find anything out at all?"

"Not much, but I can say that whatever has happened to you, it isn't because of the In Between. The only thing the In Between did to you was temporarily freeze your time. To answer your question, you're now seventeen, almost eighteen," Bookman answered.

"That doesn't make sense. I went in when I was sixteen. If the In Between stopped me aging, then what happened for a year or so?" Jayden asked.

"I'm not sure but if you could find that out, then I'm sure you'll find the reasons as to why your Abilities are losing," Bookman reasoned.

"Did you see that as well? I've only told Roderick and Liz about it," Jayden said.

"This isn't the only reason why I pulled you aside," Bookman said. "There's something else going on. I'm not entirely sure, but the way everything has been happening cannot be a coincidence. Someone is pulling the strings and putting everyone in danger."

"Okay? And why are you telling me this?" Jayden asked.

"You're the only one I trust outside of the Academics," Bookman admitted.

Jayden raised an eyebrow. "We don't know each other.

"You would be surprised. Do not trust everyone. There are certain individuals in the community whose whereabouts, associations, and associates are questionable. These individuals have influence over members of the Council so I'd appreciate it if anything that we discuss would remain between us," Bookman explained.

"Three guesses as to who," Jayden murmured.

"I have people out there looking for answers as well as doing their own investigation into the Compass Points. If you ever need help on your travels, look for this symbol and help will be given," Bookman said, handing over a business card.

The design had a four handed clock encased in two thin circles. One set of hands were pointing to eight o'clock, while the other set was to three o'clock. Each hour hand had the corresponding number engraved into it.

"How will I even know where to look?" Jayden asked.

Bookman turned the business card around to reveal a logo with the name 'Time Collectors' scrawled across it.

"You can search online for the exact address in the country you're in. When you enter the shop, present them with the card and they'll know you're an ally."

Jayden nodded and slipped the card into his wallet.

"I … actually have a question for the Academics," Jayden started. "Did the Council of 8 change or destroy history books to make it seem things went their way?"

Bookman smiled. "I'll visit later tonight and tell you what I know."

- Chapter Eighteen -

Breathing came in sharp, painful bursts as he kept pushing cramped legs into motion. The moment he glanced back, he crashed into a concrete wall and landed with a splash. When he looked at his hands, they were covered in thick red liquid.

Wide eyed, Jayden scrambled back to his feet and tried to wipe blood off his hands. He froze when a chilling roar shook the walls. Not wanting to find out what it belonged to, he bolted.

Hungry growls echoed around the corridors of the run-down hospital. He didn't know how far the beast was. All he knew was that he had to keep moving.

Until he stumbled into a crossroads.

He wasted precious seconds trying to decide which way to go. However, the thing chasing him was getting closer and that knowledge forced him to decide.

Choosing to go left, he ran until the corridor in front was shrouded in darkness. Going into an area where he couldn't see was too much of a risk and using his Abilities to create a light source would only attract the thing that was chasing him.

Jayden frowned.

How did he know that?

Before he could figure out what to do, a warm brush of foul smelling air hit the back of his neck. Eyes widened in fear, he slowly turned around. Within inches of his face, was a creature of nightmares.

A crooked mouth full of razor sharp teeth smiled at him. The eyes were sewn shut but he knew the creature would be compensating with its hearing and sense of smell. Its arms hung stiffly in front with joints dislocated at sickening angles. It was bone thin and towered over Jayden as it stretched out to its full height.

"That's enough for today."

He shook as he stared up at the monster in front of him. Neither of them moved.

"That's enough!"

The creature growled in displeasure, however, it slowly backed away and disappeared into the darkness. He waited in tense silence in order to convince himself that the beast wouldn't jump out.

Once he was sure he was safe, he turned to face his savior.

The man who had dismissed the creature wore a lab coat and tapped away on something thin. A second person dressed in tight clothing and boots stood beside the first.

No matter how hard he tried, he couldn't make out any details of the people before him.

"You've done well, Jayden. It's time to wake up."

Jayden woke up with a start and froze. Staring down at him was a blackened face with eyes sewn shut and a grinning mouth full of razor sharp teeth. Saliva dripped on his cheek and burned his skin, and he cried out.

Claws swiped against his chest as he tried to fling himself out of bed. He was pinned to the mattress and claws pierced his arm in order to keep him within reach. He managed to lodge his other arm against the thing's throat to try to keep teeth as far away from flesh as possible.

Shouting erupted in his room and a blast of air hurtled the creature into the wall beside the window. He quickly rolled off his bed in the opposite direction and tried to crawl to the door and out to safety. Clawed feet landed on the middle of his back and pain erupted along his shoulder blades.

Jayden squirmed and clawed at the floor to try to get away but the thing dug into his flesh and wouldn't let him go.

He could feel when the claws were ripped out of his back. A reptilian screech assaulted his ears and Wards were thrown around his room. All he could do was duck his head and wait for the madness to subside.

There was a sound of glass smashing and hands helped him up to his feet. He was crushed into a hug until he groaned in pain when it became unbearable.

"Sorry," Bookman said. "The thing is gone now. I'm going to put you on your bed and have a look at your injuries."

Jayden nodded against the older man's shoulder and slowly sat down on the edge of the mattress. His shirt was peeled off bloody skin and his back inspected.

Wounds burned and the pain grew in intensity as the seconds passed.

Fingers ran across his shoulder blades and a cool sensation seeped into his skin. With his back healed, he was able to lay down comfortably and close his eyes.

"We can't find where the thing went. How is he?" Balthezier asked.

"We need to warn everyone to be careful. The saliva and claws contain a caustic burning agent," Bookman answered.

Jayden opened his eyes as Balthezier sat beside him and drew a Healing Ward across his chest.

"No, wait!" Bookman objected a second too late.

The agony that ripped through him caused Jayden's back to arch, and a scream wrenched from his lips. Bookman pushed Balthezier away and wiped the Ward away to cancel the effects. Jayden gasped at the relief and tried to roll away.

"Normal Healing Wards won't work against something so dark afflicting someone like Jayden," Bookman said.

"Why not?" Balthezier asked.

"That creature isn't natural. It's a creature made with twisted Abilities," Bookman answered.

"How do you —-"

He clenched his eyes shut and focused solely on breathing. Words were filtered out and it took everything not to flinch at the sound of movement around him.

"Jay?"

He opened his eyes to find Bookman looking at him worriedly.

"I'm going to use the Healing Ward I used on your back. Okay?" Bookman explained.

Jayden swallowed the lump in his throat and nodded. As he felt a finger draw along his skin, coldness extinguished the pain and he was able to relax.

"Done."

He slowly sat up and glanced down at his chest. Apart from drying blood, his skin was unmarked.

Taking a shaky breath, he disappeared into the bathroom. He spent a few seconds leaning against the basin sink and focused on breathing. Once he was more centered, he grabbed a hand towel and cleaned himself off.

He ventured back into his bedroom, shoved a clean shirt, and picked up the whimpering pups.

Stepping through the metal door of the room in the basement, Jayden slumped in relief. Down here, he was safe. There were no windows to jump through. There was only one entry point and no monster would be able to easily come through.

Dusk slowly limped over to Jayden and curled up on his lap. Jayden ran a hand over damp fur and was relieved when only water covered his hand.

"Thank you," he said without looking up.

"They're all very protective of you," Bookman stated. "Are you okay?"

"Yeah, but I may not sleep again," Jayden answered.

"Roderick is looking over his Wards to find out how the thing came in. What are their names?"

Jayden ruffled Dusk's head. "Dusk. And these two are Diezel and Harley."

"You finally named them?" Roderick asked.

Jayden glanced up and nodded. "Figured it was about time."

"Good. While you're down here, make sure you read these damn books. I won't remind you again," Roderick said, dropping the books on the bed.

"Roderick, there isn't time for this. I leave tomorrow."

"Then make time!" Roderick demanded, storming back upstairs.

Bookman raised an eyebrow as he looked at the books.

"He refuses to tell me why, only that it'll help with the search for the Compass Points." Jayden shrugged, leaning back and staring at the roof.

"You should," Bookman said.

"Excuse me?" Jayden asked.

"These will help you. A lot," Bookman said, flicking through pages.

"What do you mean?" Jayden frowned.

"You're seriously telling me that someone with a mind like yours has not read these books or even flicked through them?" Bookman scoffed.

"Other things keep coming up. You were supposed to tell me what you know," Jayden said.

"And yet you make time to check the deteriorating border. Everything else can wait one night. Read these books," Bookman told him.

When it looked like Jayden was going to argue, the Academic added, "I'm not explaining anything until you read them. If you have any questions, I'll be in the Council Chambers an hour before the Council is due to reconvene to send the First Circle off."

Jayden sighed in defeat, got comfortable, and opened up one of the books. "Fine."

- **Chapter Nineteen -**

"Jayden?"

He looked up from the book in his lap and had to shield his eyes. The morning light streaming into the City Square was blinding.

"Koan? Is everything okay? Are my grandparents okay?" Jayden asked, quickly thinking the worst.

"Everything is fine. Your grandparents have given me the morning off but don't worry. There's a friend with them, and Leeran and Taylin already left for the day," Koan explained. "Do you mind if I join you?"

Jayden shook his head. "No, it's fine. Did you want to … go somewhere?"

Koan sat down beside him on the grass under the tree and fished out a ham, cheese, and tomato croissant. "Here."

"Oh, thanks," Jayden said, gratefully taking the food.

He closed the book and fiddled with the pastry.

He had ended up reading all night and now he was tired and struggling to wrap his mind around what he had read. At some point, he had needed to get out of The Balgaire.

"Is everything okay?" Koan asked.

"I …" Jayden bit his bottom lip as he sorted out his words in his head. "Have you ever thought you knew someone and then discovered they're a completely different person?"

"Of course. Everyone grows and changes every single day. It's life. None of us truly know one another, but we can come close to it. It can take years, and in the meantime, that person is still growing. If you care about someone, discovering another side of them shouldn't be a problem. Unless, of course, it involves toxic behavior that hurts you or others," Koan answered.

Jayden bit his bottom lip.

"Whoever you've learned something new about, talk to them. They can shed some light and help you understand," Koan added.

"Yeah," he mumbled.

Sighing, he stood up. "I should go get my things ready. Thanks, Koan. I guess I'll see you in a few weeks."

Koan hugged him tightly. "Keep in touch with your grandparents."

Jayden faltered when he swore he saw a glimpse of purple in Koan's eyes.

With a squeeze of Jayden's shoulder and a knowing look, Koan left him wondering whether or not he had been seeing things.

Jayden quickly made his way back to The Balgaire and rushed up to his room.

Balthezier and Roderick called out to him but he couldn't face either of them. He needed to straighten out his thoughts before he could address anything to do with the Adlers.

"Hey," Balthezier said, following Jayden. "Are you going to ignore us and leave without a goodbye? Talk to me."

Jayden continued to shove clothes into a bag.

"Jayden!"

Huffing, he dropped his phone and charger on his bag and glared at the blond.

"You hid something so big from me. You lied to me! You … you … I trusted you and you …" Jayden growled in frustration.

"I'm still me. Dad is still dad. We haven't changed. Jay, you know us," Balthezier said.

"You're a Compass Point, Liz. That changes everything," Jayden retorted. "Why didn't either of you tell me?"

Balthezier grimaced. "I couldn't. Keeping our true identity hidden is our number one rule in order to stay safe. I'm sorry."

Jayden studied his friend, still struggling to understand any of it.

"If none of this was happening, would you still have told me?" Jayden asked.

He took the answering silence as a no. If Szantium wasn't falling apart, he would still be completely oblivious as to who his best friend truly was. He was *not* okay with that.

After packing toiletries, he knelt down and hugged his animal companions.

"Look after them for me, please, and stay safe," Jayden said as he ruffled Dusk between the ears.

"Jay," Balthezier pleaded.

Jayden picked up his bag, phone, and wallet, and left The Balgaire.

He arrived at the Temple of 8 with two hours to spare. To waste time, he walked around, studying the array of statues. When he came back to the first statue, he sat down and took out his phone. There were three texts from Balthezier and one from Roderick. He thought about messaging Kelly and ignoring the unopened messages, but with a sigh, he pocketed his phone and closed his eyes. He was tired.

Before he knew it, he was being shaken awake. Artemis knelt down beside him while Sera and Van stood back, waiting with amused smiles.

"Is it time?" Jayden asked.

"Yeah," Van answered.

He rubbed his eyes and stretched. He followed his three companions down into the Chambers and waited for the Council to settle.

Each of the assigned pairs in the First Circle was given their destinations and told to leave with a reminder of the time restraints they were under.

Jayden glanced over to Bookman. The man was in his child form and staring down at him. He wondered whether or not Bookman already knew the truth surrounding the Adlers, and that fueled his anger and frustration over the situation. There was no time to ask.

Reid snatched his arm and they appeared in the middle of a busy London Street. To Jayden's surprise, no one stopped and made a scene about their sudden appearance.

"There's no way I'm sticking with you so we're splitting up," Reid said as he walked away.

He rolled his eyes as he hadn't expected anything else.

Unsure of where to go, he headed in the opposite direction.

London was a whole new world. The architecture was different and amazing, and everywhere he looked history melded with the new. At every chance he got, Jayden took out his phone to learn about the place he was exploring.

Once he came across a tourist attraction he recognized, he snapped a photo and sent it to Kelly with a message saying, *'Guess where I am.'*

Kelly called immediately.

"Why are you traveling when you're sick? Shouldn't you be taking it easy?" Kelly demanded.

"There are some things happening in the city that need to be taken care of and I couldn't just sit and wait. I'm out searching with some people for things that could help," Jayden answered.

"Spencer said the city was in trouble," Kelly noted.

He nodded and stopped in front of a souvenir shop.

"What's your address?" Jayden asked.

"Why?"

"I'm going to send you some cheesy postcards," Jayden answered.

"No, thanks."

"Then I'll send them to Balthezier to give to Spencer to give to you," Jayden said with a smirk.

There was silence on the other line, giving him enough time to step inside the shop and start looking at the postcard display.

Kelly huffed. "Fine. Got a pen and paper ready?"

He pulled out a notepad and pen from his stuffed shoulder bag and wrote the address Kelly gave him.

"Keep sending the photos and let me know every damn day how you're going," Kelly told him.

"Okay. I'll talk to you later," Jayden said before hanging up.

Picking out a postcard that made him smile, he then picked out a small trinket and paid for them. He was careful putting them in his bag, and then he continued to wander the streets.

He stopped for food when he got hungry and then checked into a hotel.

Once in his room, he sat on the bed and took out the books Roderick had given him. It was difficult to wrap his head around the fact that Balthezier was a Compass Point, and Roderick was his Watcher and not his father. Balthezier had lived a long life of hiding but he had managed to keep track of where all but one Compass Point was located. That last one, it seemed Balthezier had lost many years ago.

Shaking his head, Jayden shoved the books back in his bag and flopped back on the mattress.

Breathing came in sharp, painful bursts as he kept pushing cramped legs into motion. The moment he glanced back, he crashed into a concrete wall and landed with a splash. When he looked at his hands, they were covered in thick red liquid.

Wide eyed, he scrambled back to his feet and tried to wipe the blood off his hands. He froze when a chilling roar shook the walls. Not wanting to find out what it belonged to, he bolted.

Hungry growls echoed around the maze of corridors in the run down hospital. He didn't know how far away the beast was. All he knew was that he had to keep moving.

Until he stumbled into a crossroads.

He wasted precious seconds trying to decide which way to go. However, the thing chasing him was getting closer and that knowledge forced him to decide.

In a blink of an eye, the hallway turned into the remnants of a waiting room. He ran towards the front doors but they wouldn't budge and a shutter blocked the outside world. Turning back around, he frantically ran into a hallway.

Jayden came to a stumbling halt when the hall suddenly went dark. The last thing he wanted to do was venture into a place where he couldn't see what was lurking around. Using his Abilities to create a light source would only attract the thing that was chasing him.

Jayden frowned.

How did he know that?

Before he could figure out what to do, a warm brush of foul smelling air hit the back of his neck. Eyes widened in fear, he slowly turned around. Within inches of his face, was a creature of nightmares.

A crooked mouth full of razor sharp teeth smiled at him. The eyes were sewn shut but he knew the creature would be compensating with its hearing and sense of smell. Its arms hung stiffly in front with joints dislocated at sickening angles. It was bone thin and towered above Jayden as it stretched out to its full height.

"That's enough for today."

He shook as he stared up at the monster in front of him. Neither of them moved.

"That's enough!"

The creature growled in displeasure, however, it slowly backed away and disappeared into the darkness. He waited in tense silence to convince himself that the beast wouldn't jump out. Once he was sure he was sure, he turned to face his savior.

The man who had dismissed the creature wore a lab coat and tapped away on something thin. A second person dressed in tight clothing and boots stood beside the first. No matter how hard he tried, he couldn't make out any details of the people before him.

"You've done well, Jayden."

"Who ... who are you?"

"Your only true friend."

"Friend?" Jayden asked.

The one wearing skinny jeans and a tank top approached and ran a hand through Jayden's black hair gently.

"Yes. I'm the only one here for you. I'm the only one who is helping you with the big bad monster. I'll visit soon, but for now, wake up."

He rolled on to his side with a groan and succumbed to the coughing fit twisting his airways. When he managed to stop and catch his breath, there was a coppery tinge lingering in his mouth and blood spattered on the bedding. At this point, he couldn't muster the energy to panic anymore. Instead, he laid on his back and covered his eyes with a hand.

When he had his breathing completely under control, he made his way to the bathroom. In the mirror, a pale face with blood splotches stared back at him. It was a hard sight to look at.

Jayden quickly washed up and changed clothes.

He pulled the stained sheets off the bed and left them in a pile by the door. After he grabbed his things, he checked out of the hotel.

He sat in a park and rubbed his face tiredly. All he wanted to do was to go back to bed. The dreams were intensifying and for the first time since they started, bits and pieces were staying with him in the waking world.

It was horrifying to realize he was dreaming about the monster that had been stalking him in the streets of Szantium. There was something familiar about the people in the shadows, but he couldn't put his finger on it.

"Let's get coffee."

Jayden glanced up from his phone to see a recognizable face. The almond-shaped brown eyes looked at him with a gated expression. Their black hair was flipped over to the side and tips brushed along their jawline. A loose t-shirt covered them with the neckline falling over one shoulder, revealing a tank top strap. Skin tight jeans were tucked into black calf length boots.

"I know you," Jayden said.

"You remember who I am?"

He nodded. "Yeah. You gave me some advice that I ended up ignoring but you never told me your name."

"Shiro Tsukine. Let's get that coffee. I know a little café down the road."

He followed Shiro through the streets and into a pedestrian only cobbled lane. There were people coming in and out of the café, people sitting at the limited tables supplied outside, or milling around waiting to go inside and order.

Instead of waiting in the queue, Shiro slipped inside and was given two coffee cups and a paper bag straight away. No words or even money was exchanged. None of the customers questioned it or even looked towards them.

Jayden had a lot of questions about the exchange and before he could ask, Shiro held out a cup and the paper bag for him.

"Thanks," he mumbled, taking both.

He glanced inside the bag and found a blueberry muffin.

"You had another attack, didn't you?" Shiro asked as they walked back onto the main street.

He frowned at his companion. It was starting to feel like everyone knew about his condition.

"There isn't much I can't see, and I can clearly see the mess inside of you," Shiro explained.

Jayden hummed and nodded. He wondered whether or not Shiro was a part of the Academics. He'd have to remember to ask Bookman about it.

"I've searched for the Compass Points for what has felt like centuries. I came close once, but I've never found a single one," Shiro told him.

Jayden choked on his hot chocolate and stared at his companion. Why would they mention the Compass Points?

"Okay? How did you know that's what I'm looking for?" Jayden asked.

"There are certain things in motion and your loyalties will be tested," Shiro said instead of answering. "The Council of 8 are going to look like children's play toys compared to what will awaken," Shiro warned.

"Awaken? Look, I'm sick and tired, so please stop with the cryptic messages and start making sense," Jayden requested.

"Just focus on your search for now. We'll talk again," Shiro said.

"Wait a minute!"

He quickly lost Shiro amongst the flow of the crowd. Shaking his head, he sighed in annoyance and decided to find another hotel.

- Chapter Twenty -

The following morning, Jayden stayed in bed a little longer and stared at the books. He wanted to read more and focus on the words but at the same time, those words were changing everything. He needed to talk to someone about it. Bookman, maybe? The First Circle needed to know. They were all out searching for something they had no knowledge about while he was sitting on all sorts of answers.

With a sigh, he got ready for the day and went out to get breakfast. He spent a couple of hours simply wandering around until he was too tired to keep going. He grabbed some lunch and sat in a park.

He had no idea what to look for. The books only gave him vague location details, nothing exact. Babyloneous had told him to keep an eye out for old power, but he never felt any of that with Balthezier. With his friend, all he had felt was a calming warmth.

The city was huge and Jayden wasn't sure Reid was pulling his weight so he knew he'd have to be the one to check every inch of the city before moving on.

After lunch, he continued on his search. Everywhere he went, he was full of wonder. The city was fascinating. There were a few places, like a museum and a large Ferris wheel, he took photos of and sent to Kelly, telling her to visit when she got the chance.

In the evening, he headed back to the hotel with dinner.

After eating, he messaged Artemis to see how she and Sera were going.

Artemis sent back a photo with a tired looking Sera slumped against her with the message, *'Tiring. We're in Sydney, Australia, at the moment. It's hot here and there's so much to see. You?'*

Jayden replied with, *'Reid is doing his own thing. There's plenty of things to see here but no sign of any Compass Points.'*

He bit his bottom lip. He should say something about the books but he couldn't get his fingers to type that information out.

Before bed, he pulled up a map of the city on his phone and tried to figure out where he had been and where he still needed to search. It felt like he had covered most of the city already but he wasn't sure.

He pondered for a bit on what to do. He could double check and mark off the map as he went but that might slow him down and he'd miss the chance of searching the rest of the country.

Putting his phone on charge on the bedside table, he decided that in the morning he would venture away from the city. If he found nothing elsewhere, he would come back to double check before they moved on to the next country.

After breakfast, Jayden checked out of the hotel and headed towards Kings Cross Station where he managed to buy a ticket for the next train heading north.

Before boarding, he sent Kelly a photo of the station with the message, *'Heading off to magic school.'*

It wasn't long before she responded.

'Nerd.'

Followed by, *'I hope Theresa will like those books.'*

'Who?'

'I'm pregnant, nearly 15 weeks ... and I want her to be named after your mom.'

Jayden faltered. He had to read and reread the text to make sure he was reading the words correctly. Kelly was pregnant and she wanted to name her child after one of his parents. He couldn't believe it.

Before he could answer, the final call for passengers sounded off and he quickly hopped on to the train and found a compartment to sit in.

Ten minutes later, he remembered her message and sent off a congratulations with a smiley face. He hoped he would be well enough to meet little Theresa when she came into the world.

Next, he sent a message to Roderick letting him know that he was okay, and asked how Dusk, Diezel, and Harley were.

Roderick immediately called, causing Jayden to worry.

"Why won't you talk to me?" Balthezier asked.

"B-Balthezier? Why are you calling from your fath … Watcher's phone?" he asked.

"You're still angry?"

Jayden rolled his eyes. "What do you think? I need time to get my head around this. I haven't told the others yet, just so you know," Jayden explained.

There was silence on the other end.

"Why didn't you tell me?" Jayden asked.

"You know why," Balthezier replied.

"Yeah … No one can be trusted, right?"

He snapped his attention to the door as a boy wearing a navy blue sweater and shorts accompanied by an older gentleman dressed in a suit came into the compartment.

"Look, I can't talk about this now. I've got to go," Jayden quickly said.

"Call me when you can, please?" Balthezier requested.

"Yeah," Jayden absently agreed and hung up.

He stared at the darkening phone screen and sighed. It didn't sit right feeling like this about his friend. He wanted to talk to him, to sort out and deal with everything, but at the same time, he wanted space to just think and feel out his anger.

"Szantium is still growing ever unstable and if we're not found in time, it will fall across many human cities."

Jayden tore his attention away from his phone and to the newcomers.

"Excuse me?"

"Forgive me. I heard you were looking for the Compass Points," the boy said.

He slowly nodded.

"Allow me to introduce myself. I am Quentin Williams, the North-East Compass Point, fifth to be created by Thaddeus Eclipse, Ignatius

Halium, Bradlee Gaede, and Skye Wolf. This is my Watcher, Henry Williams."

The little boy had large green eyes full of old wisdom that didn't match his youthful face. His light brown hair was parted down the middle and swept over his ears. The older man's dark brown hair was brushed back neatly and his light brown eyes were focused through the window of the compartment's door.

Jayden blinked as he processed Quentin's words.

"I was told the Original families created the Compass Points. Who is Sky Wolf?" Jayden chose to ask.

"Three out of eight families participated in the creation. The others simply stood back, watched, and took credit. Just because individuals are born into certain families, does not mean they have the brain power to contribute to society," Quentin harshly pointed out.

Jayden nodded. That was another thing that was confirmed in the books Roderick had given him. It also confirmed that common Szaephian knowledge and their history books should be taken with a grain of salt unless confirmed.

"I won't say much more as I want to explain everything in one go," Quentin said.

Henry Williams stood up, and with a Ward, caused the entire carriage to go dark. Jayden felt a hand grip his arm and a swirl of air rushed around him.

Chapter Twenty-One

When Jayden was able to see again, they were standing outside of a tall red-bricked building. He glanced around, but despite the hustle and bustle, no one blinked an eye at their sudden appearance.

"A lot of humans in the United Kingdom are used to seeing the strange occurrences Szaephians cause. They tend to choose to ignore it and continue on with their normal lives," Quentin explained.

Jayden continued to watch the passing crowd, in awe of the collective acceptance of Szaephian presence in their community.

Henry tapped his shoulder and directed his attention forward as Quentin was heading inside. Above the door was a sign indicating the establishment was called 'Marvel Inn'.

It wasn't hard to spot Reid amongst the crowd inside. The guy was sitting in the middle of the pub floor, surrounded by people who were creating most of the noise.

"So, you're Reid Wyka," Quentin remarked.

"What of it, kid?" Reid asked.

Quentin raised an eyebrow. "Your parents don't have manners either. Still borrowing money to keep up your lavish lifestyle? Or was it blackmail? The Wykas never seem to know the difference."

Reid abruptly pushed away from his chair, glaring at the boy.

"You little —"

Ignoring Reid, Quentin turned to the man behind the counter watching them with amusement.

"Sorry, Scott, but everyone needs to leave."

Scott nodded. "Sure thing. Inn's all yours, sir."

As if this happened more often than not, everyone got up and left without much of a fuss.

Jayden asked, "Do you own this place?"

"Yes. Scott is the manager though. The others in the First Circle will be here within the hour," Quentin answered.

"Great. Wasting more of our valuable time," Reid huffed.

Henry, who had stayed behind Quentin in silence, stepped forward, his eyes hardening.

"Mr. Reid Wyka, in the last three days you were seen dining at high-end restaurants with other young individuals, attending Club A each night, and having both men and women accompanying you to an expensive hotel that you left for them to pay. Meanwhile, Mr. Jayden Lugian has walked all over London, bought a souvenir, stayed at two reasonable hotels, and gotten on a train to search in the north," Henry listed.

Jayden glared at the seething Reid.

"How dare you?" Reid shouted.

"Are you serious? You didn't even *bother* looking?" Jayden asked.

He was sure Reid wouldn't have made the effort but it still made him angry hearing about it.

Reid rolled his eyes. "Why would I? This crap doesn't exist."

"I see you also inherited the gene for stupidity," Quentin sighed.

Reid growled and charged at the boy with a fist raised. With a single point of Quentin's finger, the attacking man froze.

As much as he would have liked to, Jayden couldn't marvel at what was happening. He could feel his Abilities rising to the surface and slamming against the confines of his control.

Silently, he left for the bathroom. He caught a glimpse of his reflection in the old mirror and flinched. There were heavy bags under his eyes and he had a bloody nose.

Turning around to get a paper towel, Artemis was already there holding out a handful for him.

'Are you okay?' he awkwardly signed while holding the tissues against his nose.

'I should be asking you that,' Artemis replied.

She gently batted his hand away and checked his nose. There was a small nod and Artemis gently wiped his face clean.

Shrugging, Jayden signed, 'Same old.'

'Sure?' Artemis checked.

'I'll be okay. Don't worry,' Jayden replied.

'Okay. Everyone is waiting, so let's go.'

Artemis took his hand and led him to where the others had taken a seat by the fireplace.

"Why were we called here?" Van asked.

Henry sat beside Artemis and with a kind smile shared between the two, he started signing for her.

"Thank you for coming in such a timely fashion. I am Quentin Williams and this is my Watcher, Henry. I am one of the Compass Points you have been looking for."

The words hung in the air between the group and it took a moment for it to sink in. Jayden could see that none of them thought they'd actually find any of the Compass Points, let alone have one call a meeting to introduce themselves.

It wasn't a surprise when Reid was the one who broke the silence.

"Right. And I'm King Trident, ruler of the seven seas," he scoffed.

"It's best not to insult her. King Trident is not very forgiving," Quentin warned.

"She? I want to meet her!" Sera exclaimed before shaking her head. "What I think Reid meant was that you're not what we were expecting. You're a ten year old kid who barely radiates enough power to be a Level One."

"Appearance does not dictate age, nor does what I choose to share of my Abilities mean that is all I have to offer. Many choose to keep the truth about the strength of their power a secret, as Bookman does. Many others choose only to show what is expected of them, like Artemis," Quentin explained.

"Artemis?" Van queried.

"She's a high Level Eight," Quentin answered.

"No, she's not. She's a low Seven," Sera said.

"None of the Gaedes are low anything. They've always been a powerful family," Quentin said.

'He's right,' Artemis signed.

"Why did you hide it from us?" Sera asked.

'Power isn't everything to a person,' Artemis shrugged.

"I'm so attracted to you right now," Sera blurted.

Blushing, Artemis signed, 'Thanks?'

"Joking," Sera laughed. "I'm loyally engaged but you're right. Power isn't everything."

"We're getting off track," Quentin interrupted. "Eight Compass Points were created to keep your city safe. A power we know only as The Heart kept us together and steady. Over time, we developed a consciousness, then a body, and finally we created a companion, a Watcher, to protect and guide us."

"The Compass Points have human bodies?" Van asked.

"No. Only four or five of us chose a human form. Our shapes were influenced by our location and what was needed," Quentin answered. "I will take you to the next."

"Next what?" Mackenzie asked.

"Compass Point. Wouldn't it be more efficient to split us up to get this done quicker?" Sera asked.

Quentin shook his head. "Can't do that. The others may not want to approach you and that could make things harder. We will be leaving in the morning so I suggest you all get some rest."

"Where are we going?" Reid asked, folding his arms across his chest.

"Asia."

"Asia is huge! Where exactly?" Reid pushed.

Without answering, Quentin and Henry stood up and looked towards Jayden.

"Can we have a word?"

"Uh … sure," Jayden agreed.

He followed the Compass Point and Watcher upstairs and into one of the rooms.

"I take it Balthezier and Roderick gave you those books?" Quentin asked.

Jayden tensed and resisted the urge to move a hand to his bag. "What books?"

"You're a terrible liar, you know?" Quentin pointed out.

He ran a hand through his hair and sighed. "Yeah. I was told the books needed to be kept a secret."

"They shouldn't have been allowed to exist in the first place but we're past that point now. After we find the next two Compass Points, then you can tell the others about the books. I would rather have things done in order rather than have the more … problematic people disappearing on us on the pretense of retrieving a Compass Point," Quentin said.

"After Asia, it's Africa, right?" Jayden checked.

"Yes. Don't be too skeptical about the books. Make sure you talk to Balthezier like the friend he has always been," Quentin answered.

Jayden looked away and nodded.

"Good night," Quentin said.

Chapter Twenty-Two

The first country Quentin sent them to was China. Jayden and Artemis were dropped off by the bay in the midst of a bustling crowd. It was disorientating. All they had been told prior to leaving was that they would be placed in different areas of the country in pairs.

Jayden took out his phone and called Van.

"Where are you?" Jayden asked.

"Somewhere rural. Err … Sera says we're definitely in China," Van answered.

If Sera and Van were together, that meant Mackenzie and Reid had been partnered up. Nothing would be done with those two together.

"Artemis and I were dropped off somewhere along the bay in the city."

"Hang on," Van said.

He heard murmuring on the other end of the line so he took the time to take in his surroundings. Artemis had ventured off to one of those pier binoculars situated at regular intervals for tourists and was peering into one.

"Quentin sent everyone a message. Got to go. Sera's getting impatient."

The phone call ended with a yelp and thump.

With an amused smile, he checked the message and showed Artemis.

'We'll be staying at The Flower. Coordinates are in the following message. If no one can find the Compass Point in three days, we will be moving on to the next country.'

Jayden pocketed his phone and contemplated where to start searching. Artemis left the binoculars and came back to his side, pocketing her phone.

'Let's get some food and find The Flower,' Artemis suggested.

'Okay,' he agreed.

They wandered away from the bay until they agreed on a place to sit and eat. Afterward, they stopped quickly at a souvenir shop so he could buy a few things, including a postcard for Kelly.

'Who are those for?' Artemis asked.

'Kelly,' Jayden answered.

'Kelly … She married Spencer Mane, right?'

He nodded as he tucked the souvenirs in his shoulder bag.

When they eventually made it to The Flower, Quentin had settled in a booth with a cup of tea, and Henry was talking with a woman drying a glass behind the counter. No one else was in the little establishment.

"Everyone else is still out searching. We have The Flower to ourselves while we're in the country. Here are your room keys," Quentin said.

Jayden took a key and left to go upstairs to find the room and rest. His joints were aching and he could really go for a nap.

Sitting down on the bed, he opened his phone to send a message to Roderick and Balthezier. He wanted to send them an update, tell them that he was okay, but he couldn't type the words.

Sighing, he changed the recipients to Koan and Bookman and asked how things were going.

After ten minutes of no reply from either man, he finally forced himself to send the Adlers a message.

'Why did you give me those books? Why not someone else?'

'You needed to know,' Roderick answered. *'You're the one who we trust.'*

Jayden bit his bottom lip, the guilt over his reaction growing.

Everyone was seated and in the middle of breakfast by the time he managed to convince himself to get up and get ready for the day.

He signed to Artemis that he was going for a short walk and stepped outside. He needed to clear his head after having a restless night. A brewing headache threatened to blow up every time he was jostled around as he moved through the peak morning crowd.

When Shiro fell in step with him, he groaned.

"There is something worse than the Council of 8 almost here," Shiro warned.

"Okay? How do you know?" Jayden asked.

"Once you've been around for as long as I have, you start seeing patterns in the way society twists and turns. There's a possibility that the Council of 8 weren't an independent entity like everyone had believed, or something else could be happening," Shiro explained.

"That's unfortunate," Jayden murmured.

From the corner of his eye, he could see Shiro studying him.

"You've lost something," they noted.

Jayden raised an eyebrow. "Excuse me?"

"Remember that while the past can still hurt and forgiveness can't be given, the future can still happen."

In the second it took for him to turn to Shiro, they had vanished.

He huffed in annoyance. He was getting fed up with the cryptic messages.

Fingers linked with his and Artemis gave him a smile. She gave him a paper bag and when he looked inside, there was a scrambled egg sandwich.

'Thanks,' he signed.

Artemis flashed him another smile and led him to a nearby park bench.

'What's wrong?' Artemis asked.

He lowered his breakfast and thought for a moment. There was a hesitation about mentioning Shiro.

'I have … a feeling that something bad is coming,' Jayden answered.

Artemis frowned. 'Like what?'

'No idea. It's just a feeling,' Jayden shrugged.

'It'll be okay.'

He nodded, not really sure if he believed that.

'Let's start looking around.'

'Eat up first,' Artemis signed.

Jayden quickly ate his breakfast and tossed his rubbish in a nearby bin.

'Did Quentin tell you what … who we're looking for?'

'He said only that we'd know when we see them,' Artemis said.

Jayden scowled. 'Let's go.'

Without knowing what they were looking for, wandering the streets of the city felt like a waste of time. No matter where they walked, their search came up empty.

Despite that, he and Artemis were amazed by the sights. They walked from a futuristic looking tower with two balls attached to its frame, to gorgeous gardens with traditional buildings. In the gardens, he took a deep breath and basked in the peaceful atmosphere. When he remembered, he took a couple of photos and sent them to Kelly.

By the time they left the gardens, Jayden needed to lay down. His body was aching and the headache from the morning had worsened.

Artemis took pity on him and transported them back to The Flower. She helped him to his room and into bed. When he apologized, Artemis simply shook her head with a kind smile.

Days two and three went pretty much the same as the first. When all groups came back to The Flower on the afternoon on the third day, reporting they either found nothing or powers they came across only belonged to other Szaephians, Quentin took them to their next destination – Japan.

They decided to check into a hotel, and with a two day deadlines, Sera and Mackenzie were given the north to search, Van and Reid were given the south to search, and Jayden and Artemis were to focus on the remaining area in between both groups.

Jayden went straight to his room and curled up on the king single bed that was closest to the large floor to ceiling window and furthest away from the doorway. It was early afternoon and all he wanted to do was sleep.

There was a faint tap on the door and Artemis stepped in with a couple of bottles of water and a bag of snacks. She was going to be his roommate.

'Are you okay?' she asked.

'Tired,' he answered.

She placed the shopping bag down on the small square table that stood against the opposite wall the beds were lined along and sat on the edge of his bed.

'Get some rest,' she signed and squeezed his calf reassuringly. 'I'll wake you up for dinner.'

- Chapter Twenty-Three -

Jayden stretched as he left the bathroom. He'd had a good night's sleep with no dreams, he was hungry, and he actually felt good for a change. He was ready to proactively help with the search.

As he stepped into the room, he found Artemis paging through one of the books he could have sword he had left hiding in his bag.

"Artemis!"

He stormed up to her and tried to snatch the books away but Artemis held them out of reach.

'Where did you get these?' Artemis asked.

'Give them back,' Jayden quickly signed.

'No. Why didn't you tell us about them? All of the answers we need are here and you're letting —"

'Artemis! No one can know. Not yet,' Jayden interrupted.

'Why?'

'Roderick said they had to be kept a secret and Quentin didn't want anyone else to know about them just yet,' Jayden explained.

She studied him for a moment before holding out the books. He snatched them from her and proceeded to put them back into his bag. Jayden knew he should have been more careful but he hadn't thought anyone he travelled with would have gone through his belongings.

Artemis reached over and squeezed his upper arm a little to get his attention.

'I'll keep silent about this but maybe we can see if any information in these books can actually help us out,' she signed.

Jayden stared at his bag and grimaced. His anger and distrust was misplaced.

'Let's get something to eat and then we'll start searching around,' Artemis suggested.

He nodded and followed her out into the streets. They decided to get breakfast from a nearby convenience store and ate while they wandered around.

"At least I get to cross off travelling before I die," Jayden murmured.

Artemis tilted her head after seeing his lips move.

Shaking his head, he pointed to a shop and asked her if she wanted to have a look.

Jayden ended up buying quite a few things for not only Kelly and her unborn child, but for Roderick, Balthezier, his grandparents, and Artemis. After paying, he held up the necklace and little keychain for his friend. She smiled gratefully with a small blush and took her gifts as she kissed his cheek.

Stepping back out into the street, he glanced up at the clear sky. There was a sense of anticipation in the air and it made him nervous.

They stopped by the post office so he could send everything and then continued through the streets for the next hour until he needed to stop. He was frustrated about becoming a hindrance, especially since he had started the day feeling great.

'Are you okay?' Artemis asked, helping him to a seat.

He nodded and buried his face in his hands.

'I'll get you some water,' she signed once she managed to get his attention again.

Jayden buried his face again and sighed.

Artemis was back before he knew it with a cold water bottle. As he sipped at the refreshing drink, she gently rubbed his back.

'Pushed it a bit?' Artemis asked.

'Yeah.'

'Let's go back,' she said.

A Transport Ward engulfed them and they were standing in front of the hotel. He stumbled back when they reappeared and was grateful to have his friend there to help keep him steady.

Quentin was on the phone in a heated argument when they stepped up to the entrance. Jayden didn't catch anything being said, but once Quentin caught sight of them he walked away. He couldn't help but roll his eyes and continue to his room. He wasn't interested in eavesdropping on anyone's conversation.

Jayden slipped out of his shoes, placed his wallet, phone, and room key on the bedside table, and laid down.

Breathing came in sharp, painful bursts as he kept pushing cramped legs into motion. The moment he glanced back, he crashed into a concrete wall and landed with a splash. When he looked at his hands, they were covered in thick red liquid.

Wide eyed, he scrambled back to his feet and tried to wipe blood off his hands. He froze when a chilling roar shook the walls. Not wanting to find out what it belonged to, he bolted.

Hungry growls echoed around the maze of corridors in the run down hospital. Jayden didn't know how far away the beast was. All he knew was that he had to keep moving.

Until he stumbled into a crossroads.

He wasted precious seconds trying to decide which way to go. However, the thing chasing him was getting closer and that knowledge forced him to decide.

In a blink of an eye, the hallway turned into the remnants of a waiting room. He ran towards the front doors but they wouldn't budge and a shutter blocked any glimpse of the outside world. Turning back around, he frantically ran into a hallway.

The shrill ring of a phone caused him to jump with fright. Cautiously, he approached the front desk.

A loud roar froze him on the spot. With fearful wide eyes, he glanced back, expecting to have been caught. Seeing nothing in the waiting room with him, he ignored the ringing phone and ran.

Every office he passed, a phone rung. Terrified the noise would attract the monster towards him, he darted into the next office and answered the phone.

"Hello?"

"Jay? We've been evacuated. There are ... monsters coming out."

He frowned. "Kelly?"

"Yeah. Spencer has —"

A low rumble behind him chilled his blood. Slowly, he glanced at the door.

The beast had found him.

Long sharp fingers attached to deformed arms gripped the door frame as a head with an open mouth full of razor sharp teeth appeared.

He didn't know what to do. He couldn't move. He was trapped.

"Jayden!"

The monster lunged and he ducked, clenching his eyes shut and expecting the worse.

Hands gripped his shoulders, shaking him awake. Forcing his eyes open, he gasped in an attempt to feed starving lungs. Before he could regain his breathing, a rough coughing fit erupted and he could taste blood.

Jayden was forced forward and his back was rubbed soothingly. It took a moment before his body calmed and he slumped against the person beside him in relief.

"You okay?" Van asked.

"Yeah," Jayden rasped.

He shakily took the offered cup and in between small sips of cold water, Sera wiped away the blood covering his skin.

Shuffling and clattering stole his attention. The room was an absolute mess. The walls were sliced up and cracked open. Blood had been smeared across the wall his bed was now shoved up against, and Artemis's bed was currently blocking the door to the bathroom. The bedside table he had placed his belongings on had been smashed and the pieces littered the floor by the door to the room.

He spotted the remnants of his phone on the floor as Artemis swept the mess up with a Ward.

"Sorry."

"It's okay. Must've been some dream," Van said.

"He lost control. Again. It's not okay," Mackenzie stated. "He can't be here. He's not even contributing to the search."

Jayden glared at his twin.

"We should be helping the city and not wasting time cleaning up this mess. Father said the quakes are getting worse and we're running out of time," Reid piped up.

"Shut up, both of you!" Sera snapped. "Go get dinner."

"Excuse me?" Reid asked, eyebrow raised.

"Out!" Sera reiterated. "You, too, Mackenzie."

Seeing the sparks fly off Sera's hand, Reid didn't argue any further but Mackenzie hung in the doorway. She growled and stepped towards him. Thankfully, he finally listened and left.

"Please give Jayden and I a moment alone," Quentin requested. "Van and Sera, please make sure they actually do get dinner for all of us."

Sera nodded and led Artemis out by the hand. Van helped ease Jayden against the headboard and followed the girls.

"How are you feeling?" Quentin asked once the door was closed.

"Peachy," Jayden rasped.

"Tell me about your dreams."

"Why?"

"Curiosity."

Jayden sighed and licked his lips. He could still taste blood.

"I'm running through an abandoned hospital and the … the thing that was chasing me in the city, it's chasing me in my dreams. Um … this time, a phone started to ring and when I answer, it's Kelly. She tells me they had been evacuated because of monsters but then the creature found me and …" Jayden trailed off.

Quentin hummed.

"At this rate, you will be hospitalized and unable to leave in a matter of weeks," Quentin noted.

Jayden ran a hand over his face.

"I know, but while I can do something, I will," Jayden said.

The boy nodded. "Clean yourself up and come to my room. We'll be having dinner there."

He watched Quentin leave before glancing up to the ceiling with a heavy sigh.

When he forced himself out of bed, his legs wouldn't hold him up and he fell to his knees. Gritting his teeth, he used the bed to help him stand back up. Thankfully, he stayed standing and he was able to shuffle to the bathroom.

The mirror revealed a pale face still covered in flecks of blood and dark shadows underneath his eyes, highlighting how much weight he'd lost in his face. He could barely recognize himself.

He took off his sweaty shirt and found skin splotched with new bruises, long scratches, and a rash along the left side of his chest.

This wasn't good.

His phone was destroyed so he couldn't consult with one of his doctors and he would rather avoid the questions that came from asking one of his friends to borrow theirs. That conversation would have to wait until tomorrow when he'd be able to buy a replacement and get their numbers again.

Taking a deep breath, he washed up and changed into fresh clothes.

Dinner was already in full swing by the time he made it down the hall to Quentin's room. The room was more like a studio apartment. There were two single beds, a kitchenette, a bathroom, and a small dining table.

He took a seat beside Artemis and Quentin. Artemis passed over a small bowl of soup and he smiled at her in thanks. The soup was more than enough and he would have been satisfied with half of the amount given, but he didn't want anyone to worry even further.

After dinner, it was decided that they'd practice sign language. For Sera's sake, they started off with the basics and went from there.

"What a waste of time," Reid huffed.

"Is that all you can say? Seriously, man. Give it a rest," Van said.

"Useless and stupid are wasting everyone's time. We should be in Szantium helping with the evacuation, not on this pointless trip. Even if the kid says he's a Compass Point, who's to —-"

Van was abruptly on his feet and swinging his fist at Reid.

"The only faulty one here is you," Van growled as he punched him.

"Sit down, Van," Quentin ordered.

Van glanced back at Quentin and growled. Despite clearly wanting to keep hitting Reid, he flopped down beside Sera and crossed his arms over his chest.

"Seeing as how you can't say anything intelligent, you won't be saying anything at all until we move on to the next destination."

"Excuse —-"

With a wave of his hand, a symbol for a Ward Jayden didn't recognize was created and slapped against Reid's throat. For a few entertaining seconds, they watched him struggling to speak.

Confusion turned to rage. In a silent fit, he lunged at Quentin. Van and Sera scrambled over each other to get out of the way. Henry was in front of Quentin and slammed Reid down in a matter of nanoseconds.

"Apparently you won't be moving either. At least not until tomorrow. Use this time to think about your behavior and attitude," Quentin said.

The boy stood and drew a symbol along Reid's back, causing him to go stiff and his movements ceased.

Sera and Van stared in awe.

However, Quentin wasn't finished.

"One more word from you," he said as he pointed to Mackenzie, "and you'll be joining him."

Mackenzie glanced over to Reid and Jayden before holding his hands up in front of himself in surrendering peace.

"I'm going to bed," Mackenzie said.

Jayden watched him leave before turning his attention back to what was happening around him. Van had found a permanent marker and was busy drawing on Reid's face to the amusement of everyone else.

Day two in Japan started out as bad as how day one had ended.

Jayden woke up stiff and sore. He shivered from the cold sweat clinging to his skin. Getting to the bathroom was an effort but he managed to shower and dress without falling over.

When he stepped out into the hall, he was knocked back into the door. Reid didn't waste time glancing back at him as he continued towards the elevator. The guy was obviously angry about how last night ended for him.

"Are you okay?"

He looked around to find his twin standing there. With a sigh, Jayden pushed away from the door and ventured to the elevators.

"Jayden, wait."

"It's our last day here, Mackenzie. We don't have any more time for your lectures," Jayden said.

"I know but … I have a bad feeling about today so I —-"

"Give it a rest and stop playing the caring brother. Just save your breath," Jayden snapped.

Clenching his fists, he stepped into the elevator and closed the doors before Mackenzie had the thought of stepping in with him. Downstairs, he grabbed a glass of juice from the breakfast bar and sat down with the others.

"Hey man, you okay?" Van checked.

Jayden glared at him.

"Never mind. You look fine," Van quickly said.

"If you're all done with breakfast, I want you to finish searching your areas and be back here by three," Quentin instructed.

'You should eat,' Artemis signed to Jayden.

'Juice is enough. Let's go,' he replied.

Without finishing his juice, he stood up and left.

Once they turned on to a main road, he regretted getting out of bed and leaving the hotel. There was something very wrong and as he struggled to breathe, his vision went hazy.

"Artemis …"

Jayden stopped and tried to focus on breathing. Black figures were popping up and crawling over buildings around him. He couldn't work out if he was hallucinating or not, and he didn't want to wait around to find out that answer. He gasped out in an effort to tell someone, anyone, to look and see what he was seeing.

He reached out for a blurry figure he hoped was his friend.

"Art … mis …"

When he took a step forward, the world tilted sharply and he could feel himself fall into darkness as his eyes closed.

Chapter Twenty-Four

Sniffing, Jayden wiped his wet eyes and cheeks as someone stepped into his room. He had been left alone for what felt like hours and he didn't like where his mind was taking him.

Quentin took a seat on the edge of the bed while Henry stood by the closed door.

"How are you feeling?" Quentin asked.

"I …." Jayden didn't know how to answer.

He slowly eased himself up. Henry stepped over and wedged a pillow between him and the headboard.

"The others wanted to take you to a hospital, but considering you're currently a human and a Szaephian medical mystery, I made the call to avoid any unnecessary questions. The matter of your Abilities was also a factor. They were … sorry, I should say 'are' going haywire," Quentin explained.

Jayden clenched his eyes shut and took a shaky breath. He tried not to let the overwhelming panic take over.

"Are?" he managed to ask.

"Think of it as a leak," Henry said. "Whatever control you had over them means nothing at this point. The holes are currently small enough to not be noticeable right away or have that much of an effect, but they are there and they will grow."

Jayden couldn't take it. Breathing became a struggle and he felt like he was being crushed.

Henry eased him forward and rubbed his back soothingly.

"All is not lost, Jayden," Quentin said.

He glanced over to the boy, gasping for air with tears in his eyes.

There was something calming about Quentin that convinced Jayden to try and center himself. Taking a deep breath, he leaned back against the headboard and exhaled slowly. He tried to focus on something else until he felt brave enough to face the problem again.

"We can monitor the output and employ the others to help contain your Abilities as the leak worsens," Quentin offered.

"But?" Jayden asked.

"It would be best to go back to Szantium to make preparations. They might be able to help prolong the inevitable, but at this point you have about three and a half weeks left," Quentin said.

Jayden bit his bottom lip. Three and a half weeks wasn't that long.

"My Abilities … I was told they were trying to fight for me. To … make things better," Jayden said. "How can they lose like this?"

Quentin grimaced and shook his head.

"What do you want to do?"

He thought for a moment. There were people he wanted to see before it was too late, but on the other hand, he felt responsible for seeing this search through to the end. He bit his lip as he weighed all of his options.

"Don't send me back," he pleaded.

Quentin nodded. "As you wish, but only if you rest and keep Artemis, Henry, and I in the loop on how you're faring."

Jayden nodded.

"Get some rest."

He laid back down and closed his eyes. He was tired of fighting.

Sitting in the middle of the reception of a rundown hospital, he saw the beast watching him from the entrance of a hallway. His first instinct was to run, however, even in his dreams, he was exhausted. If the creature wanted to rip him apart, then so be it.

He rubbed his eyes tiredly and sighed.

"Giving up already?"

Two people stood in the shadows with the creature. The one closest reached up and petted the creature on the head.

"Who are you?" Jayden asked.

One of them stepped into the light to reveal tanned skin, black hair flipped over, a loose top with skinny jeans, and boots. The person was familiar, but Jayden couldn't place a name to the face.

"A friend."

"A friend?"

A hand ran over his cheek and through his hair.

"Yes. We gave you a gift to give to everyone, but they twisted it into something that's causing you pain. I'm going to give you another — one that they can't take away from you, but I need to know something first."

Jayden tilted his head in confusion.

"What?" he asked. "What gift?"

"Where are the Adlers?"

He frowned. "Liz and Roderick? Why?"

"They're old friends I haven't seen in a while and it's about time we caught up."

Jayden rubbed his eyes tiredly as he tried to think through the slugging fog creeping over him.

"They're ... they're at The Balgaire."

"Where's that?"

He leaned his forehead against the shoulder of his friend.

"It's ... um ... it's in the side street ... the alley ... Red Lane. Near Café 8," Jayden managed to say.

"Thank you, Jayden."

He was gently pushed back against the chair. It was getting harder to stay awake.

"It will be over soon."

Jayden squinted in an attempt to make out facial details of those in front of him.

"Turn ...er?" Jayden asked in uncertainty.

"Don't worry. You won't remember."

Once Jayden was awake and dressed, they all left Japan. When they arrived at their new destination, he stumbled and was grateful Van was there to keep him upright.

"Where are we?" Mackenzie asked.

"Oh! I know," Van exclaimed in excitement. "We're in South Korea. My brother works here."

"Can we crash at his place?" Sera asked.

"Our accommodation has already been organized. The fewer people who know where we are looking, the better," Quentin said.

Jayden didn't miss the way he flashed a look towards Reid and Mackenzie.

"Okay," Van grumbled.

"Henry, we will need a car suitable to fit all of us," Quentin said to the older man.

The Watcher nodded and left the group.

"Where are we going?" Sera asked as they waited.

"To the place we will be staying in," Quentin answered cryptically.

"Where though? Why do we need a car when we could just use a Ward to get there?" Sera pressed.

The boy didn't answer and focused on his phone until Henry returned with a van.

After piling inside the vehicle, and ignoring a grumbling Reid, Jayden leaned his forehead against the window and watched the passing scenery.

The city turned into suburbia and properties became larger and hidden behind high fences. Jayden yawned and wished he had a phone to use to pass the time with.

When the van stopped outside of a fence, he sat up straighter and glanced around. Quentin held out a small device and the gate opened to reveal a spacious property.

As they pulled in, he couldn't believe how immaculate the gardens were. Trees, plants, statues, and other garden bits and bobs were placed in a way that promoted space and complimented the house nicely.

"Whoa," Van gasped.

The group spilled out of the van and stared at the traditional looking house.

"Who's the rich guy?" Sera asked.

"Remember to be respectful while we're here," Quentin informed them. "There are enough rooms for everyone to have one, but before you step inside, take off your shoes."

Jayden slipped off his shoes and slowly walked through the massive house, taking everything in. Artemis took his hand and led him to a set of rooms that were side by side. She signed that the rooms would be theirs.

"Hey, guys. We're having home cooked meals while we're here. Van and I will be cooking so we're going shopping. Need anything?" Sera asked.

A home cooked meal sounded great. "Thanks. Hang on."

He started to sign to Artemis but Sera stopped him.

"Wait, let me practice," Sera said.

Poking her tongue out a little, she slowly managed to ask Artemis if she needed anything or if she would like to go with her and Van. Artemis smiled and nodded. When both girls turned to Jayden, he shook his head.

'I don't need anything except rest,' he signed.

Artemis gave him a quick hug and left with Sera.

Alone, he ventured out to the deck and took a deep breath. It was quiet and peaceful. They were in their own little world on this property.

"No. We're in South Korea somewhere. Yeah, no. I can't get him to use them. He's always with that –- Hang on. A Harbinon is eavesdropping."

Reid stepped around the corner and glanced at him. He rolled his eyes as the guy quickly walked past and went back inside. Jayden was tempted to follow and listen but before he even stood up, he had second thoughts.

Henry knocked on the doorframe and ventured out to the decking where Jayden stood waiting.

"Your sim card hadn't been damaged so I've inserted it into a new phone I bought before getting the car," Henry said.

He couldn't believe his luck. "Thank you so much. How much do I owe you?"

Henry shook his head. "Don't worry. Money is not an issue. I suspect there are people who wish to hear from you."

The older man squeezed his shoulder briefly before going back into the house.

With the new phone and a list of contacts at the ready, the first person on his list to get in touch with was Balthezier. When the call wasn't answered, he tried Roderick. Again, his call went unanswered.

With a frown, he sent both men a message.

'It's Jay. Please call me back. I'm sorry for, well, everything. Just call me back.'

Afterward, he decided to call Koan.

"Hello?" Koan answered.

"It's Jay. Are you busy?" he asked.

"Kind of but I can spare a moment," Koan said.

Jayden bit his lip. "I'll call back later."

"No, no. Sorry. I didn't mean it like that. I can talk," Koan quickly said.

He nodded and fiddled with the fabric of his pants. Now that he could talk to someone, he found the words refusing to come out.

Thankfully, Koan prompted the conversation.

"Jay, what's wrong?"

"It's not good. I can't get in touch with Liz or Roderick," Jayden explained.

"I'll see if a friend can get to The Balgaire. I can't go myself until I'm finished with what I'm doing," Koan said.

Jayden instantly felt guilty. He knew Koan was busy, not just with his grandparents but with whatever other duties he had.

"No, it's okay. I'll be sent back soon enough so I'll check then," Jayden dismissed.

"You sure?" Koan checked.

"Yeah. Those books you had me reading since I came back … they all had conflicting information to what was available in the Great Library," Jayden stated.

"A lot of our history was rewritten by the Council of 8. Anyone who objected had been killed until eventually, no one knew any differently," Koan explained.

"That … that's problematic and sad. No one knows their history," Jayden said.

"Some of my friends have been working on correcting it but it's slow going," Koan said.

There was a muffled voice on the other end of the line and Jayden felt his heart sink.

"Sorry, Jayden. I have to go," Koan apologized.

"It's okay. See you," Jayden said.

"Keep in contact, okay? Talk to you later," Koan said before hanging up.

Jayden lowered his phone to his lap and ran a hand through his hair with a sigh. He was tired but he still had people to check in with.

The next person he called was Bookman. It felt weird contacting the Academic since they barely knew each other, but he did have something to ask.

"Hello?"

"Jayden? Everything okay?" Bookman greeted.

He couldn't help but flinch at the question.

"Not really. I'm going to be sent back soon and Liz and Roderick aren't answering me," Jayden explained.

"I can —-"

"No, it's fine," Jayden interrupted.

"You sure you don't want someone to check in with them?" Bookman checked.

"Yeah."

He fell silent and his eyes wondered over the garden before him.

When he couldn't think of anything to say, he sighed and said, "I should —-"

"How bad?"

"I … have less than a month left," Jayden said.

Bookman cursed.

"Yeah. When I get back —-"

"Let me know and I'll be there, okay?" Bookman interrupted.

"Yeah, okay. If I give you a name, will you be able to tell me if they're with the Academics?"

"Okay."

"Shiro Tsukine."

There was silence on the other end for a few seconds before muffled voices could be heard.

"They're not with us," Bookman said.

"Oh. Okay …" Jayden trailed off.

"Where did you hear that name?" Bookman asked.

He shrugged and when he remembered Bookman wouldn't be able to see the motion, said, "Just a friend, I guess. Can you … talk to me about anything?"

"Are you okay?" Bookman checked.

"No. What are you up to?"

"There are more rips exposing the In Between. Now Shadows are coming through. It's nothing bad at the moment so Hunters are able to deal with them quick enough. My team is working around the clock to figure out how to close the rips."

Jayden ran a hand through his hair in frustration.

"Sounds like a mess," he remarked.

"Yeah," Bookman agreed.

"Do you know why this is happening?"

"I suspect it's in response to the worsening stability of Szantium," Bookman guessed.

They were moving too slowly for the city.

"So we don't have as much time as we thought."

"No. We still need to –- Sorry, babe. I have to go. Message me," Bookman said.

Jayden frowned in confusion. "Babe? What?"

"Love you, too. Bye," Bookman said.

"Right. Bye?"

He stared at his phone, wondering what had prompted such a weird end to their conversation.

Chapter Twenty-Five

After a filling lunch, Quentin sent Artemis, Sera, and Mackenzie off together, and to Van's dislike, he was stuck with Reid. Jayden couldn't help the smile as he heard Van start getting creative with his threats if Reid even said a word about how much they were wasting his time.

He watched everyone leave, feeling useless for no longer being able to help. Not sure what he was supposed to do in the meantime, he ventured back outside with Roderick's books.

When Quentin sat next to him, he closed the book and fiddled with the cover.

"The Human Plane is being ripped apart and Shadows are coming through. Hunters are dealing with it but …"

"We're running out of time," Quentin finished for him.

He nodded.

"Artemis knows about the books but I got her to agree to not say anything to the others."

"Do you trust her?" Quentin asked.

"Yes," Jayden answered without hesitation.

"Okay. What's on your mind?"

"Even if we find the other Compass Points, none of this will matter if The Heart can't be found," Jayden said.

"Don't worry about The Heart. It's never far from us and once we're all assembled, it should be easy to find," Quentin said.

As the boy spoke, Jayden frowned as a series of messages bombarded his phone, distracting him.

"Should?" Jayden eventually asked.

He pulled out his phone as more messages came through. All of them were from Kelly. The most recent one said, *'I'm beyond peeved at you right now. Call. Me!'*

"Is everything okay?" Quentin asked.

"Yeah," Jayden answered, going through the messages.

"I will go get us some snacks and a drink," Quentin said.

He shook his head. "I'll pass, thanks. I need to go stretch my legs."

He stood up, grabbed a coat, and made his way to the front door. He left the property and ventured out into the street. Along the way, he tried to call Balthezier and Roderick again. When neither answered, he bit his lip in worry. Why would both of them ignore him? Did his reaction make them believe he didn't want them in his life anymore? Were they hurt from his anger and needed space?

After sending a message asking if they were okay and to call him back, Jayden called Kelly.

"Dude!" Kelly answered. "Why the hell did you hang up on me before? Why haven't been answering my calls or messages?"

"I'm sorry," Jayden murmured.

There was a moment of silence on the other end and he knew Kelly was running through possible reasons.

"You've gotten worse, haven't you?" she asked.

"Yeah. Why were you calling me?"

"Are you coming back?"

"Not yet."

"Where are you now?"

"South Korea," he answered, looking down the street.

"Are —"

"Are you safe?" Jayden interrupted.

He didn't want to talk about what he was going through anymore. Just once he wanted to ignore his problems.

"Yeah. Spencer moved us in with his parents."

"In Szantium?"

"Na. They have a place in Vancouver."

"What happened?" Jayden asked.

"There was a small quake and this giant crack that stretched up into the sky opened up in the park close to home. Low level Shadows started coming through and people started to freak out. Spencer said the crack exposed the In Between and that's how the Shadows are getting through," Kelly explained.

Jayden winced. He should have been there to help her.

"Sorry."

"For what?"

"Is Spencer around? I'd like to ask him a favor," Jayden said.

"Sure," Kelly answered, dragging out the word. "Hang on."

He stopped walking when there was a break in the fence line. A small park broke the monotonous street. There was a small playground with a pathway and a couple of benches. Skeletal tree trunks stood tall in the grass. It would be a nice place to hang out and walk through during the warmer months.

Right now, only the grass was thriving.

A white speck slowly floating down caught his attention. He looked up to the gray sky and was pleasantly surprised to see that it had started snowing.

While he waited for Spencer, he took a seat and switched hands holding his phone in order to keep them from turning blue.

"Hi, Jayden. What can I help you with?" Spencer greeted.

"I need you to go to The Balgaire and tell Roderick and Liz to call me back ASAP."

"Just send them a message."

"I have!" Jayden exclaimed. "Neither of them have answered."

"Maybe they're busy, just like the rest of us," Spencer sighed.

Jayden growled in frustration.

"Tell them to call me back!"

He ended the phone call and paced around the park. He had a bad feeling and it was growing worse.

Running a hand through his hair, he glanced at his phone and decided to head back to the house.

Once back, he made himself comfortable on the deck and tried to read. However, he found himself watching the snow slowly fall. When that led to being too cold, he moved inside and kept trying to read.

By evening, he had read the same paragraph multiple times and had no clue what he had read. Spencer hadn't gotten back to him and his phone battery was running low after checking it so many times.

He couldn't sit still and more than once, he contemplated asking someone to send him to The Balgaire. If Spencer couldn't or wouldn't check on the Adlers then Jayden would have to. The bad feeling had been nagging him all day and it was close to boiling over the edge.

When the others came back, Artemis tried to get him to sit with her and it had worked for all of five minutes. Van and Sera tried to help distract him, but again, it only worked for a brief time before he was checking his phone.

"It's time … yes. We don't have time to keep this up. I have a bad feeling they've been taken, possibly by those who took her. The Heart is … okay. I'll see you soon," Quentin said.

Quentin pocketed his phone and addressed the group watching him.

"We're going to The Balgaire," Quentin announced.

Reid huffed in annoyance. "Really? You lot pressed for this damn search and now we're bailing out? I'm sick of our time being wasted when we sh —"

"The only waste of time, Wyka," Quentin growled, "has been dealing with your self-entitlement. Just because you were born with a certain surname, does not give you the right to assume you can walk around like you own the place."

"Excuse —-"

"The Wyka's are nothing more than a blip in history and if you continue on living your borrowed privileged life the way you are, you *will* have a rude shock when you find yourself alone. I suggest you start reevaluating yourself."

Quentin crossed his arms, a red tinge brightening his cheeks after the tirade.

Van gaped in disbelief. "Dude!"

Before anyone could say anything else, Henry stepped up and transported them en masse to The Balgaire.

Chapter Twenty-Six

Heat and heavy smoke caged Jayden in from all sides. Roaring fire licked up the wooden walls and chewed through pillars. He broke away from the group and frantically tried to get through the burning destruction.

He ran to where the staircase should have been, and instead found a fallen support beam and the remnants of the staircase burning away. There was no other way he'd be able to get to the top floor.

It was getting harder to breathe through the thick smoke, however, he needed to find his family.

Hands grabbed his shoulders and arms, but he pulled away. There was one place he had to check so he headed for the basement entrance.

"Liz!" Jayden shouted.

Arms wrapped around him before he could take the first step down. Thick smoke turned into daylight and clearer air. He gasped and coughed. He struggled against the hold to go back in but he was forced to watch in horror as The Balgaire continued to burn.

Other Szaephians stood in intervals around The Balgaire, streaming water into the fire. Jayden shoved the person holding him back and stormed over to the closest firefighter.

"Where's Liz and Roderick?"

The man barely spared a moment to look over to him.

"Don't know. No one knows. Last few days there's been crazy fighting and by the time anyone could get close enough to help, the place was burning down, and no one was here," the Szaephian answered.

The ground shook as a thundering snap assaulted their ears. All attention turned upwards. Above The Balgaire, a crack was splintering through the air. It stretched high into the sky and ended in the ruins of the pub and hotel.

He clenched his shaking fists and stared at his burning home in fear and panic. The Balgaire was gone. Balthezier and Roderick were missing. Dusk and the twins were who knows where.

With the added rip, things were going from bad to worse.

The earthquake worsened and grew in strength rapidly. Pieces of earth rose around him. He didn't even try to stop his Abilities. Blood dripped from his nose and white tendrils of power stretched out of him.

Arms wrapped around his waist and a soft glow surrounded him. A voice urged him to breathe and reminded him that it would be okay. Chunks of rock crashed into the ground as his Abilities were calmed down. He was taken from The Balgaire and to his Anchor.

Artemis kept her arms around him, gently rocking back and forth until he was calm and the shaking in his hands ceased.

Jayden turned around in those arms and hugged back. He was happy to stay there until he was certain he could stand on his own.

'Thank you,' he signed.

Behind him, Babyloneous approached. Dusk hobbled beside him and the twins stuck close to the Linstonate.

"You're all okay," Jayden whispered.

When they saw him, the pups whined and raced over. He was on his knees and gathering them up in a tight hug. Dusk was close behind them and he brought him into the embrace. He ran his hands over each of them, making sure they were okay.

'Balthezier managed to get them here,' Babyloneous told him.

"What happened?" Jayden asked.

The serpent shook his head. *'I am unsure.'*

Babyloneous looked troubled as he leaned down and nuzzled Jayden's cheek. He snapped his head away from Jayden and sniffed the air.

'There are others trying to come in. Do you allow them access?' Babyloneous asked.

Jayden nodded. "If they're a part of the group I'm with, then yes, they're allowed."

His travelling group appeared behind him. Immediately, their attention was drawn to the giant serpent watching them.

"You have a —"

"Dude!" Van shouted. "What the hell are you keeping here?"

Reid conjured a Ward and ran to attack Babyloneous. Harley and Diezel cut him off and as he stumbled back in surprised, Harley latched on to his ankle. Colorful language erupted from the guy and he tricked to kick the winged pup off.

"Harley!" Jayden shouted.

"Oh! You found the twins already?" Quentin remarked.

Quentin knelt down and pried the pup off of Reid's ankle.

"What?" Reid asked dumbly.

Quentin stood with Harley in his arms and rolled his eyes. "Not you. Jayden."

"What?" Jayden answered distractedly.

He glanced around nervously. Something was wrong. Something was trying to pull his control apart and pester his Abilities into reacting. Jayden clenched his fists as they shook.

Reid glanced up from checking his ankle and Jayden saw his lips curl into a small smile.

Wind whipped around him. He let out a shaky breath and swallowed the lump in his throat. This couldn't be happening. His control was slipping out of his hands and he could do nothing about it.

"What … what are you doing?" Jayden gasped, staring wide eyed at Reid.

"Jay? What's wrong?" Sera asked, worried.

He rubbed his eyes with the palm of his hands. When he looked back to his friends, he watched them step back with uncertainty.

'Your eyes, they're blue,' Artemis signed.

Breathing became labored and he stared at his hands as white tendrils of power rose out of them. A grainy glow pulsated around his body and he stepped back in alarm.

"No …"

Babyloneous rushed over to the group and wrapped his body around them moments before Jayden lost complete control.

He doubled over in pain and screamed as his Abilities violently ripped out of him.

Earth flew everywhere and vegetation disintegrated into ash. A panicked reptilian cry echoed through the Anchor, but every second was drowned out by the rush of burning Abilities.

When it finally ended, he fell to his knees. Bright blue eyes faded back to his normal black. His body spasmed as he gasped for air. He barely felt the pain brought on by deep cuts bleeding across his body.

In his mind's eye, he could see the flat grassy fields, Kalarney's tree house in the forest, and all the way over to the pavilion across the bridge. He could see thin, white glowing spider webs growing along the ground, pushing in deeper. The ground shook and groaned as it began to split apart.

Babyloneous uncurled his burnt body, revealing scared pale faces.

Sera, Van, and Artemis rushed over to Jayden.

"Jay!" Sera called out.

His mind fluctuated in and out of consciousness. He was aware of hands touching and grabbing him. The scenery changed in the blink of an eye and words were barely recognizable. Someone nearby said the Anchor had broken apart, while another added that the creatures living there had been safely evacuated thanks to Mackenzie but —-

Everything else became lost.

- Chapter Twenty-Seven -

Angry words anchored Jayden back to the world around him. He groggily looked around and found Reid arguing with Doctor Turner and someone he could only guess was one of Reid's older relatives.

"The Anchor was destroyed in minutes! It was ripped apart while I was right there. If he's in Szantium when —-"

"Reid, you will do as ordered," the stranger said.

"We're supposed to be saving the city and our people!" exclaimed Reid.

"Still naïve," Doctor Turner sighed. "You have your orders. Obey them or there will be consequences for you and yours."

Jayden must've made a sound as the three turned to look at him.

"Don't cause trouble for our family, Reid. Or you will be alone," the relative warned before leaving.

Reid glared at Jayden and stormed out.

"How are you, Jayden?" Doctor Turner asked from beside the bed.

He glanced from where the doctor had been standing in front of his bed to where he was now, confused.

"Okay?" Jayden hoarsely answered.

Doctor Turner raised the head of the bed as a way to help him sit up.

"What —-"

He blinked and when he looked to the doctor again, the man was busy tapping away at his tablet.

"The IV attached to you has blocked your Abilities. It's a last measure type drug and only to be used for a short amount of time as it has a high risk of causing more harm than good. One of the side effects is a distorted sense of time. Once we know you won't put the hospital or anyone else in danger, the IV will be removed," Doctor Turner explained.

Jayden frowned at the IV and sighed. "Right."

"Tell me what happened," Doctor Turner requested.

"What do you think?"

"What I think and what the truth is can be two different things," Doctor Turner pointed out.

"Lost control."

"Why?"

He started up at the ceiling and thought about it. He had gone through so many strong emotions so quickly but Artemis had helped him calm down. Why hadn't he stayed that way?

"I … don't know. I started losing control when we found The Balgaire on fire but I … a friend helped me calm down at the Anchor. There was this weird tugging feeling and the next thing I knew, my Abilities were going haywire and it hurt," Jayden explained.

The doctor nodded and tapped away at his tablet. Once he was done, he fished out a pill bottle from his lab coat.

"I want you to start taking these. They're a refined version of the first tablets I gave you. Take one every morning," Doctor Turner instructed as he handed them over.

Jayden stared at the bottle in disdain and wondered whether or not he should tell the doctor there was no point.

"Come see me in two weeks," Doctor Turner said.

He nodded and was left alone.

He wondered if the doctor knew he only had weeks left, maybe less now. But none of that mattered now. Kalarney was still missing. The Adlers were now missing. The last thing he wanted to do was waste any more time. He needed to focus on the search for his missing friends.

As he swung his legs over the edge, a nurse stepped into the room.

"What do you think you're doing? Get back in bed," the nurse ordered.

Jayden shook his head. "I'm leaving."

"Not for another couple of hours. Doctor Turner's orders."

He sighed in annoyance and sat back to stare at the ceiling tiles.

The next thing he knew, he was alone and the sky was darkening. He rubbed his eyes tiredly. He hoped he hadn't lost too much time because of the drugs.

Once again, Jayden started to get out of bed, needing to get up and do something.

"Dude, seriously? Lay back down," Sera demanded, coming into the room.

"I'm leaving," Jayden said as he managed to stand.

"No, you're not," Sera argued.

"I'm going to look for my friends and family."

"You don't even know where to start looking," Mackenzie pointed out.

"I'm not waiting around for someone else to disappear!" Jayden snapped.

Van put his phone in his pocket and stepped closer. "Bookman has sent scouts to look for Roderick and Balthezier."

"What about Kalarney?" Jayden replied.

"Who?" Van blinked, confused.

"A friend who's been missing for years," Jayden answered.

"Being friends with you seems to be more hazardous by the day," Reid remarked.

"Lucky you don't have to worry then. Do you have friends or were those people you were constantly with bought?" Van asked Reid.

A young woman with short pale gray hair framing a familiar face with a set of familiar blue eyes let herself into the hospital room, followed by Quentin and Henry. She wore a cream colored knitted sweater with a collared black shirt poking out with dark jean leggings and black high top sneakers.

"Ah, hi?" Van greeted.

"I'm Clara Waters, Kalarney's sister and —"

"Kalarney doesn't have any siblings," Jayden interrupted.

"It's ... complicated," Clara said.

"Complicated? Her ... Your parents abused her because she's a Ricornon!"

"We don't have any parents," Clara quickly said. "Kalarney is the eldest Compass Point and I'm her Watcher. Five years after we settled down in human forms, she was stolen from me."

"Hold up!" Jayden demanded. "Kalarney … No. She can't be. She only has earth based Abilities. She told us!"

"She is," Quentin confirmed.

Jayden couldn't believe it. Why did Kalarney say she was a Ricornon? Did she not know or was it because the whole business had to be kept a secret? The books hadn't indicated anything about her at all, and even Babyloneous had referred to her as a Ricornon.

He shook his head in a bid to push past all the demanding questions.

"She hasn't been missing. She told me Leeran and Taylin saved her from abusive parents and left her on the Anchor," Jayden informed them. "She disappeared when we snuck into the Great Library nine years ago."

Clara frowned. "I couldn't sense her."

He rolled his eyes. It hadn't been hard to figure that much out.

"So you're useless then," Jayden said.

"Don't be rude. Did she tell you who her parents were?" Sera asked.

Jayden shook his head. "Wasn't told."

"Then we should find that out. From there, we might be able to find a lead as to where she is now," Sera suggested.

"Liz spent years trying to find her," Jayden pointed out.

"We need a starting point," Sera argued.

She folded her arms and stared at Jayden, prepared for an argument.

"Question," Van spoke up, raising his hand. "How does a Compass Point disappear from their Watcher?"

"Incompetence," Jayden murmured.

"Rudeness isn't going to get us far. We already have to deal with those two, so back off," Van growled, indicating Mackenzie and Reid.

Jayden looked down at his hands and clenched his fists tightly. He was struggling to understand any of it. More and more of his friends were turning out to be someone he didn't know. Did he really know anyone?

"It's fine. Not being able to find who created me tells me that someone with a lot of power knows what Kalarney is and they know how to block the link between a Compass Point and their Watcher," Clara said.

'Who would have that type of knowledge and power?' Artemis asked.

Henry translated for those who didn't know sign language and there was a moment of silence while they thought about it.

"Someone from the Original 8, like the grandparents?" Jayden guessed.

"In case you haven't noticed, the old geezers don't use their Abilities, and if they do, it's only basic and simple Wards. Bodies can't cope with the strain when they're old and frail. Simple logic, idiot," Reid pointed out.

"Whoever is involved wouldn't be a part of the Szaephian community," Quentin said.

A sudden thought had Jayden biting his bottom lip.

"A Harbinon," Jayden said.

"You've just implicated yourself and your brother," Reid replied with a raised eyebrow.

Jayden shook his head. "A Level 8 might be able to do it if they're on the high end of it, but more than likely, it's a Harbinon."

"So you're saying … there's another?" Sera checked.

"When I found out I was a Harbinon, I was told there had been three –- One was destroyed when they defeated a Shadow, and two didn't have happy endings," Jayden explained. "Apart from Mackenzie and I, how many other Harbinons have there been that any of you know about?"

He watched them all think about the answer and Reid checked his phone.

"I'm not dealing with this stupidity," Reid huffed and left.

He sighed. Patience for that man was running paper thin.

"One other. They were the reason the laws against Harbinons came about. They wanted to prove themselves so they went after old and powerful Shadows. If they're the same one you were told about then they weren't destroyed. They did survive the Shadow but they … uh … also didn't," Van explained.

"What do you mean?" Mackenzie asked.

"From what I've read, the Shadow and this person kind of melded into one being. They pretty much lost their marbles and started accusing Szaephians of turning their backs on them. It got pretty messy. A lot of people died and the city was partially destroyed. They were arrested, but how do you contain a crazy Harbinon? You can't really," Van informed them. "Unless you put them in the In Between."

Jayden tensed. The In Between appeared harmless and the light show it created could have been mistaken as an Aurora, but he knew the frightening truth. It was cold and uncaring. If he wasn't dreaming about the hospital, then he was dreaming about the In Between. It lulled him into a false sense of security.

Whoever chose to use the In Between as a prison, they were monsters.

Sighing, he tried to get out of bed for the third time.

"Whoa! Hang on a moment. The doctor hasn't discharged you and you still need to be assessed," Van tried, trying to stop him.

"Because I'm oh so dangerous? Sorry, but I can't keep sitting here wasting time," Jayden growled.

"Leave Kalarney to me," Clara said.

"Like hell I will!" Jayden snapped.

Artemis stood in front of him, arms crossed, glaring.

"Once you're discharged, we will meet up to discuss what we'll be doing from here on out," Quentin said.

"I'm looking for my friends," Jayden kept trying.

"No, Jayden Lugian. Other people are dealing with —-"

"Liz is one of the —-"

"We'll discuss *all* of this later," Quentin interrupted with a pointed look.

The boy glanced out of the door and frowned.

"Henry and Clara, it's time to go," Quentin said.

Without explaining why they needed to leave, the three of them disappeared. A moment later, Doctor Turner came into the room.

"I'd like to talk to my patient alone," Doctor Turner requested.

Artemis squeezed his shoulder before following Van, Sera, and Mackenzie out of the room.

The doctor closed and locked the door behind them. Jayden sat up straighter and frowned. Being locked in the room with the doctor set him on edge.

"While we were impressed with the extent of what our gift caused to the Anchor even while tainted, it was not good enough. For our plans to work, we'll need to make some adjustments. In the meantime, I need you to keep searching for the Compass Points," Doctor Turner said.

Jayden's frown grew deeper, and when he realized what the doctor was admitting to, he scrambled out of bed and tried to edge as far away as the room allowed.

"Y-you … You did this to me?" Jayden accused.

Doctor Turner adjusted his glasses and closed in on Jayden. When he reached out, Jayden flinched but all the doctor did was gently run his hand through his black hair. The touch caused his mind to go fuzzy and he slumped against the man.

His body was picked up and laid down on the bed. When he looked over to Doctor Turner, he caught sight of blue eyes in place of his usual dark shade in the reflection nearby glass offered.

"Don't worry. You'll be able to give them our gift soon enough. Just be patient," Doctor Turner said.

Jayden slowly nodded.

"The tablets will stop your Abilities from acting on their own so make sure you take them. When you have all the Compass Points, stop taking them and call me," the doctor instructed.

Jayden nodded again.

He laid there as Doctor Turner signed the forms to allow him to be released from the hospital.

"Listen to the brat and keep what you know to yourself," Doctor Turner ordered before leaving.

Left alone, he blinked and struggled to understand what had just happened. It felt like something had briefly taken over and he had only wanted to obey. Had he and Doctor Turner met before he had been brought in to investigate his sickness?

When Artemis came back into the room with a bag, he shook his head and managed to give her a small smile.

'I can leave now,' Jayden signed.

She tilted her head with a slight frown before slowly nodding. The way Artemis was watching him was confusing and it made him falter.

'Here's a fresh change of clothes. I had to guess your size though so I'm sorry if they don't fit,' Artemis said.

He nodded and slipped out of bed as Artemis left to give him privacy to change.

- Chapter Twenty-Eight -

Caution tape surrounded the burnt out husk of The Balgaire. It was hard to look at and even harder to walk through. There was hardly anything of the hotel left and the pub floor was barely recognizable. It broke his heart to see his home reduced to charred rubble.

A woman in overall shorts was in the midst of tossing a ball with the pups when they arrived. Dusk swerved his head around and watched them come in.

"It's about time you got here," the woman remarked.

"There were more important matters to attend to. Forgive me," Quentin said.

Bypassing Quentin and the woman, Jayden took the twins over to Dusk off to the side. He placed Harley and Diezel down and hugged his Linstonate friend.

When he pulled back, Dusk swayed in closer and sniffed. He met Jayden's gaze and tilted his head. Grimacing, he ruffled Dusk's head.

"Jayden, I'd like to introduce you to the Compass Point of the East, second to be created, Jiang Xiaoxing," Quentin introduced.

"Just call me Jet."

He didn't look away from his animal companions and murmured, "We've seen each other before."

"A little rude, aren't you?" Jet remarked.

He sighed. He needed a breather from everything, at least for a minute. He still hadn't had the chance to ask about Babyloneous and the other serpent who had lived in the lake.

"Jayden, please come over here. We all need to talk," Quentin called out.

He begrudgingly went over to the others. Dusk followed and, much to Jayden's appreciation, pressed against his leg. When he stopped walking, the pups took a seat on his feet.

"Where's Reid and Mackenzie?" Sera asked, glancing around.

"They're busy," Quentin answered.

"Shouldn't we wait for them?" Sera checked.

"Why bother? Reid thinks we're only wasting time and Mackenzie is questionable at best," Van said.

"Never mind them. With Jet, we only have three Compass Points left to find before we try and locate the two that are missing," Quentin said.

Van frowned. "There's another Compass Point missing aside from Kalarney?"

"Liz is a Compass Point," Jayden said. "So are Harley and Diezel."

"How do you know?" Sera asked.

He fished out the books from his messenger bag and held them out for the group to see.

"Roderick gave them to be a while ago. One is a journal and the other contains information on the Compass Points –- nothing indicating the exact who or what but just enough information to give some sort of idea," Jayden explained.

"Are you serious? You had this information all this time? Why didn't you tell us?" Sera demanded.

"I told him not to," Quentin answered.

"Why not?" Sera growled.

"Those books put us in danger and I needed to know who could be trusted," Quentin reasoned.

'We've found Quentin, the pups, Jet, and we know Kalarney and Balthezier are Compass Points. Who are the last three?' Artemis asked.

He shoved the books back in his bag and tried to ignore the glares he was getting from Sera and Van. Having the books was frustrating, and knowing what was contained on their pages had made things even worse. If he had told them sooner, he knew he wouldn't have been able to convince them the books were factual because *he* hadn't believed what he had read.

"There's a Compass Point in Africa, one in the Amazon, and one in the sky," Henry answered.

Van tilted his head in confusion. "The sky?"

"A meteor shower will happen on August eighth in Australia," Quentin clarified. "We will be going to Africa first, then to the Amazon, and by the time we have found those two, it will be time to head to Australia."

"We have to be careful. Someone is taking Compass Points so I will be taking those two pups into hiding until Quentin contacts me," Jet added.

Jayden glanced down at the two pups crawling over each other by his feet.

"Harley and Diezel … Take Dusk. He'll help," Jayden said.

The aforementioned animal nuzzled his leg.

"Okay," Jet agreed.

"Do you know who is after you guys?" Sera asked.

"No. The one giving orders has stayed hidden and there are many loyal followers," Jet answered.

Jayden frowned. "The Wyka's are a part of this."

"Reid is a jerk, but really? They're trying to help save the city," Van reasoned.

He shook his head and glanced out of the ruins of The Balgaire.

"In the hospital, Reid and a relative were talking to … to someone … about what I did to the Anchor."

Why couldn't he remember specifics? He was sure on the details until he had started talking.

Shaking his head to clear it, he continued, "Bookman also warned me about the Wyka's and Mackenzie earlier," Jayden continued.

"You're in touch with Bookman?" Jet asked.

He nodded.

"Good. What else has he said?"

He thought for a moment before answering. "Cracks are appearing in the Human Plane and Shadows are coming out. He and his team are investigating while Hunters deal with the Shadow problem."

"Quentin, you'll need to hurry," Jet warned.

"I'm aware."

"What do we do about Reid and Mackenzie?" Sera asked.

"Nothing for now. We will watch and wait," Quentin said.

"Really? And if something happens because of them?"

"Henry will be there to help, and if worse comes to worse, I'll go back into hiding. Artemis will take Jayden to find Bookman, and Sera, you and Van will split up. You two will need to make sure you aren't being followed before going to the places I will give directions to," Quentin explained.

Jayden glanced up at the crack hovering in the space where the first floor had been. It was an uneasy sight. He could feel a number of Szaephians surrounding the crack, and he wondered how many Shadows had already come through.

When his phone buzzed with a message, he pulled the device from his pocket and read the text from Bookman.

'Leeran and Taylin have disappeared. Keep an eye on Mackenzie and be careful. Talk more later.'

Jayden swore.

"Jay?"

He ran a hand through his hair. "That was from Bookman. Leeran and Taylin had disappeared and Mackenzie needs to be watched."

"It's time to leave then. Sera and Van, please go get Reid and Mackenzie. Do not mention Jet or anything we have discussed, only our first destination," Quentin instructed.

Jayden knelt down in front of Dusk. "I need you to keep looking after the terrors for a little bit longer."

Dusk licked his cheek and nuzzled him in understanding. Jayden wrapped his arms around the Linstonate and took a deep breath.

He pulled away from his friend, ruffled the fur between Dusk's ears, and left The Balgaire.

"Jayden, are you okay?" Quentin asked, following him out.

"Balthezier, Kalarney, Harley and Diezel have turned out to be Compass Points. It can't have been a coincidence. Why did you seek me out instead of any of the others?"

"Don't go down this thought pattern. You're not ready," Quentin warned.

"Not ready for what? What aren't you telling me?" Jayden demanded.

"We need to find these Com —-"

"No!" Jayden shouted. "What we need is for you to tell me."

"Hey, we're all here and ready to go," Sera interrupted.

Without a word, Quentin went back inside. Jayden placed hands on hips and growled in frustration.

"You okay?" Sera asked, worried.

"Just great," he murmured before following the boy inside.

Jet, the twin pups, and Dusk were already gone. Quentin and Henry were in a hushed conversation that stopped when they realized they had company.

"Time to go," Quentin announced.

Arriving in Africa, they were shrouded in nighttime darkness with only the luminescence from the stars above lighting the way.

"We will make camp here for the night, and then in the morning I will take everyone to where the Compass Point is," Quentin instructed.

"Why can't we use our Abilities and go now?" Mackenzie asked.

"We could be locked up or escorted away. Plus, it's rude," Quentin answered.

Jayden knew Mackenzie and Reid were rolling their eyes but neither said a word about the matter.

- Chapter Twenty-Nine -

Quentin had them moving as soon as the sun began rising. They walked through the wilderness, keeping a respectful distance from any animals they spotted. Jayden remembered to snap a couple of photos, and noticing the signal bars were gone, pocketed his phone with a mental reminder to send them to Kelly once they were in cell service range.

To their right, he caught sight of something that made him squint with uncertainty. Something was kicking up a lot of dust and heading straight towards them.

"Does anyone else see that?" Van asked.

"Yeah," Jayden answered.

"What is it?" Sera asked.

They stared at the dust storm, and when he realized a stampede was fast approaching, he turned around in panic.

"Run!" he shouted.

Without looking back at where the others were going, he bolted.

The rumbling behind him was getting louder and louder. Jayden frantically looked around for somewhere he could hide or climb up to safety.

He spotted an opening in the earth widening to the left, and taking a chance, he ran towards it. He dropped to the ground, slid inside, and distanced himself from the entrance as much as possible.

Not long after, something else slid in, forcing him to turn his face away from the airborne dirt with a cough.

Jayden groaned when he realized it was Reid.

Before either of them could remark on the other's presence, the ground rumbled with deafening thunder.

He clamped his hands over his ears, body tensed and curling in on itself, until there was quiet. For a moment, everything was still. When he went to move to leave, Reid grabbed his arm and placed a finger to his lips.

He was going to ignore the guy and leave, but large paws stepped past the opening to their hole. More walked past and the nose and mouth of a large cat poked into view. Jayden froze as the predator sniffed. When the mouth full of sharp teeth receded, he sighed but the relief was short lived. A paw swiped into the hole, narrowly missing his chest.

Jayden scrambled back as claws and teeth continued to try and reach them.

Reid drew a Ward into the dirt and the wall they were leaning on was pushed back, giving them more room to remain safe in. All they could do was watch and wait.

He glanced over to his companion and realized his shoulder was soaked with blood. Without saying anything, he pushed Reid forward to have a look.

"Hey!" Reid shouted.

"You're hurt so shut up," Jayden said. "Take your shirt off."

It was a surprise when Reid did as told.

He fished out his small first aid kit and cleaned the scratches on Reid's shoulder and back. The well-dressed guy hissed and jerked forward in pain.

"Sorry," Jayden mumbled.

Reid stayed quiet the entire time he was being tended to. After finishing up, Jayden sat back to allow him to put his shirt back on.

After a moment, Jayden said, "I know you were the reason why I lost control."

"Don't know what you're talking about," Reid murmured.

"I heard you talking about pushing me to use my Abilities. Your … I don't know, father? Both of you want me to destroy Szantium."

Reid visibly tensed. It was different from the usual confident and demanding presence he usually carried himself with.

He inwardly flinched at his carelessness for mentioning it. Stuck in a hole with Reid was not how he wanted to have this conversation.

"No one has to follow in their family's footsteps," Jayden said.

"Stop talking like you know anything," Reid growled.

"I'm related to someone who shares my looks and killed the people I called family. Leeran and Taylin keep insisting I do as I'm told and forget about the ones who actually mattered to me. The only blood relatives who care and respect my choices and who I am are my grandparents," Jayden explained.

"Boohoo. Who cares?" Reid mocked. "Just because you heard one measly conversation doesn't mean you know what's going on."

"Then tell me," Jayden said.

Reid's silence had him sighing. All he could hope for was that this little conversation might make the guy reconsider what choices he had.

Their makeshift roof was removed and Jayden prepared for the worst. He was relieved at the sight of his friends staring down at them.

"It's safe now," Quentin said. "Let's go. We're staying in a nearby village."

Reid didn't waste a second to climb out while Van reached down and help Jayden up. A woman with her black hair tied in a bun, thick necklaces draped over her neck, and wearing a sleeveless dress smiled at him when he caught her eye.

Stepping away from Van, he swayed a little. Hands grabbed his shoulders until he nodded that he was okay.

"Are you alright?" Van asked.

He nodded. "Yeah. I just got a little dizzy."

Artemis took his hand and they followed their guide to the village.

Cheering and laughing kids of all ages ran up to greet them once they were closer to the small village that consisted of mud, stone, and straw made huts. A couple of kids took the guide's hands, one took Sera and Artemis's hands, and the rest led them to the fire pit in the center. Each child hugged the group's guide before running off again.

"Your phone will not work here," the woman said, smiling knowingly at Reid.

Reid grumbled, "I gathered."

"Please sit, eat," the woman said.

Jayden took a seat beside Artemis and accepted a bowl from an old lady with kind, welcoming eyes.

"It's good to see you. Everyone, this is Nuru, the Southern Compass Point. With me is Jayden Lugian, Artemis Gaede, Sera Quiroz, Van Bixlar, Reid Wyka, and Mackenzie Laiyfe-Rain," Quentin said.

"It is good to see you, too, Quentin, and it is a pleasure meeting everyone. Forgive me for my English. I know many languages but it has been a while since I have used this one. Please eat your soup and then I wish to show you something," Nuru said.

Jayden glanced down at the bowl in his hands. There were vegetables and an unknown type of meat floating in steaming hot herbed water.

Reid, Mackenzie, and Sera put their bowls down without touching the food. Jayden raised his bowl and sniffed. It smelled appetizing and when he took a mouthful, found it rather tasty and refreshing. However, his appetite was nonexistent and he couldn't will himself to eat.

Once everyone was ready, Nuru led them away from the village. They walked through the wilderness and he was surprised the animals they passed either barely paid them any attention or came up to Nuru for a small pat.

The further away they walked, the more he noticed how quiet their surroundings were getting. It made him nervous.

A crack hovered meters above the ground. It was equally as high as it was wide. The ripped space made the one at The Balgaire look tiny.

"It's massive!" Sera gasped.

"Just wait," Nuru said.

They watched the giant crack pulse with the river of the In Between. He glanced over to the woman. Even though they weren't at risk of being pulled in, the sight of the In Between kept him on edge and all he wanted to do was run in the opposite direction.

The earth shook as a black mass pulled itself out and dropped to the ground with a loud bang.

"What —"

A black humanoid shape stood up and smiled at them with squinting white eyes and a mouth full of razor sharp teeth. Its skin bubbled and its movements were jagged.

"What is that?" Van asked.

"A Shadow," Nuru answered.

"Shadows don't – Oh, jeez!" Van cried out, flailing around in fright.

The humanoid Shadow charged towards them at lightning speed. Its arms were flung back and it howled in hungry anticipation.

Sera and Van tripped over each other trying to get away, while Reid and Mackenzie readied themselves to fight back with Wards.

Jayden took a step back, trembling. The creature held a resemblance to the monster that had been chasing him in his dreams and through Szantium, but unlike that thing, this Shadow had wide white eyes.

Before the Shadow could reach them, it slammed into a barrier that rippled and shimmered from the impact.

They stared in horror as the Shadow tried to claw its way through. It snapped sharp teeth and growled at them savagely. Apart from the thin silhouette, there was nothing else that made it human.

"Shadows like this have been coming through since the air split open. An entire village had been wiped out before I realized what was going on. I managed to find and destroy the Shadow, and put up a barrier to stop any more deaths from happening," Nuru explained.

She held out her hand and released a Ward. The symbol wrapped around the Shadow tightly. It screamed and struggled for freedom until its body exploded in a puff of black sand.

"We have to warn the others!" Sera exclaimed.

"No, we don't. We don't have time to worry about things happening here or there. Our priority is to retrieve the Compass Points so that's what we need to focus on," Mackenzie argued.

"People are dying! Our responsibility has always been to protect humans," Sera growled.

"Our responsibility is to *our* people," Mackenzie said.

Before she could retort any further, Jayden grabbed her wrist. When Mackenzie rolled his eyes and focused on taking a photo of the crack, Jayden took the opportunity to shake his head. Sera stared at him for a moment before sighing and nodding.

There was no point in arguing. He knew Mackenzie didn't care much for humans, but it still grated on his nerves hearing the remarks. He hoped Quentin would allow at least one of them to go back home to warn everyone.

"We need you to stay hidden until I contact you. We have two more Compass Points to find and then I will send out a message for everyone to gather. But be careful, Nuru. Someone is stealing us," Quentin warned.

"I am aware," Nuru nodded. "Jayden, we need to have a word before you depart."

Confused, he jerkily nodded. "Okay."

He followed Nuru away from the group in silence. A thousand questions ran through his mind and a thousand more scenarios played out as he tried to think why he'd been singled out.

"It is good to finally meet you after all this time," Nuru said.

Jayden frowned. "Excuse me?"

"I am the Calming Ward Balthezier uses to help you," Nuru explained.

He blinked and repeated, "Excuse me?"

Nuru smiled and took his hands.

"My primary form is any Ward I can think of. Once Balthezier met you, he knew, and I volunteered to help him make sure you remain okay," Nuru told him.

"Knew what?" Jayden asked.

"Have you started to question why we gravitate towards you?"

Jayden let out a shaky breath. "I tried to ask Quentin before we came here but he told me to focus on finding the Compass Points."

"There would be more to that, I imagine. He is protective. I promise all will be revealed soon. Do not trust that male doctor and the medicine he gives you. He already has control over a part of you and your Abilities," Nuru advised.

"Doctor Turner …" Jayden trailed off.

"I will give you a Ward that will help fight against the influence over you long enough to see the end of what must be done," Nuru offered.

He nodded and forced himself to keep his questions to himself. Everything was becoming too complicated and he was too tired to try and untangle it all.

"Thanks."

She lifted up his dirty shirt, revealing skin covered in bruises and rashes. A finger ran over his stomach and a faint green glow blossomed before fading away.

He shivered as he felt the Ward settle in.

Nuru cupped his check. "Trust your Abilities, and take time to reflect and communicate with the core of who you are. It may be the thing that saves you."

"Jayden, we need to go. We're stopping in a city close to our next destination for supplies. Nuru, be careful," Quentin interrupted.

"You, too," Nuru replied. "Jayden, it will be okay. Do not be afraid."

- **Chapter Thirty -**

Quentin took them to the outskirts of a bustling city with buildings and landmarks Jayden didn't recognize.

"Get supplies and meet back here in half an hour. Jayden, stay here," Quentin instructed.

'I'll stay as well,' Artemis volunteered.

'Go with Sera. I'll be okay. Can you get me something to eat and drink, please?' Jayden asked.

He fished out his wallet and held it out for her. However, she held her hand up and shook her head with a smile.

'Don't worry about it. Are you okay?'

Jayden nodded. 'Yeah.'

"We'll be back," Sera said with a tired smile.

He watched the group split up as they walked into the city. He didn't miss the Reid and Mackenzie immediately take out their phones.

"We will be splitting up once we are in the Amazon, but I must confess, I have a bad feeling about this trip," Quentin admitted.

"Why?" Jayden asked.

"I'm not sure."

Jayden watched the activity in front of them and sighed. There were a lot of people going in and out of buildings or approaching stalls lining the streets.

"Doctor Turner is giving the Wyka's orders. Nuru told me he has control over the part of my Abilities that have lost and I'm pretty sure they're trying to get me to destroy Szantium like I did with the Anchor," Jayden told Quentin.

"Where is this coming from?" Quentin asked.

"Nuru gave me a Ward and I guess it's helped clear my head. When I woke up in the hospital, I saw Reid, Doctor Turner, and who I guess was Reid's dad, talking together. Plus, I heard Reid talking on the phone when we were in South Korea."

Quentin nodded and rubbed his chin as he thought about it.

"While it's just us, I would like you to call Bookman in order to pass over an update on what we saw in Africa," Quentin eventually said.

Jayden was taken aback. He didn't understand why the matter was brushed aside for something else.

"Okay," he said, taking out his phone.

It came as a bit of a surprise when Bookman answered rather quickly.

"Jay, hi. I was about to try and call you again. Where have you been?" Bookman asked.

"Sorry," Jayden said as he walked away from Henry and Quentin. "We were in Africa without reception."

"I see," Bookman murmured.

"Is everything okay?"

"Yeah, well no. We're struggling to find a way to fix the breaches and stronger Shadows are coming through."

Jayden grimaced. That was not news he had been wanting to hear. "Szantium?"

"It's … stable enough right now. Which is something, at least. Once you are all back with the Compass Points, the Council wants you to lead the negotiations with the human council, the uh … United Nations," Bookman said.

"Why?" Jayden asked.

"You grew up with humans," Bookman pointed out.

"I wish people would stop using that as an excuse. Other Szaephians have lived in the Human Plane so why can't they do it," Jayden said.

"It's not the same. Szaephians don't know how humans think. We may look the same but our society is too different. We're going to need to let them know a new city will either appear or be built, and explain what has been happening recently."

Jayden ran a hand through his dirty hair. There was too much to do and it was causing stress to become overwhelming.

"Jay, breathe. I'll help you with this. You won't be alone," Bookman said, interrupting his spiraling thoughts.

"Y-yeah, thanks," Jayden managed to say. "I rang to tell you there's a massive crack in Africa and humanoid Shadows are coming out. Nuru pretty much dealt with the issue with a barrier, but …"

Bookman cursed. "I was hoping those reports were false."

"Reports?"

"I've received one or two reports about humanoid Shadows appearing, but the sources were sketchy at best so I didn't put too much thought into it with everything else going on. Are you alone right now?" Bookman said.

He glanced over at Quentin and Henry and at the people passing him by the main road leading out of the city.

"We're outside of a city and only Quentin and Henry are with me right now," he answered.

"Give them the phone," Bookman requested.

Frowning, he went back to the duo and held out the phone.

"Bookman wants to talk," Jayden said.

Henry took the phone from him and greeted, "Hello, Henry speaking."

When then older man went silent then gave Bookman their location, Jayden tilted his head in curious confusion.

The phone call ended and he received his phone back without explanation.

It only added to confusion when Bookman popped up next to him.

The leader of the Academics grabbed his wrist and pulled him into a tight hug. Jayden found himself relaxing in those arms and returned the hug.

"It is good to see you again," Bookman said, pulling back.

"You, too," Jayden mumbled.

"How long do we have?" Bookman asked Quentin and Henry.

"Eighteen minutes," Henry answered.

Bookman nodded. "Okay. It's time to tell you what I should have told you weeks ago."

Jayden frowned. He didn't have time to ask before Bookman was taking his hand and engulfing them in a Transport Ward. They reappeared on a piece of land big enough to give the two of them enough room to move around without bumping into each other. Above them, the clear blue sky was splintered and shards were missing, revealing a river of blue and green swimming above them.

He cautiously stepped closer to the edge and nervously took a look. In an instant, he felt like he was back in the nightmares he had after coming back where the In Between was trying to lull him into a false sense of security.

In a panic, he scrambled back and crashed into his companion.

"I've got you. Are you okay?" Bookman asked.

Jayden nodded. "Yeah. The In Between feels like it's trying to pull me back in with the promise of never ending safety."

"I'd expect it'd have some sort of effect on you after spending so much time within, but this is the only place I knew where we could talk in private," Bookman said.

"It's okay. It's fine. What did you want to talk about?"

"Do you know where we are?" Bookman asked.

"No," Jayden answered.

"The remnants of your Anchor," Bookman said.

He glanced around, horrified. He wouldn't have guessed that was where they were. Unless you looked up at the cracked sky or over the rocky edge, there was nothing to distinguish their location. As far as he could tell, Bookman had taken them to an extremely small private island.

Bookman swiped his hand through the air and the space around them changed. The sky crumbled away and revealed a full view of the In Between. Fragments and chunks of earth floated around like space junk.

"No ..."

"You destroyed it. Your Abilities went into the core of the Anchor and ripped it apart with an explosive force."

He went wide-eyed and pale.

"I knew ... I knew I ..."

"Jay, focus. I'm telling you this because the power I found in the remnants here, I have found in sections of the city," Bookman said.

"What ... what does that mean? I'm already destroying the city?" Jayden asked in disbelief.

"This power is sick, almost like it's rotting and it's being manipulated."

Jayden swallowed the lump in his throat. Letting out a shaky breath, he closed his eyes and thought for a moment. He knew Doctor Turner was manipulating his Abilities, but he hadn't thought that what was happening in Szantium now was linked to what was happening to himself.

"Is it possible that whatever or whoever changed what I am is using the parts of my Abilities that have already lost to cause Szantium to destabilize?" Jayden asked.

"It's highly possible," Bookman answered. "When I was younger, I took a great interest in the Compass Points and I spent years searching everywhere for any answers or clues. Eventually, I met Balthezier and Roderick. You'd never believe it, but back then they were cold and distant. They warned me to stop my search but my need for answers and knowledge is why I was invited into the Academics. I ended up finding those books Balthezier and Roderick had hidden and I managed to read quite a bit before being discovered. Balthezier can pack quite a punch."

Bookman rubbed his ribs in memory before continuing. "I never told anyone the information I had learned, never really did anything with it. I had some of the answers I wanted so I was content. I guess they were watching me, and the human versions of the Compass Points started approaching me. I gained their trust slowly and they began telling me a few more things."

"So you knew? All this time and you knew Liz was a Compass Point and you never said anything?"

Bookman nodded. "I knew about Quentin and Henry, Jiang Xiaoxing and her black cat, Minis, Kalarney and Clara, and Nuru and the tribe she lives with."

Jayden clenched his fists tightly.

"Why didn't you say anything?" he asked through gritted teeth.

"All I was permitted to do was to instruct you to read those books. I worked hard gaining their trust and I wasn't going to ruin it."

He almost deflated from Bookman's words. It was understandable and he could respect Bookman's silence.

"Did you learn anything about The Heart?" he asked,

"That was the one thing all of them refused to talk about," Bookman said, shaking his head.

When Jayden was reunited with Balthezier, after hugging him and making sure that he and Roderick were okay, he was going to start demanding answers.

"Don't be angry. I, and those that follow me, swore an oath to keep our knowledge safe from those who would use it to cause harm. That's especially true for sensitive information like that of the Compass Points."

"I understand," Jayden sighed. "I kept those books a secret as well until recently. It's just … frustrating to have things hidden, even if I understand why. I can confirm, though, the Wyka's are taking orders from Doctor Turner."

"Doctor Turner … that makes sense. After you asked me about Shiro, I started to dig around and found links to a Doctor Misha Turner. There isn't much about them, only that they were banished from the community a very long time ago," Bookman said.

Jayden frowned. He wondered if they were the same ones he knew.

"Is there anything else that needs to be talked about?"

Bookman thought for a moment and shook his head. "No. If anything else does come up, I'll message you."

"Okay."

When Bookman reached out to take his hand, Jayden took a step back. There was one thing he wanted to ask before being sent back.

"Do you think I'll survive this?"

The Academic studied him for a moment. He could see in those purple eyes that Bookman wanted to say yes, but the man was about facts and the fact was, there really was no hope."

"I will do everything in my power to make sure you do," Bookman eventually said.

Jayden grimaced and took the older man's hand.

They were back with Quentin and Henry with minutes to spare before the others were due to be back. Bookman said a quick goodbye to the Compass Point and Watcher before leaving them.

"We got you three something to eat, drink, and a little sugary snack for a boost of energy," Sera said.

"Thank you," Quentin said as he and Henry accepted a bag of food.

With a murmur of thanks, Jayden shoved the food into his shoulder bag.

'You're not hungry anymore?' Artemis asked.

'I'll eat a bit later,' Jayden answered.

Artemis took his hand and squeezed reassuringly.

"Our next destination is the Amazon Rainforest. We will be splitting up again as this search will be … a little different and troublesome. This time we need to look for one particular tree," Quentin informed them.

Reid raised his eyebrows in disbelief. "We have to look for a single tree … in a forest?"

"Yes," Quentin answered. "This particular tree will be one of the oldest. It's tall and will resonate with more power than any other plant."

"What are the pairs?" Van asked.

"Jayden and Reid, myself and Mackenzie, Sera and Van, and Artemis and Quentin," Henry answered.

Jayden glanced over to Reid and Mackenzie. The way they were watching him was setting off his anxiety. He would have preferred to be partnered up with someone who wasn't trying to use him. Whatever Quentin was up to by deciding on that pairing, he was dreading the outcome of the search, more so since the boy had expressed concern about upcoming events.

"It's July twenty-eighth. Ideally, we will leave the Amazon on August seventh in order to make it to Australia in time for the meteor shower. If the tree isn't found by then, we'll be back after collecting the fragment we need," Quentin said.

"Meteor shower?" Mackenzie asked, frowning.

Jayden grimaced as he nodded.

They were down to the final two Compass Points before they could turn to focusing on rescuing his missing friends.

- Chapter Thirty-One -

High humidity drenched them in sweat within seconds after Jayden and Reid arrived in the Amazon Rainforest.

He fanned his shirt collar for some relief as he took in their surroundings. It was dense with trees that stretched high up in the sky and thick underbrush. Animals, reptiles, and insects sung in every direction. It was loud and overbearing.

"We need to be careful," Jayden said.

"Why?" Reid asked, raising his eyebrows.

"There's a lot of deadly things here — snakes, jaguars, poisonous frogs, bugs, and even some of these plants will make you really sick," Jayden informed him.

"Right. Those things may be deadly to you but I'll be fine," Reid scoffed.

Jayden rolled his eyes and remained silent. He watched Reid try to swat away mosquitos that were swarming around them. There was no use arguing with someone who wasn't going to listen. He'd learn soon enough.

Growling in annoyance, Reid grabbed his arm and pulled him closer as he drew a Ward in front of them. The symbol grew and encased them in a bubble. Insects hovering around them fell away and they were free from others taking their place. It was a better solution than measly bug spray.

At least that was on thing they didn't have to worry about.

Satisfied, Reid pushed Jayden away and walked off.

By late afternoon, Jayden was ready for a shower and sleep. However, he couldn't simply pick a spot and curl up for a nap. A lot of what lived in the rainforest waited until after the sunset to come out in order to avoid the heat. The safest place for them to rest would be up in a tree, and he was running out of energy to climb.

He began looking at trees and determining which one would be best to climb and also offer the best kind of shelter and safety for the night. Every time he stopped or strayed away from where Reid was heading, the guy growled with impatience once he realized and was forced to stop or follow.

"What in the hell are you doing?" Reid growled.

"Looking for a tree we can climb up and stay in tonight," Jayden answered as he stared up at a tree.

"Excuse me?" Reid asked in disbelief.

"It'll be the safest place to sleep," Jayden explained.

"No," Reid rejected without hesitation.

He shrugged. "Your choice."

Ignoring Reid, he kept searching until he found a tree suitable enough. Before he started climbing up, he glanced over to Reid and contemplated whether it was worth trying to persuade the stubborn guy to join him. Just because they didn't get along didn't mean Jayden wanted him to get sick or hurt.

Right now, though, Jayden didn't have the energy to get into an argument, so he focused on hoisting himself up through the sturdy network of branches.

Birds and marsupials flitted through the canopy around him but didn't come close. He sat back and watched the activity. He was surprised at how peaceful he felt and how easy it was to relax. It was nice.

Below, Reid set up camp at the base of the tree with a small floating fire.

Yawning, Jayden closed his eyes.

It felt like mere minutes had passed when he was jolted awake. The dark night was broken up by a small ball of fire hovering next to him. When he looked down, he could see Reid climbing up.

"Shut up," Reid grumbled.

It was easy to hide his amusement with the cover of night.

"Didn't say a word," Jayden mumbled.

Reid hoisted himself on to the next branch up and said, "I will push you out of this tree if you do."

He snorted as he rolled his eyes.

Jayden and Reid walked through the humid rainforest in silence. Fabric and hair clung to their skin. Their water bottles were running low and Jayden was pushing himself to keep going despite the dizziness and pain coursing through his body.

Gradually, the roar of crashing water filled the air until it dulled out every other noise. They changed direction and when the body of water was in sight, they both agreed to stop and rest.

"Give me your bottles," Reid said, holding out his hand.

Jayden fished his water bottles from his shoulder bag and handed them over. He watched Reid create a small floating fire and boil a bubble of water from the river while he nibbled on a biscuit.

"How do you know this place is dangerous?" Reid asked.

"I read," Jayden answered.

Reid raised his eyebrows. "You read about things like this Amazon?"

He extinguished the fire and divided the boiled water into each of their bottles.

"Yes," Jayden confirmed, taking back his bottles.

"Why? Got no friends?" Reid provoked.

Jayden sighed. Just when he thought that maybe Reid could hold a conversation without insulting someone, the guy had to go and prove him wrong.

"I do have friends and what I do in my spare time is better than continuously attacking someone I don't know," Jayden growled.

Not wanting to hear anything else, he continued walking along the river.

By the time he was settled in a tree for the night, he was exhausted and grumpy. The temperature had barely dropped and the stickiness of his skin and clothes made it hard to fall asleep. Every time he started drifting off, he was pulled back into the waking world again. The nocturnal sounds grated on his nerves ceaselessly.

At one point in the night, he turned to find Reid staring at his phone. He couldn't see what he was looking at but Jayden was tempted to snatch the phone away and toss it.

"Go to sleep," Reid huffed, finally putting the device away.

That was easier said than done.

In the end, they were climbing down and moving forward before dawn had lit up the forest floor. Words were barely passed between them as they dragged their feet through the crowded ground. Dark circles lined their eyes and their bodies craved rest.

The path they took led them up an incline and out on to a rocky ledge free of trees. Waterfall after waterfall broke the river and misty spray filled the air.

Despite being out in the sun, he was starting to cool down. It was a nice break from feeling crowded in and he took a deep, relaxing breath.

He followed Reid as they continued along the river. He wondered what the guy was thinking. There was tension running through his shoulders and it was the longest stretch of silence he had every witnessed from him.

When Reid suddenly stopped, Jayden walked right into his back.

"Sorry," Jayden said. "Why'd you —"

Reid whipped around and with wide eyes, clamped a hand over Jayden's mouth and shook his head.

He frowned and glanced past the scared guy.

Taking a drink from the river on a rocky outcrop not far from where they stood was a large spotted cat.

As they stepped back, both attempted to grab the other and in turn began slapping hands away. When the cat glanced over towards them, they turned around and ran.

Jayden clambered up to a rocky ledge and only turned to look back once he reached the top. Reid was no longer behind him. He looked down from where he had come from and towards the trees.

"Reid?" Jayden shouted.

He glanced over the edge and scanned the water. When a head popped up, he sighed in relief. However, that relief was short lived. Reid flailed his arms around and struggled to keep his head above the surface.

Cursing, he dived into the water. He swam the short distance and helped Reid stay afloat.

"You okay?" he asked.

Reid nodded and coughed.

When he tried to pull him to shore, he was met with resistance. The current was too strong and the waterfall behind them was pushing them further downstream. Jayden tried harder, tried to swim forward at an angle, however, they still didn't get any closer to the shore.

"Look!" Reid shouted.

In front of them, the river vanished and another waterfall was fast approaching.

"Reid, use a Ward to get us out!" Jayden demanded.

As he tried to draw a Ward, Jayden was ripped away and enveloped in a rush of bubbles. He was pushed further down and dragged along with the fast moving current. Jayden kicked out and waved his arms around until he was able to right himself up and swim to the surface.

Air filled his lungs and he brushed hair and water away from his eyes. As he looked around, panic began to build.

Reid hadn't resurfaced.

"Reid!" he shouted.

He took a deep breath and dove back under. Looking through the murky water proved difficult but he kept searching until his lungs were burning.

Gulping down air, he dived back under the surface and once at a depth he believed he would be able to see the bottom, started to draw a Ward.

Fingers wrapped around his wrist and tugged. He let out a gargled cry in surprise. He pushed his body back towards the surface. It was slow going dragging another body with him but they finally made it.

All he took was a few seconds to breathe before he pushed his body to move again. This time, he had no issue getting to shore.

Once he was able to stand, he wrapped his arms around Reid and dragged him to solid ground. The guy wasn't conscious. Worried that he hadn't found his companion in time, he checked for a pulse and leaned down.

Jayden cursed and wracked his mind on how to perform CPR. With shaky hands, he began compressions. When he thought he did enough, he pinched Reid's nose and pushed air in through his mouth.

It didn't work. Reid was still not breathing so he tried again, pushing back his rising panic. Halfway through the second mouth to mouth set, Reid coughed and gasped.

"Oh, thank god," Jayden murmured.

He sat back and eased Reid up, rubbing his back.

"You okay?"

Reid nodded.

After taking time to focus on breathing, Reid stood up and trudged into the line of trees.

Sighing, Jayden followed.

To his surprise, he had cleared a patch of land and was in the process of using a Ward to create a barrier. Jayden hesitated momentarily but stepped inside. Reid stood opposite him, held out a hand, and a small burst of fire sprung to life.

"Branches are low enough for our clothes to dry on," Reid grunted.

He nodded as he dropped his bag. After stripping down to his boxers, he hung his clothes on one of the low hanging branches and sat down to sort through his drenched belongings.

Thankfully, none of the water had breached the plastic covering his food. There was edible fruit in the rainforest but he wasn't sure if he'd find anything he would have been able to recognize and he wasn't going to eat something that could potentially make him sick.

The books Roderick had given him were ruined. Pages were soaked through and he didn't know any method or Ward that would save them.

Sighing, he put the books aside and took out the gifts and postcards he still had to send off to Kelly. Once dry, the postcards would at least serve as food for the fire. Everything else might be salvageable once dried.

"Who were those for?" Reid asked.

"An old friend from high school," Jayden answered.

"Aren't postcards old fashioned?"

He shrugged. "Maybe, but I wanted her to have things to help her remember me as I am and what I've done, and not the sickness that killed me."

For once, Reid had nothing to say.

Jayden sat back. There was nothing left to do except wait for everything to dry.

"Jay?" Reid spoke up, combing fingers through his ash white and red hair. "Than —"

He looked up at his companion. The guy had gone rigid and wide-eyed. It was all the warning he had before a hand clamped over his mouth, fingernails digging into his cheek, and he was dragged to his feet.

Leeran stepped around into view, looking unimpressed. Which meant that the one holding him was Taylin.

"Useless as ever, Reid. We will be taking him now," Leeran sneered.

Reid shook his head and stood up. "This … this wasn't the plan!"

Jayden struggled against Taylin but hands clamped down harder and one of his arms was pulled behind his back sharply.

"Now, now, son," Taylin hushed.

He tried to call out, to get Reid to react and help him, but the hand was pressed too firmly against his mouth.

Reid was obviously torn about what to do but when he stepped around the fire, Jayden found himself hoping he'd help.

"Let him go. We still have two Compass Points to find. Doctor Turner —"

Leeran slapped him away with a Ward Jayden didn't recognize. He crashed into a tree trunk hard and struggled to get back up.

"Your doubt has caused this change of plans. Oh, your father wanted us to deliver a message," Leeran said, kneeling down. "Consider yourself an orphan."

The woman slammed another Ward against the fallen man, and this time, Reid didn't get up.

Jayden kicked out his legs and cried out but it was no use. Taylin was stronger and bigger. Leeran stepped in front of them and held out a hand. The last thing he saw was a Transport Ward stretching over them.

- Chapter Thirty-Two -

Jayden was disorientated from the moment he opened his eyes. He was no longer in the humid, overcrowded forest and instead, he was freezing and in the remnants of a waiting room at a hospital all alone.

Goosebumps riddled his skin, and he wrapped his arms across his bare chest in a bid to retain as much body heat as possible. His boxers and hair were still damp and it added to the cold he felt.

Simply stepping near the entrance sensors didn't open the doors and he couldn't push them open. Even if he did somehow get the automated doors open, there was a shutter blocking the outside world.

Growling in frustration, he turned back to the waiting room. Chairs were strewn across the stained floor and at the reception desk, there were discarded papers and a computer that wouldn't turn on. When he tried the phone, there was silence.

He needed to find a way out, but if he couldn't do that, then maybe there was a working phone somewhere that he could use to call for help.

Jayden stood in the middle of the waiting area and looked left to right. There were two hallways he could choose from but no way of knowing which led to safety and which led to whoever Leeran and Taylin had left him for. In the end, he chose to go left.

Before entering the hallway, he stopped to stare at the wall. Claw marks had been carved out of the plaster. He ran his fingers over a set and dread settled heavily in the pit of his stomach.

"Have I been here before?" he murmured to no one.

Continuing on, he cautiously ventured down the hallway and went into the first unlocked office he came across. Inside, the desk had been left cluttered with a broken computer, files, stationary, and a landline phone. However, just like at the reception, the phone was dead.

With a huff, he searched the office for anything that would be useful. Amongst the faded paperwork, there was a pair of rusty scissors. If he came across anything unsavory, he would be able to defend himself with them long enough to make a run for it.

To his luck, there was a coat hanging on the back of the door. He shook it out, sneezing from the plume of dust that rose in the air, and pulled it on. At least he wouldn't freeze as quickly.

He found a crinkled old piece of paper covered in dried blood in one of the pockets with a message scrawled in his familiar handwriting.

'Run. Hide and don't make a sound.'

Jayden glanced around the office, confusion growing exponentially. Why would there be a note in his handwriting in an abandoned hospital? As far as he could remember, he had never been here before.

Shaking his head, he discarded the note and left the office.

As he walked further into the hospital, he ducked into any and all unlocked rooms he came across. However, every phone that had been left behind was either broken or did not work. It appeared there would be no way to call for help.

The next door he stepped through caused him to freeze. It was large and smelled of stale air. A single chair had been situated in the middle of the room and he could see leather straps in the spaces where wrists and ankles would sit. The floor was stained with something dark, and the windowless walls were damaged with scratches, holes and burn marks.

He couldn't be here.

Jayden backed out of the room and into the hall until he met with the wall.

"No ..."

The clink of scissors hitting the floor was loud. It startled him into moving.

He ran down the hall in a frantic bid to find an unlocked exit. Bare feet slid across the floor when he tried to turn down another corridor, and he collided into the wall.

He needed to keep moving. He needed to get out.

Instead of finding a way out, he ended up finding Taylin standing next to the misshapen creature that had been haunting him with a chain around its neck. Its attention snapped towards Jayden and when it tried to advance, Taylin tugged it back.

"Do you remember yet, Jayden?" Taylin asked.

"R-remember what? What are you doing?"

He stepped back, shaking.

The creature licked its lips and tugged more insistently on the chain. He could see exactly what Taylin was about to do and he silently pleaded for it not to happen.

A month ago, Taylin had been pushing him to make more of an effort to be a part of the family and now …

"Taylin, what's going on?"

Without answering, his biological father released the creature.

Wide-eyed, he briefly glanced over to Taylin in disbelief before twisting around and running back the way he had come from.

He darted through as many corridors as possible in a bid to lose the creature.

Breathing came in sharp, painful bursts as he kept pushing cramped legs into motion. The moment he glanced back, he crashed into a wall. Legs gave way and he landed with a splash.

For a moment, he kept his eyes clenched shut in order to stop his head from spinning.

When he opened his eyes, he saw his hands covered in thick red liquid.

He scrambled to his feet and tried to wipe the blood away. A chilling roar shook the walls and it was enough to get him moving again. He didn't know how far away the beast was. All he knew was that he had to keep moving.

Until he stumbled into a crossroads.

He wasted precious seconds trying to decide which direction to go in. In the end, it was approaching sounds that forced him to move and he darted into the hall on the right.

Dizziness caused him to stumble and he found himself falling to his knees in the waiting room.

Jayden looked around for any other option but before he could do anything, sharp pain pricked around his neck and he was flung into hard plastic chairs.

For a moment, he saw stars and the pain in his head rattled him. He pushed away chairs that had toppled on top of him as he sat up. With a shaky hand, he touched his neck and hissed. His fingertips came back bloody.

Heavy breathing mixed with a growl reminded Jayden of the danger in front of him. He wasted no time getting to his feet and clambered over the pile of chairs. The creature tried to follow but he knocked a chair in front of it at the right time and it tripped into the mess of furniture.

He ran out of the reception area and into the office he had gotten the coat from. Immediately, he pushed the desk and filing cabinet against the door.

Jayden ran a hand through his hair and backed up against the far wall, panting. How was he going to get out of this?

He jumped when a loud bang rattled the door. A second bang and a thin arm shot through. He looked for a vent, a window, anything that he could climb into to escape as more of the door was shredded.

There was a tense brief moment as he wondered if he was safe when the arm retreated. However, he watched through the hole as the blackened sickly thin body threw itself against the door. The desk shot towards him from the force and pinned him against the wall while the door slammed opened and the doorknob became embedded into the plaster.

He struggled to keep his breathing even as he tried to get the desk to budge.

The creature sniffed as it stepped into the office. Murky drool dripped from its jaw, causing the floor to hiss where it touched.

It jumped on top of the desk and slashed claws across his chest. He cried out in pain but his cry became mangled when teeth sunk into his shoulder.

Jayden's eyes burned blue and his Abilities ripped out of him. The creature was thrown back into the hallway along with the desk. He slumped against the wall, watching blood drip to the floor as he took a moment to breathe.

It felt like he had blacked out for a second as his Abilities came to his rescue.

Taking a shaky breath, he pushed away from the wall and shuffled out of the office. He passed the beast trying to wrestle its head out of the wall and forced himself to be as silent as possible as he walked further into the hospital.

Jayden needed to keep a hand against the wall in order to remain steady and on his feet. He had pushed his body too much and the last thing he needed right then was for the dizziness to get the better for him.

Unfortunately, he didn't get far before he was slammed against the wall.

Claws dug into his back and teeth came close to his cheek. He gagged from the foul stench emanating from the monster's mouth.

Seconds dragged by agonizingly slowly as the creature took its time sniffing. Jayden thought that if he was going to be ripped to shreds, he wished it would happen quickly.

To his surprise, the creature leant back, gripped his bitten shoulder, and dragged him down the hall. He kicked his legs out, twisted his body, and waved an arm around in a bid to be released. He screamed to be let go, for someone to help him, but no one came and those claws only dug in deeper.

After a while, Leeran and Taylin fell in line behind them and, of course, ignored his pleas.

The creature burst open a door and he almost suffocated from the musty air. He glanced around and started to shake.

"No, no, no!" Jayden shouted.

He was hoisted up and thrown down on to the chair. He took the chance to try and push his way out, and even went as far as using his Abilities. His attempts backfired and he coughed up blood. His body burned in places where flesh had been torn and it was hard to concentrate on anything else.

Taylin ripped the coat off him and strapped his wrists and ankles down as Leeran tied a piece of fabric over his eyes.

The immediate darkness was enough to snap his attention back to the forefront. Jayden panted in panic as he tried to strain his hearing to keep track of where everyone was what they were doing. There was a jingle of a chain, and then the thump and click of a door closing. Afterwards, silence pressed against him.

Forcing himself to take slow deep breaths, he tried to calm down and pulled against the cuffs. He wondered if he could command his

Abilities to free him and keep him safe but he knew that wasn't possible. He didn't have the amount of control it would take to do something like that without risking hurting himself.

When footsteps echoed in the room, he clenched his fists tightly and braced himself.

"L-let me go," Jayden stuttered.

"I cannot do that. There's something blocking our gifts and our connection to you. It's a little ahead of schedule but we will begin taking the final steps to ensure Szantium is destroyed," Doctor Turner said.

Jayden tensed. The Ward Nuru had placed on him had made him feel better than he had in weeks. It was the only thing that was keeping him as normal as possible.

"No! I'm … I'm not going —-"

He screamed as his body was assaulted with unbearable pain. Muscles seized up and his back arched up off the chair. A faint red glow could be seen along the edges of the blindfold but it didn't give him any idea as to what was happening. He didn't know if he was being cut open, burned, or if a Ward was being used. It felt like a combination of everything all at once.

He screamed and screamed until his voice went hoarse, and he kept screaming until his voice was completely gone.

"Jay …"

Eventually, the pain eased up and footsteps walked away from him.

He struggled to stay awake. He couldn't move. His couldn't think. All he was aware of was the numbness running down his body and the jagged sound of his breathing.

"Jay, it'll be okay. Just hold on."

Jayden groaned and slowly shook his head. All he wanted was to be left alone.

"Just hold on."

- Chapter Thirty-Three -

Time was broken up into two periods — the time where pain was allowed to numb down and he was left to rest, and the time of blinding white hot pain. His throat was raw from screaming, but that nuisance only blended in with everything else he experienced.

Jayden could feel Nuru's Ward trying to fight back, but bit by bit it was hacked away. He tried to hold on to it, tried to get his Abilities to obey him just this one time to help and protect him, however, it was futile.

After that first session, no one spoke to him. He knew Doctor Turner was there. When the pain was allowed to die down, Jayden concentrated on the sound of fingers tapping on something that he could guess was the man's tablet. The man was obsessed with his notes even while torturing someone.

He wondered whether or not Leeran and Taylin were there, watching. He wondered why they didn't stop this. What would turn a parent away from their child's pain, even if they had a strained relationship?

If Leeran and Taylin were here, did that mean Mackenzie was here as well? What if Mackenzie were in his position, would they stop what was happening then?

Thinking about Mackenzie turned his attention to Reid. He hoped the guy was okay. The fact he tried to do the right thing, to get him away from the Laiyfe-Rain's, meant a lot. He wondered if Reid had tried to follow them or maybe he had gone to find the others.

Was anyone looking for him?

Thoughts tumbled in and out, and he tried to grasp at any of them in the hope of distracting his mind from what was happening to his body.

Jayden struggled to open his eyes. His body felt weightless and sluggish. The last thing he could remember was running towards the enemy, wanting the fighting to end.

When he finally managed to open his eyes, he found himself floating in a sea of blue and green. As a wave brushed against him, he was left feeling like he was being nudged back to sleep. At first, he wanted to listen but fear stopped him.

He fought against the calming effects as long as possible. Just as he was beginning to lose the energy to keep resisting, a bright light erupted in front of him. It was warm and felt alive, and he wanted it. He pooled his remaining strength together and he clawed his way towards the light.

When he got to it, he kept going. He climbed into the light and tumbled down on to something hard. A soft breeze of fresh air washed over his skin and the chill he hadn't realized clinging to his bones, melted away.

Jayden shivered. His skin felt like it was on fire and yet he was freezing as he laid there in only his boxers. When something brushed against his skin, he flinched away.

A blanket was draped over his body and the comforting weight was welcomed. He wanted to curl up and cry into the fabric.

"Let us in, Jayden."

"Who …" he managed to whisper.

A hand gently ran across his forehead, pushing away his grimy hair.

"A friend trying to help. Let go of everything and let us in."

"No!"

He slowly shook his head.

"Let … m … go."

There was a sigh and the blanket was taken away. He whimpered and tried to follow.

His head was yanked down and the pain was back. It stretched from his collarbone and down to his stomach. Liquid ran down the side of his ribs. Breathing hurt. He could feel something moving across his chest and it felt wrong.

There was a tug on something inside of him, but it was met with resistance and he struggled to breathe.

He stared at the dirty and stained ceiling, trying to remember what had happened. He could hear dripping sounds in the distance. When he tried to sit up, he was met with distance. Hands, ankles, and his chest was strapped down to what he was laying on.

"What's going on?" he asked.

A figure stepped up beside him but didn't answer. Instead, he was met with so much agony. No matter how much Jayden tried, he couldn't get away from it.

He didn't understand what was going on. He dug deep and urged his Abilities to help him. There was a burst of energy around him and the pain was suddenly gone.

He panted and turned to watch the figure use the wall to stand up again.

"Interesting," the man murmured.

Jayden used his Abilities to rip off the restraints and slid off the reclined chair. He tried to stand but it was a struggle and he needed to use the chair to stand.

"It's good to see you using your Abilities, but unfortunately you're using them against the wrong people," a newcomer said.

He glanced over to the doorway. The newcomer had dark hair and wore a tank top and fitted jeans with boots.

"I'm protecting myself," Jayden retorted.

"We are not the enemy, Jayden. Szantium is."

He rolled his eyes. "I'm going home."

"Home? That no longer exists for you."

"What do you mean?"

"You've been gone for seven years. They all think you're dead, but don't worry. We'll send you to Szantium in order to give them an extra special gift for a most sacred day."

A Ward wrapped around his body and lifted him off the ground. He was pinned back on to the chair and strapped down.

"What are you going?" he demanded.

"Turning you into what they perceive us to be — a living bomb."

It was very easy to lose track of hours and days. Occasionally he was given a sip of water but that was as far as any kindness went.

When he woke up next, it was of his own accord for once. It felt weird. Normally, he would have been woken up by sheer agony returning.

"There is *something* odd about him," Doctor Turner said.

Jayden turned his attention to the voices around him.

"Explain."

"It's something I noticed before but since I couldn't find answers, I simply put it aside. I do know that we are not dealing with a Harbinon," Doctor Turner said.

"He's something more? What?"

"Unsure. But it doesn't matter. I've broken through that pesky Ward so stage two will begin in two days," Doctor Turner said.

Jayden frowned. If all this pain was stage one, what would stage two involve? Who was the doctor talking to? The voice sounded like the one who kept insisting they were a friend but he had a hard time pinpointing it to a name.

Thoughts began fading away as his mind clouded over.

He licked his dry lips and tried to fight off the urge to sleep. He wanted to hear more.

Thoughts on the conversation slipped away and turned to the dreams he had been having. It felt like he was remembering a distant memory.

If he was starting to remember what had happened prior to arriving back at Szantium, then what he was currently going through had already happened. Doctor Turner had held him hostage for almost two years, forcing him to change into something that would destroy Szantium.

A strangled noise rumbled in his throat at the thought of that. No one had known what was happening to him then but maybe, just maybe, people would be looking for him now and would be able to stop this.

"You're conscious? Good. It's time to get to work," Doctor Turner said.

Day in and day out, he was pushed beyond his limits. Pain was all he knew and no matter how much he fought back, it wouldn't stop.

Eventually, he stopped fighting back. He stopped screaming. All he had the energy to do was lay there and send his mind elsewhere.

Once he stopped reacting, the restraints were removed and he was helped to his feet. He recognized and wondered why Leeran and Taylin were there, helping him regain strength in his unused legs. However, he didn't trust his mind. At that point, he wondered whether or not he was seeing things, after all shadowy figures were watching them silently and no one else seemed to notice they were there.

When he was able to stand and move on his own, he was directed to stand in front of a wall with a giant 'X' painted on it.

"Use your Abilities to hit the center of the X," Doctor Turner instructed.

The first attempt missed by a long shot.

"Keep going. We won't move on until you can aim correctly," the doctor said.

Jayden shot his Abilities at the wall. Gradually, he started to get closer to the target and eventually managed to hit the center of it. He was commanded to hit it again and again in order to make sure the first hit wasn't a fluke.

Afterwards, he was taken to a cell and left there with a cup of water and a roll on a plate. He stumbled over and dropped on to the hard bed lining a brick wall.

He was beyond exhausted.

Aiming practice took over his days. It was a nice reprieve from the pain. When Doctor Turner was satisfied with the damaged wall and his aim, he was directed to hit random items found throughout the hospital. His control over his Abilities grew and became more refined.

Outside of aiming practice, he was left alone in the cell. He was able to sleep peacefully and uninterrupted, and he was given better food to eat once a day.

However, hitting inanimate objects soon wasn't enough.

He stood in front of a disjointed creature that had been chained to the wall. The thing had its eyes sewn shut. Gangly arms jutted out at sickening angles that ended with long claws.

He didn't want to be anywhere near the thing.

"Use your Abilities," Doctor Turner instructed.

"And do what?" he asked.

"Hit it," Doctor Turner clarified.

"No."

"Excuse me?" The doctor raised his gaze from his tablet and stared at him.

"N-no," Jayden repeated, stepping away.

Doctor Turner sighed.

"This is disappointing."

The doctor stretched out his hand and slammed a Ward against him. He was knocked back and slumped against the floor.

He woke up back on his hard bed in the cell, body aching. When he sat up, he realized he wasn't alone. The creature was being held against the bars on the opposite side by Taylin.

With a nod from the doctor, Taylin let go.

Jayden scrambled out of bed and barely managed to avoid a swipe of claws.

"What are you doing?" Jayden shouted.

He darted around the small cell as he tried to avoid getting sliced open as much as possible, however, it was easy for the creature to get the better of him. It jumped on his back and bit down on his shoulder. Claws dug into his ribs and he fell as he cried out.

The burning pain almost caused him to black out but he didn't stop that from trying to crawl away.

Taylin pulled the creature off him by the chain. He clenched his eyes shut as he panted through the pain. There was a squeak of the cell door opening and the jingle of a chain, and once again, Jayden was alone.

Doctor Turner knelt down in front of him. There was a soft white glow and the pain and burning disappeared.

"You better learn quickly," Doctor Turner warned.

He stood up and left Jayden lying on the floor.

They left him to rest again before coming back to take him to the chained creature.

"Use your Abilities," Doctor Turner said.

He swallowed the lump in his throat and shook his head.

"No."

Doctor Turner gave him an unimpressed look. He held out a hand and Jayden automatically flinched. However, the bespectacled man didn't

aim his Abilities at him. The burst of power hit the chain and the creature was free.
"Run."

- **Chapter Thirty-Four -**

Jayden forced his mind to focus on his dreams and the memories they were revealing. If his dreams were right, then stage two involved throwing his Abilities around to improve aim and then attacking the blinded creature. If he didn't, punishment would be dealt.

He now remembered it was Doctor Turner who had changed who he was and the man was doing it all over again in order to meet certain goals.

Thoughts were broken as pain surged through his body again. He was tired of going through this rollercoaster. All he wanted was to be left in peace, even if it was to die alone.

"Jay, listen to me. You need to hold on."

He could barely understand the words. The voice was heartbreakingly familiar.

When the pain began to ease, he was left panting and whimpering.

"You'll be able to rest soon, Jayden Lugian," Doctor Turner informed him before leaving.

He sobbed in relief.

"Jayden, please listen to me."

He let out a shaky breath as he struggled to hold back tears.

"Hold on and remember who you are, little brother. Help is coming."

He stared at the ceiling of his cell. He felt broken and defeated. Three times he had been chased through the hospital and had skin torn and bitten into. Each time, the doctor had left him to suffer longer and longer before getting Taylin to chain the creature back up and healing his wounds.

There were three things Jayden was sure of:

No one was coming for him.

No one would stop this.

There was no point in resisting any further.

With a tired sigh, he closed his eyes as he resigned himself to his fate.

Once again, he was taken to where the creature had been chained up.

"Use your Abilities," Doctor Turner ordered.

Taking a deep breath, Jayden closed his eyes. He was close to shaking his head. The word 'no' was on the tip of his tongue. But he was tired. He couldn't fight back anymore.

He didn't want to fight back anymore.

Without looking, he shot his Abilities at the chained creature and tore off an arm. It screamed horrendously loud.

After, something inside of him felt different.

He raised his head and had his Abilities tear the creature into four more pieces. When it didn't stop screaming, he slowly closed his hand into a fist. The action sent a Ward to the creature's head. There was a sickening squelch and there was silence in the room.

This wasn't ...

"Well done, Jayden Lugian," Doctor Turner congratulated.

He looked over to the older man. In the reflection of the man's glasses, he saw his eyes fade from a startling shade of blue back to normal.

"Let's move on to different targets. We'll have them moving around the hospital so you'll need to go hunting," Doctor Turner said.

Jayden nodded.

In a split second, he felt the splintered core of who he was shatter into pieces.

Jayden was awakened by claws digging into his mounded shoulder. All he could muster was a sob as his body was pulled off the chair and dragged across the floor. Multiple footsteps followed them. The floor was cold against his bare skin and by the time they stopped, his sore body was shivering uncontrollably.

Claws retracted from his flesh and he curled up on the floor. Whining metal caused him to flinch. Rough hands grabbed him and maneuvered him around until he was seated on a barely cushioned surface. Rough fabric was wrapped around his shoulders and he was ushered to lay down.

Once again, the whining of metal filled the air, followed by the sound of a lock clicking into place. He laid there, unwilling to move in case the straps were put back on or he was hurt again.

Hours went past and when nothing happened, he allowed himself to relax enough to fall asleep.

This time, he didn't dream and when he opened his eyes, it felt like he hadn't rested at all. He wanted to sit up and remove the blindfold but he couldn't muster the energy to do anything but lay there.

"Hungry, son?" Taylin asked.

Without waiting to get an answer, Taylin came into the cell and helped him into a sitting position. Every touch caused him to flinch, and every flinch only caused more pain to ripple through his body.

"Open your mouth. You need sustenance," Taylin said.

Jayden tried to turn his head away and refuse. The older man roughly grabbed his jaw and forced his mouth open. Water was slowly poured into his mouth and he had to swallow or choke.

When Taylin finally let go of his jaw, he coughed and groaned. He barely had thirty seconds to catch his breath before his jaw was pried open again and water was poured down his throat.

"There's a tray of food by your bed. Make sure you eat. We need you to keep your strength up," Taylin said before leaving and locking him in.

Jayden laid down and tried to get back to sleep.

Eventually someone came back for him. The door to his cell opened and he was lifted up out of bed and carried out. Warmth radiated from the person carrying him and eased his muscles, relaxing him almost to the point of falling back to sleep.

He was dumped on to his feet, and when he heard growling, he tried to move away. As chains rattled, he took a shaky breath, expecting to feel claws or teeth.

Foul breath washed over his face and panic threatened to bubble over.

"Shadows crave one thing –- power. This makes them easy to manipulate. Dangle what they want and they'll come to you, no matter what dangers lay in wait. Normally, their shape is determined by the amount of power they have. However, there is one form they will never take. Do you know what and why?" Doctor Turner asked.

Jayden jerkily shook his head, breathing hard.

"Human. They think it's beneath them to look like us. In their eyes, they are the superior race and we are the cattle."

An ear splitting screech filled the room.

Doctor Turner pulled off his blindfold, revealing three black figures chained to the wall by their neck. Jayden scrambled back in fear. They each had a set of large white eyes, gangly arms and legs, and jaws lined with sharp teeth snapping in frustration. What he was seeing looked exactly like the thing that had clawed its way out of the crack in Africa.

"My pets have been refined. They're stronger, faster –- better than ordinary Shadows will ever be. Once tamed, they won't hesitate to follow orders. All those loyal have been assigned tasks. These three have been the most troublesome," Doctor Turner said. "Destroy them."

Wide-eyed, Jayden glanced over to the doctor with horrifying realization. The strange Shadows in front of him, the thing that had appeared in Africa and what was being reported to Bookman –- these weren't appearing because Szantium was breaking apart or because cracks were opening up. Doctor Turner had created them and set them loose.

"Destroy them," Doctor Turner repeated.

"Why?" Jayden asked hoarsely.

Doctor Turner cast a Ward around Jayden's body and caused him to seize up.

"Destroy them," Doctor Turner repeated.

Jayden shook his head. Again, he was bombarded with pain.

This was the task that would change everything. He knew that what he did now would determine whether or not he would be able to stay as himself or become the puppet the doctor wanted.

No matter what happened, he was not going to give in this time.

Over and over again, he refused and was punished. His body spasmed as he tried to force his limps to move and crawl away. But after a certain point, he couldn't even lift his head.

Doctor Turner sighed in annoyance. "Take him back."

The blindfold was tied back around his head and hands dragged him along the ground. He was dumped on to his makeshift bed and left alone.

Jayden had no idea how long he had been left alone, but it had been long enough for another dreamless sleep. When it was time, Leeran and Taylin took him out of his cell and through the hospital. The blindfold was yanked off and he needed to blink a few times before he was able to make out shapes.

When he realized the humanoid Shadows were in front of him again, he whipped around in an attempt to escape. Leeran and Taylin were waiting behind him with a sneer and barred the doorway.

"Destroy them," Doctor Turner ordered.

Again, he refused, and again he was punished.

Every time Doctor Turner gave the order to destroy, Jayden refused. On and on it went until he couldn't get back to his feet.

"If you do not obey, you'll be the one who is destroyed," Doctor Turner warned.

He groaned his objections.

Doctor Turner shoved his tablet into a pocket and unlocked the chains to the nearest Shadow. Jayden's breath hitched in panic and he pushed himself up on shaky arms.

The Shadow spared a glance to the doctor and cautiously stepped forward. When nothing happened, it charged towards him.

He braced himself and clenched his eyes shut. If he died, then no one would ever be able to use him again.

In the second it took for the Shadow to close the gap between it and Jayden, he swore he heard Balthezier urge him to keep fighting.

Answering his call to live, Abilities blasted out of him. Wide and flat golden spears shot out and pierced each of the Shadows. They screeched and clawed at the spears but all three exploded into ash.

Each of the spears clattered to the floor and in the silence, the sound echoed.

He used the wall to ease himself up. For once, he didn't feel weak or light-headed, and he hadn't lost any blood from using his Abilities. It was strange.

Moving away from the wall, he stared at his hands.

Something was different.

He approached the fallen spears. In the golden surface, he could see his eyes had turned blue and for once, he didn't care what that meant.

All he wanted to do was live and protect those important to him.

The Council of 8 couldn't stop him and neither would Szantium.

- Chapter Thirty-Five -

"Do you know what's in front of you?" Doctor Turner asked.

Despite the blindfold still covering his eyes, Jayden knew it wasn't a Shadow, not even one of the doctor's hybrids.

"You've met before. Even recently. You and everyone else see him as a monster. He had been one of the first to be blessed, however, he and the other Council of 8 members took our gifts, and ignored their true duty. This is the cost of betrayal," Doctor Turner explained.

The blindfold was taken off and Jayden was confronted with the misshapen creature he had been running from. It was already bleeding from several cuts along its body. Arms were chained to the wall but barely stopped it from lunging forward.

"The last time both of you were here, you took pleasure in ripping him apart. Unfortunately for him, I wasn't finished with him. Now it's time for you to kill One again," Doctor Turner ordered.

Jayden tensed and shook his head. He couldn't do that again. Even if this thing had hurt him before or even if it had once been one of the Council of 8, he couldn't obey.

Doctor Turner sighed impatiently and warned, "It's either you or it."

He shook his head.

"I won't … I won't kill anymore," he managed to say.

He turned around and pushed past Leeran and Taylin. He ran through the hall, wanting to get as far away as possible.

Moments later, something collided with his back, sending him to the floor. Without glancing back, he tried to crawl away.

Claws dug into his calf and he cried out in pain. He twisted around and tricked to kick the creature off but it bit down on his attack foot.

Tears pricked the corner of his eyes as he punched and pulled at the thing's head. He could feel the edge of who he was, of who he wanted to be, start to unravel.

"Please," he quietly begged.

The part of his Abilities that Doctor Turner already controlled began stirring.

"Listen to your friend, Jayden Lugian," whispered a voice beside his ear.

He jumped and shook his head.

"Kill the thing and everything will be okay. Trust and let go. It's the only way you'll survive."

Again he shook his head.

"Don't you want to save them? If you listen and obey, we'll take you to see her," bargained the voice.

"Her?"

"I believe she called herself — Kalarney."

Jayden went wide-eyed. He couldn't believe it. Could they really take him to see her? She was still alive and now was within reach?

"Those that betray us, don't deserve to live. Kill it and I'll take you to your precious friends."

Friends …

"Don't forget — we have a gift to give everyone afterwards."

That's right, he thought slowly. The gift …

He took a slow deep breath and his eyes turned blue. Everything around him was drowned out at the thought of this gift they wanted him to give.

"Kill it," Doctor Turner urged.

He held out a hand and a golden sword shimmered into his grasp. He hesitated for a second. A reasonable voice whispered that he shouldn't give in, he needed to keep fighting. Did he really want to do this? This wasn't who he was … was it?

He raised the sword. Gold was slowly washed away by black, spreading from the hilt and stopping half way up the blade. In between one breath and the next, he slammed the sword into the creature's back. It was sliced in two and the force carried along the floor for meters.

The two halves of the creature fell away as he eased himself on to his feet.

Ignoring the voices around him, he focused on the body at his feet. It wasn't over. Claws started to twitch, and red and black sparks of power began to sew flesh back together.

Wanting all of this to be over, wanting to bury the fear he had of this monster, Jayden smashed the sword down over and over again. Blood splattered along the walls and covered his skin. He didn't stop hacking at the creature until his arms were too heavy to move.

Afterwards, he stood there panting and watching.

"Interesting weapon."

He glanced up at the doctor and tilted his head.

"Wide golden spears and now a sword …" Doctor Turner murmured.

"Jayden, show me the spears you used," the voice behind him demanded.

He glanced back. The dark haired person standing there was familiar. He'd seen them in his dreams. He'd seem them in London and before fighting the Council of 8. They were the one who gave him advice so why were they here now?

"Shi … ro?" he asked hoarsely.

"Show us the spear, Jayden."

He frowned and jerkily nodded.

The sword disappeared with a single thought. He held open his empty hand and a moment later, the spear appeared. Just like the sword, the gold was partially washed away by black.

Shiro leant forward and studied the weapon. They hummed and straightened up with a smile.

"Jayden, show us all of the weapons you have access to," Shiro requested.

The spear floated away from his hand and stood up straight in front of him. The sword appeared beside the spear, followed by a pair of daggers, a bow, dual pistols, a trident, a shield, and a scepter. All eight hovered around him. They appeared before them gold but a black stain grew across all eight.

"Doctor Turner, I'd like to introduce to you The Heart," Shiro stated.

Jayden didn't understand. How could they know from the weapons?

"What makes you certain?" Doctor Turner asked.

Shiro raised an eyebrow. "Jayden, show him the eight links."

Thin black chain links came into view. They connected him to each weapon. Two of them had splintered links and were barely holding on.

"Try to move the sword," Shiro said.

Doctor Turner stepped closer and tried to grab the weapon. To Jayden's surprise, the doctor's hand went straight through with no effect on the sword.

"Interesting."

"Each weapon symbolizes each Compass Point. As long as those chains remain intact, there is hope for Szantium. But if The Heart is attacked directly, then Szantium will rain down on those filthy humans," Shiro said.

Jayden faltered and his weapons faded away. Szantium wasn't the only thing at risk. Humans … Humans needed to be protected.

He held his head as pain overloaded his senses.

"Let's get him back to the lab. Now that I know what I'm dealing with, I can adjust what I've done already," Doctor Turner said. "Leeran, Taylin, take him to the lab."

Hands gripped his arms tightly and forced him to move. He could feel himself regain control over his body and mind, and he struggled harder against his birth parents. He didn't want to go back to that room. He didn't want to be a weapon.

With a sore throat and barely a voice, he yelled out that he wasn't The Heart and he didn't need to go back to that room. He begged and pleaded but it all fell on deaf ears.

Arms and legs were bound to the reclined chair and he shook in fear.

Doctor Turner stood beside him and tapped away at his tablet. Once he was finished, he pocketed the device and rolled up his lab coat sleeves.

"It seems we have picked the right child for our plan. Mackenzie has proven to be obedient and easily controlled with his weak mind. It would have been better to use him as he has tamed powerful Shadows thanks to the Council of 8's training. However, he's also been proven to be useless. I'd never imagine The Heart would have been born as *their* child. Do you understand what this means?" Doctor Turner asked.

"Please," Jayden begged. "I'm not … I'm … I'm only a Harbinon!"

"Didn't you ever wonder why the Compass Points came to you first?" Doctor Turner asked.

"They …"

Jayden couldn't deny that. He had befriended Kalarney and Balthezier years ago. Granted, other factors brought them together. Quentin had sought him out on a train in London instead of one of the others. The pups had been found in Szantium. Jet had visited The Balgaire and —

Thoughts were derailed as agony bombarded his body. He screamed until he could not scream any more. He lashed out with his Abilities. The floor and walls were ripped apart. White static snapped around the room but none of it those inside.

"I've found the true core," Doctor Turner said.

"Show me," Shiro requested.

A golden orb was raised out of Jayden's chest and left to float there. A chain kept it attached to his body, but some of the links were splintered and coming apart.

He panted as he clenched his eyes shut. He reopened them, hoping that what he had seen was a delusion.

It wasn't. When others had spoken about his core, he had always assumed it was a metaphorical thing, not literal.

"A compass? Makes sense," Doctor Turner murmured.

Cracks ran across the entire thing and the pointer was aimed south and barely hanging on. Chips of glass were missing from the face of the compass, but its appearance wasn't what Jayden was focused on. Small white threads of static wrapped around less than half of the core while the majority was covered in black and red static. A jagged thread of black static arched up and shot towards the white bundle. The two clashed midair in a small explosion. It was a fight of dominance and the white side was slowly losing.

"Don't destroy the remainder. Simply cage it," Shiro instructed.

Doctor Turner reached out to the core but what little static there was, it wouldn't let him near it. The doctor wiggled his fingers a little and reached out again but he was still stopped.

Shiro sighed. "Now, now, Jayden. We've already made you healthy. Let us at least protect the remainder of who you are."

Shiro held both hands on either side of his core and encased it in a dark bubble.

Jayden cried out. His back arched and he couldn't breathe.

Seconds of gasping and clawing at the arm rests ended when he blacked out.

- **Chapter Thirty-Six** -

Jayden was barely conscious when he became aware of hands digging into his arms and his feet dragging along the ground. The blindfold hadn't been put back on and he could see where he was being taken to.

When he was released, his legs gave way and he struggled to raise his head. Whatever was happening now, he didn't want to deal with it.

Heavy chains scraped across the floor and hissing caused the hair on the back of his neck to stand on end.

"Kill them," Doctor Turner ordered.

Jayden tensed and didn't move. If he did, he was scared of what he'd do.

Thundering feet shuffled across the floor. There was heavy breathing and menacing growls. No matter the type of sounds he heard, he refused to raise his head to see what his next opponent was.

"The rabid beasts haven't eaten in weeks," Doctor Turner informed him.

Jayden's heart pounded against his chest. Breathing became rapid and his mind raced through sluggish thoughts as he desperately tried to figure out what to do.

"Kill. Them," Doctor Turner reiterated.

When he didn't move," the doctor sighed.

"He still isn't taking orders," Doctor Turner said.

Jayden rubbed his tender chest and swallowed the lump in his throat. It was taking everything he had to remain in control and he was so close to losing.

"Release the black one," Shiro ordered.

Something heavy fell to the floor, sending his blood stone cold. A reptilian roar shook the building. There was snapping teeth and a heavy foot stepped closer to him.

"Jayden, our gift will be lost if you're eaten," Shiro said to him gently.

He stopped shaking as his mind clouded over. The gift was important. It needed to be delivered.

He slowly stood up and faced the approaching black and red serpent. Its wings were torn and trailed behind it. Blood sluggishly dropped to the floor, but whatever injuries it had now, the serpent wasn't going to stop.

Jayden held out a hand in front of him and shot out his spears. Not one of them missed. They pierced scaled flesh and the serpent cried out. It snapped out at him, teeth missing mere inches from his face.

As the serpent reared its head back to strike, Jayden yanked the spears out. They swirled around him and arched upwards. The weapons hurtled forward and pierced the tender flesh of the serpent's neck.

The beast moaned as it collapsed. With its final breath, the serpent's body turned to ash.

There was another heavy clunk of metal landing on the floor. The ground shook as a second serpent charged towards him. Its light green-blue tail whipped around and slammed through a wall closest to Jayden. His shield shimmered around him, protecting him from the flying debris, but through the chaos, he'd lost track of the serpent.

The moment he dropped his shield, something slammed into his back and sent him hurtling through multiple walls.

He spent several seconds unsure whether or not he had stopped moving. Everything hurt and he coughed from the dust falling down around him. Groaning, he shook his head. He was buried underneath remnants of cement and plaster, but it wasn't a problem for his Abilities to clear off.

Blood dripped from his fingertips. He couldn't move his arm. The pain he felt from broken skin and bone were nothing but an inconvenience he could push through.

His body appeared beside him with an arrow notched. Beside it was his awaiting sword. On his other side were the spear and dual pistols. There was no way he was going to let this crazed beast take away the gift.

The serpent charged. Jayden waited.

When the serpent was close enough, he fired his readied weapons.

The serpent was hit by bullets and an arrow, but it used its tail to bat away the bladed weapons. It wasn't enough to stop it.

Jayden shot out his Abilities and commanded the sword and spear to rise from the floor. He cried out as he bombarded the serpent with all that he had as it charged towards him.

Teeth bit into his chest and back. It could have taken off his head but instead had angled its jaw to the side. Why?

'Do not forget who you truly are, Jayden Lugian.'

Jayden faltered. He knew that voice.

A warmth spread through his body, pulsating from his chest.

Teeth slowly retracted from flesh and a tongue wrapped around his body briefly. He stayed stock still, frozen by shock until the tongue was gone and he was gently nuzzled.

He couldn't believe what he had done. He trembled as tears fell down his cheeks.

"No," Jayden hoarsely whispered. "I'm … I'm sorry. I'm sorry! Please … don't leave. I can heal you. I'm so sorry, Babyloneous," he cried.

Through uncontrollable shakes and blinded with tears, he tried to get his Abilities to work and save his friend.

'It's okay. Save your energy,' Babyloneous said gently. *'Listen to me, Jayden Lugian. Listen. My brother and I are not the last. There is another — a girl who has learned the harshness of this world too early. A shifting serpent … Please find her for me, Jayden. Do not let her be alone anymore.'*

Babyloneous dropped his head weakly to the floor with a groan.

'This … was not … your … fault.'

Jayden stared wide eyed before tentatively reaching out. He nudged the serpent's snout, hoping to get a response.

"Ba … Babyloneous?"

He nudged his friend more insistently. He couldn't be dead. This wasn't happening!

"No …"

He took a shuddering breath as he watched Babyloneous's body turn into a river of clear blue water. Something small floating in the water caught his attention as if reflected light. He watched it float towards him and when it was closer, he reached in and pulled it out. Once he did, the river collapsed, soaking him.

A single small blue scale had been left behind. He clenched his eyes shut and leant his forehead against the scale.

"Well done, Jayden," Doctor Turner said.

He tensed. That's right. He had done this for them. Doctor Turner and Shiro had broken him down to turn him into a killing monster all for the sake of delivering some gift.

If that's what they wanted, then so be it.

Out of anger and devastation, he commanded his Abilities in a way he hadn't done before. White-hot static stretched out of him and snapped over to the doctor.

"Enough!" commanded Shiro.

The attack froze and he glanced over at them. He would never let them control him again. He'd rather die.

"You can't control me anymore," he whispered.

Panting, he pushed and pushed against the pressure of the command. There was a crack and a white explosion ripped out of him. The run down hospital was shredded and burned into nothingness.

There was a thundering noise from above and a crack in the air slammed into the ground in front of him.

He dropped to his knees, body weakened even further but that didn't stop him from pushing his Abilities out.

A green glow filled the air and the warmth eased his attack until it stopped completely. Small orbs floated around him. Calm radiated everywhere.

Jayden shook his head, desperate to stop the influence. He didn't want to feel any of those things.

"Jay …"

Weakly, he looked back and saw four people he didn't think he'd ever see again. Artemis had tears in her eyes as she kept an injured Balthezier standing up, and beside her, Reid carried the thin form of Kalarney.

Both of his travelling companions had heavy bags under their eyes. Their clothes were tattered and dirty and burns smudged their skin.

For a brief moment, Jayden wondered whether or not he was hallucinating. Fear and panic had him thinking this was yet another test.

Artemis eased Balthezier down next to Reid and rushed over to Jayden. When she went to touch him, he flinched back.

The action caused her to bite her bottom lip but it was quickly turned into an understanding expression.

'It's okay, Jay. We're going to take you somewhere safe,' Artemis signed.

He stared blankly at her before shifting his gaze back to the puddle. Why would he go anywhere after what he did? No one was safe.

A hand slid along his bloody back and he was transported out of the remnants of the hospital and on to the soft carpet of a warm house.

Hands immediately grabbed hold of him and he was carried away. He struggled and fought back. His efforts became desperate when he was pinned down. There was no way he was going back to that cell or restrained.

"Jay, you're safe. Calm down so we can help you."

Not understanding the words after days of agony, he forced his Abilities into action. Everyone was forced back. Alone, he curled up on his side, clenching the serpent scale sharp enough to break skin.

"Jay, you're safe."

A Calming Ward engulfed the room and his body relaxed.

"Time to sleep now. Everything will be okay."

Chapter Thirty-Seven

A soft steady voice gently coaxed Jayden awake from a nightmare. He stared at the wall until he was able to make our words.

Balthezier was in a wheelchair reading aloud from a book. The guy had a bandage covering one eye, an arm in a sling, and a knee in a brace. There were hints of bruises and bandages poking out from underneath his loose clothing. Despite the hurt and what he had been through, Balthezier still managed to give him a smile when he realized Jayden was staring.

"Hey, how are you?" Balthezier asked.

He shifted his gaze to the ceiling and didn't answer.

"Jay?" Balthezier asked, frowning.

From the corner of his eye, he could see Balthezier reach out for him and he shied away. Hurt and concern flashed across his friend's face. Jayden swallowed the lump in his throat and kept his focus up.

Balthezier pulled out a phone from his pocket and tapped away at the screen. Not too long after, Doctor Gray came in, pocketing her phone.

The doctor took a seat on the edge of the bed and gave him a reassuring smile.

"How are you feeling, Jayden?" she asked.

Just like with Balthezier, he didn't respond. He couldn't. His throat was sore, but beyond that, he had nothing to say.

"I expect you'd be feeling pretty crappy. You've been asleep for a few days with a drip to rehydrate and provide much needed antibiotics. For some reason Healing Wards wouldn't work so I've wrapped a cast around your arm, stitched up nasty cuts and what looks like stab wounds, and bandaged everything else. You'll be sore and some movements will be hard to do in the meantime, but you're going to make a full recovery," Doctor Gray explained.

He didn't care how badly he was hurt. Why wouldn't they just leave him alone?

At the lack of reaction, Doctor Gray grimaced. "Try to rest a bit more."

From the corner of his eye, he could see his two companions share a worrying look.

"I'll come back to see how you're doing later," Doctor Gray advised before leaving the room.

The blond watched him for a bit and idly scratched at his chest.

"Dad is gone. I … he sacrificed himself so I had the strength to keep living. He wanted you to know that he thought of you as a son and that he's proud of you," Balthezier said.

Jayden couldn't stop a tear from falling down. He didn't know how much more of this heartache he could take.

"I'm sorry we didn't tell you that you were The Heart. I'm sorry we kept it all a secret. Maybe if we had told you, things could have been different … You'd be more protected. The Heart had never taken form before, but when you came into our lives, Dad and I wanted to keep it all from you so would be able to enjoy a normal life. We had hoped it would keep you safe. You wouldn't have had to worry whether or not people … None of us imagined that something like this would happen."

With effort, Jayden rolled on to his side so his back was to his friend. He didn't want to hear any more of it.

Balthezier sighed and resumed reading out loud.

Jayden continued to lay in bed in silence. He was relieved no more restraints were used and no one else tried to touch him. No matter how many times he woke up, there was no fresh pain. It was a relief but he didn't want to believe it would last.

When he was awake, he stared at the scale in his hand. Balthezier kept coming in and reading to him, and Doctor Gray was the only other visitor he had. It was more than he could take. He was forced to keep their company during waking hours and while he was asleep, he was plagued by what he had done.

When the door to his room opened and he didn't hear the sound of a wheelchair or heels moving along the floorboards, he tensed.

"Gray said you've shut down," Reid stated as he sat down on the chair next to the bed. "You were right, you know? There are more important things than family loyalty, especially if that loyalty leads to … a friend getting hurt."

Reid huffed at the ongoing silence and scratched his head. "Look, just don't give up."

At that point, Balthezier was wheeled in.

"What are you doing in here, Wyka?" Balthezier growled.

Reid sighed and stood up. "Just leaving."

The door clicked closed and Jayden was left with Balthezier and whoever brought him in.

Balthezier gently took his hand and his thumb gently caressed the skin along the back of Jayden's hand. The longer that hand was touching his, the worse he shook. Touch was bad. Touch meant pain. Without a word, Balthezier released his hand.

"A lot has happened since you were taken. The Compass Point who took the form of a tree is now a sapling in the backyard with its Watcher — a little blue and yellow bird. Sera, Van, and Henry retrieved the meteor without any problems. Kalarney is healing well considering what she's been through. Quentin and Clara haven't left her side and they've been able to gradually heal her. Dusk, the twins, Jet, and Nuru are also here," Bookman explained.

Jayden didn't know how to react. Everyone was doing okay, they were all safe and healing, and that was good, but he felt empty.

"Jay, whatever they did to you …" Bookman stopped and glanced to the injured blond. "There's no simple way to put it. A chunk of Szantium was broken off."

He let out a shaky breath. Shiro and Doctor Turner were winning no matter what he did. If he gave in, Szantium would be destroyed and humans would pay the price. If he fought, the city was still in danger.

"With Nuru's help, Szantium has been given a little more time, and most people have already been evacuated. Those that stayed behind are trying to save as much of our culture as possible. We need the First Circle to talk to the United Nations," Balthezier added.

When his attention barely shifted from the ceiling, both men shared a concerned look.

"Give us any indication that you understand us," Balthezier requested.

Balthezier and Bookman studied him in silence.

"This isn't good … Jay, we know you need time to heal and we'll be —-"

"We can't save Szantium without you," Balthezier interrupted. "We can't have gone through all of this just to give up in the end."

Jayden rolled on to his side and stared at the wall, ignoring the flare of pain in his shoulder. He couldn't help. There were others who would be able to pick up the work. There would have to be.

"Okay," Balthezier sighed. "Get some rest and we'll be back later."

Opening his eyes, he was confronted with the chair he had been strapped down to. He scrambled back in fear. Struggling to breathe, he ran out into the hall. As he tried to turn a corner, he miscalculated and crashed into the wall.

Breathing heavily, he leant against the wall and emptied his stomach.

After wiping his mouth, he focused on breathing and calming his pounding heart. He needed to find a way out.

Slowly, he continued walking and eventually, he came across a room with blood pooling out into the hall. He couldn't breathe. The bodies of two serpents were laying in the room, but their heads had been removed and stuck on the wall like trophies.

Jayden closed his eyes and let out a shaky whimper. This wasn't right. This wasn't how anything had been left. Why had they become so twisted?

Footsteps echoed behind him and he couldn't bring himself to look.

"Such a pity. They were the last."

He tensed and trembled. No …

"Don't worry. We may not have you but we still have your core caged. You'll never be free of us. I'll see you soon, Jayden Lugian," Shiro said.

An agonized sob was strangled in the back of his throat.

No matter what his friends said or needed, he couldn't help them anymore. Doctor Turner and Shiro had made sure of that.

Something heavy slammed into his back and forced him forward. In an instant, his muscles seized with incredibly blinding pain.

Jayden woke up hoarsely screaming, his Abilities going haywire, and hands trying to hold him down. There were muddled voices all around and the hands trying to pin him to the bed seemed to multiply. He struggled and fought for his freedom.

A lukewarm feeling washed over the room and he watched as a symbol draped over him like a blanket. He kept fighting and managed to break the Ward with his Abilities.

"Everyone, get out! Now," Bookman demanded.

Bookman pushed hands away from him and ushered everyone out of the room. Jayden sobbed as he curled up. He clamped hands over his ears and scrunched up his eyes.

He was pulled up and arms wrapped around him. He struggled to breathe and he clawed at Bookman's back in a bid to be released.

"Jayden, listen to me. I know you can't stand being touched but … You're safe, okay? We're in the Human Plane and no one will take you away from us again. Try to time your breathing with mine. Slow and steady. In two, three, four. Out, two, three, four," Bookman tried.

He let out a mangled cry and a harsh breath.

Slowly, he was able to follow Bookman's count and regain control over his breathing. The world gradually realigned and the panic numbed down. The clawing eased up to fingers scrunched into fabric and he turned his face against Bookman's neck and sighed.

When the older man went to lay him down, Jayden's hold tightened and he shook his head.

"Okay. We'll stay like this for a bit longer," Bookman said gently.

- **Chapter Thirty-Eight** -

Jayden waited until he was finally alone to sit up. His muscles had stiffened up and he could feel the pull of stitches. Shivering a little, he awkwardly pulled the blanket up around his hunched shoulders.

He needed to get out of the house and away from these people who pushed him to be right and looked at him as if he were a broken disappointment.

As if they knew what he needed and wanted, his Abilities drew up a Transport Ward and he disappeared from the bedroom.

He had no idea where he had ended up but it was cold. He didn't have shoes on and the only source of warmth he had was from the blanket he had wrapped around himself.

He stood in front of a small house on a quiet street. Taking a chance on his Abilities doing something right, he knocked on the front door and waited. After a few minutes and no one answering, he sighed and took a seat by the door, hugging his knees.

He was tired. It might not have been the best decision to have left the house but there was no other way he'd be able to get away from everything.

Eventually, a car pulled into the driveway and two people stepped out. At first they didn't seem to notice him sitting by their door, but when they walked up with grocery bags in hand, they stopped in confusion.

Jayden glanced up, teeth chattering from the wintery chill.

"Jayden?"

The man in front of him had short, wavy brown hair and wore smart clothing. His warm eyes took him in worriedly. There was a hint of familiarity but his tired mind couldn't put a name to the face.

"It's me, Nick."

Recognition dawned on him. His childhood friend had grown up into a mature, fine looking adult.

"You're … you're alive," Nicholas whispered.

Jayden used the brick wall to ease himself up. He clenched his eyes shut as he swayed with dizziness.

His old friend rushed over and kept him upright while the brunette woman unlocked the front door and led them inside. Jayden was eased on to the couch where he was able to focus on breathing and trying to stop his body from shaking.

Another blanket was draped over him and he pulled it closer.

"Jay? Are you okay? What happened?" Nicholas asked, sitting on the coffee table in front of him.

Licking his lips, he whispered, "You … you remember me?"

Nicholas grimaced and nodded. "Yeah. Roderick did a pretty rush job on making us forget. It all came back within the year. Why are you here? How come you look the same, but more … like you've been through hell and back?"

Jayden bit his bottom lip.

"Sorry … I just … needed to get away," he whispered.

"Kelly said you were dead," Nicholas stated.

He went to open his mouth to speak but thought otherwise. Getting the words out was tough. His throat was too raw and he didn't have the energy to keep going.

"I've organized a bath for you so you can warm up," Nicholas's companion said. "There'll be lemon and honey tea, and a note book and pen waiting for you when you come out."

He nodded his thanks.

"You remember Bailee, right?" Nicholas checked.

The name did sound familiar. The more he looked, the more he remembered. Her light brown hair was tied up in a messy bun and she wore rounded glasses over her brown eyes. She was dressed in jeans and a soft looking turtle neck jumper.

He could remember Bailee was the one able to return Nicholas's smile after his grandfather's funeral, the one who he liked and wanted to be with once Jayden's priorities and focus had shifted. It was nice seeing them still together.

He wondered how Silena and Adam were doing. Were they still together or had they went separate ways? Were they in school or focusing on jobs now?

As he tried to stand, Nicholas was by his side instantly. Jayden flinched when he was touched again and it took everything within him not to jerk away completely. Bailee took the blankets away and didn't follow as he and Nicholas headed towards the bathroom.

"Do … you need help?" Nicholas asked, uncertain.

Jayden bit his bottom lip. He didn't want Nicholas to see his body, but at the same time he wasn't sure if he'd be able to get his shirt off alone.

Sighing, he nodded.

'Just don't ask,' he shakily signed.

Nicholas frowned in confusion. "Sorry, I don't understand."

Jayden let out a strangled noise of frustration.

"D…don't … ask …w-what … happened," Jayden managed to get out.

"Oh. Sure. Tell me if I hurt you, okay?" Nicholas compromised.

The brunette helped him out of his clothes, and Jayden could see the need to ask grow. However, Nicholas kept his word and didn't say anything. As gently as possible, he unwrapped the bandages around Jayden's ankles and wrists and covered everything else with water resistant coverings.

Jayden flinched at the feeling of hot water against his skin but gradually, he relaxed. He hugged his knees and focused on breathing.

"Jay, I'm sorry I wasn't there for you and I'm sorry I blamed you for Ron and Theresa's death," Nicholas blurted out.

Jayden blinked in confusion. He didn't understand why Nicholas was apologizing. Those days felt like a lifetime ago.

Slowly, he nodded, unsure of how to react.

"I turned my back on my friend because I was scared. I shouldn't have done that," Nicholas added.

Swallowing the lump in his throat, he tried to indicate that he was scared as well by pointing to himself and holding up two fingers.

"You, too? You're scared?" Nicholas checked.

Jayden nodded.

"It's real bad, huh?"

Again, he nodded.

"I've seen the news. I can't imagine what it's been like for your side of things," Nicholas said. "Tip your head back and I'll wash your hair."

Jayden did as asked and Nicholas used the tap hose to wet as much of his chair as possible while trying to avoid hitting his injuries with the water. Nicholas worked quickly and gently to wash and rinse Jayden's black hair.

"Okay, all done. Let's get you dried and dressed," Nicholas said.

He nodded and with help, eased himself out of the tub. A towel was handed over and he was given a bit of privacy to dry his body.

Nicholas led him to the master bedroom and he was dressed in warm clothing that was slightly too big for him. Afterwards, they slowly made their way back to the living room where he wrapped himself back up in a blanket.

Bailee came out carrying a large first aid kit and sat down on the coffee table next to the steaming hot cup of tea, bottle of water, and a strip of painkillers.

"Take two of these and I'll help deal with those injuries that need to be recovered," she said.

He gratefully took the tablets and yawned. As he struggled to stay awake, he was vaguely aware of Bailee applying a cream over his tender skin and covering it all with fresh bandages.

"Why don't you get some sleep?" Nicholas suggested.

He shook his head and put his mug back onto the coffee table. Awkwardly, he wrote, *Don't want to dream. I'm sorry for dropping in. I'll leave.*

"Nonsense. You're more than welcome here, right Bailee?" Nicholas said.

The kind faced woman beside his old friend nodded. "Stay as long as you need."

Thank you, he wrote.

"I know you don't want to dream, but you clearly need rest. So lay down. I'll be here," Nicholas said gently.

Jayden hesitated before nodding and easing himself down. The blanket was adjusted and he was given a cushion to rest his head on.

Jayden sat up abruptly, panting. His heart pounded against his chest. Remnants of dreams full of cracking land falling apart beneath his feet filled his vision, making him forget where he was.

A hand reached out for him and without thinking, he slapped it away and scrambled to the other end of the couch.

"Easy. It's just me," Nicholas said.

He took a shuddering breath and stared at his old friend. With a slow, deep breath, he was able to slowly convince himself to calm down.

"I've brought you some soup if you're hungry," Nicholas said.

He ran a hand through his hair and stared up at the ceiling. For a moment, he simply concentrated on filling his lungs and exhaling slowly. His dream made him wonder whether or not he was dreaming about what had happened to Szantium while he was with Doctor Turner and Shiro or was he dreaming about something that would happen to the city soon?

"Nightmares?" Nicholas guessed.

Jayden hummed.

"Did you … want to talk about it?" Nicholas asked.

This time, he shook his head.

"Oh …" Nicholas said, disappointed. "Okay."

Jayden tapped his thigh as he thought. He couldn't talk about what had happened. He wanted nothing more than to stop thinking about it all and he wanted to be able to stop reacting like it was still happening. However, at the same time, he knew that if he talked about it, it would help and others would be able to help him through it better.

He shakily picked up the notebook and pen again.

'I went travelling with some friends to find some things to help the city. It was okay but I …' He stopped writing and showed Nicholas the note.

"But?" Nicholas prompted.

'I was taken and …'

His hand started shaking and he clenched his eyes shut as he breathed in harshly.

"It's okay, Jay. I get it. It's okay. You don't need to say anymore," Nicholas reassured.

Jayden dug his hand into the pants pocket and frowned. The scale wasn't there. He moved the blanket around and slipped his hand between the couch cushions.

"Where is it?" he asked frantically.

His breathing sped up and Jayden was close to pulling the couch apart in order to find the scale.

"Where's what?" Nicholas asked.

"The … the scale!"

"Easy, Jayden. I've got it," Bailee said, coming into the living room.

He looked towards the brunette woman with wide eyes.

"While you were in the bath, I turned it into a necklace so you wouldn't lose it," Bailee explained.

She held out the newly made piece of jewelry for him and he snatched it away from her. His hand shook as he stared at the necklace. A hold had been drilled in the rounded side of the scale and a black ford threaded through.

He clasped it in between his hands and leant forward, head bowed. His body shook with relief and he couldn't stop the tears falling.

"I'm sorry, Jay. I didn't … I'm sorry," Bailee quickly apologized.

Jayden shook his head. He took a moment to let the emotion out, to let himself feel the overwhelming loss, before turning to focus on easing his breathing and gathering himself.

"Oh! I was given these when you vanished," Nicholas said.

He got up and disappeared into the master bedroom. In the meantime, Jayden eased himself upright and wiped the tears staining his rosy cheeks.

"I don't know why Balthezier gave me these, but …" Nicholas shrugged.

He glanced up to find Nicholas holding out a bracelet made out of midnight colored beads flecked with silver. Nicholas sat on the coffee table and gently placed the bracelet over Jayden's bandaged left wrist. The calming effects were instant.

Jayden set the scale necklace over his head, joining Dale's old dog tags.

'Can you call Kelly? I should go back since I didn't tell anyone I was leaving and they might think I've been taken again.'

"Sure."

Jayden could see that Nicholas wanted to press for more information. The guy must have an increasing amount of questions but he remained silent.

'If I survive after everything is dealt with, I'll explain what's happened, okay?'

Nicholas went to squeeze his shoulder but thought better of it and left to go get his phone.

- Epilogue -

While he waited, Jayden closed his eyes and sorted through his thoughts. He didn't want to go back and be coddled. He didn't want to be told over and over again that he was needed. The Compass Points were waiting for him. His friends and the people of Szantium were all counting on him to save them. Doctor Turner and Shiro needed him to bring about their plan.

It was too much. He wanted to be back living in The Balgaire peacefully with Roderick, Balthezier, and Dusk.

"She's coming to pick you up. Jay, you okay?"

He blinked and realized his eyes were wet with tears. He wiped his cheek, sniffed, and shook his head.

"I want to help," Nicholas volunteered.

'Thanks but ... it's too dangerous,' he wrote. *'It'll be okay, Nick.'*

There was a knock at the door that stole their attention. Bailee was the one who went and answered the door.

"Hi, Kelly ... and Spencer," she greeted.

Bailee was left standing with an apologetic Kelly.

"What do you think you're pulling?" Spencer growled, storming in and heaving Jayden off the couch. "Why would you disappear like that after everyone had finally gotten you back?"

Jayden stumbled as he was shoved towards the door. He tried to fight off Spencer but his efforts and lack of words only made the blond angrier.

"We searched for you for weeks and this is how you thank us!" Spencer shouted.

"Spencer!" Kelly shouted.

"Stop … touching … me!" Jayden shouted hoarsely.

Spencer ignored him, grabbed his arm tightly and dragged him out of the house. Jayden stumbled and cried out in pain. His breathing was becoming heavy. Past and present melded together and he was back in the run down hospital being dragged back to that chair. He didn't want to go.

White tendrils stretched out of him. No one was going to make him go back into that chair again.

The power wrapped around Spencer and forced his hand off of Jayden. The blond was tossed across the front yard. Even though he was free of the hold, he wasn't finished.

"I will not be used!" he growled ominously.

Jayden ploughed his Abilities into the ground. They shot up around Spencer and caged him in.

"Jayden, enough! Don't hurt him," Kelly pleaded.

He doubled over as pain racked his body. It felt like he was being ripped open. The earth shook and he fell to his knees. His Abilities faded away and Spencer was free. The trembling grew stronger, setting off car alarms, dogs, and people screaming.

"Jay, breathe. You're safe," Kelly tried.

A thundering crack had everyone flinching and covering their ears.

Jayden took a shaky breath and forced himself to look up. In a jagged motion, the air was splitting in two. The edges peeled back slightly and he was staring at the In Between. The end of the crack slammed into a house, tearing it and its neighbors apart.

"Holy shi —"

He couldn't help but wonder if it was his fault this was happening here and now.

A rock shot out of the crack and crashed into the street in front of them. Asphalt and earth sprayed everywhere until it came to a complete stop.

"What's going on?" Bailee shakily asked.

He couldn't pry his eyes away from the boulder. There was something wrong with it. A dark, hungry power was radiating from the rock. It was a power he horrifyingly remembered.

Overwhelmed with fear, he shook his head and backed away. Those things couldn't be here. Not now. He wasn't ready.

A bony arm shot up and clawed fingers slammed into the rock. Large white eyes stared over the edge, taking them all in.

"No," Jayden whispered.

"Jay?"

A gangly black humanoid body climbed on top of the rock. The Shadow glanced around at its new surroundings and released an ear splitting screech.

COLLIDING WORLDS:

REUNION

Book 3

COMING IN 2021

ABOUT THE AUTHOR

D. Henry hails from Melbourne, Australia. When he isn't writing, he's drawing, and when he isn't drawing, he's probably doing something in the name of procrastination. He writes Young Adult Fantasy and enjoys letting his imagination run wild with ideas of magic and new worlds.

You can find him on:

@willowispstudios

@willowispstudios

@willowispstudio

ko-fi.com/willowispstudios

www.ingramcontent.com/pod-product-compliance
Lightning Source LLC
Chambersburg PA
CBHW021142110726
47900CB00002B/441